THE
39 STEPS
AND THE POWER HOUSE

D1332235

THE 39 STEPS

AND THE POWER HOUSE

JOHN BUCHAN

This edition published in 2019 by Arcturus Publishing Limited
26/27 Bickels Yard, 151–153 Bermondsey Street,
London SE1 3HA

Typesetting by Palimpsest Book Production Limited

Cover design: Peter Ridley
Cover illustration: Peter Gray

AD001533UK

Printed in the UK

Contents

Introduction

The son of a Calvinist clergyman, John Buchan was born on 26 August 1875 in the Scottish town of Perth. His childhood was spent largely in the rural countryside that was to feature strongly in his fiction. At seventeen, having received a scholarship, he began studying classics at the University of Glasgow, later transferring to Oxford. Buchan was a student when his literary career began. His first book, an edited collection of writings by Sir Francis Bacon, appeared before his twentieth birthday. He graduated as an award-winning author with six volumes of history, poetry and fiction to his credit. Given this record, it is not surprising that much of Buchan's adult life was to be spent in the employ of publishers Thomas Nelson and Son.

The Thirty-Nine Steps was written and published during the early months of the First World War. An early thriller – or, to use the author's term, 'shocker' – it introduces Richard Hannay, the protagonist of Buchan's most popular novels, including *Greenmantle* (1916) and *Mr Standfast* (1919). *The Thirty-Nine Steps* would prove to be Buchan's most enduring work; such was its popularity that it was published in book form before *The Power-House*, a previous 'shocker' that featured his other great heroic creation, Edward Leithen.

A commercially successful author, Buchan's fame was given a further boost with Alfred Hitchcock's 1935 adaptation of *The Thirty-Nine Steps*. That same year, having been created 1st Baron Tweedsmuir, he became Governor General of Canada.

Buchan died in Montreal on 11 February 1940.

TO
CAPTAIN THOMAS ARTHUR NELSON
(LOTHIAN AND BORDER HORSE)

My Dear Tommy,

You and I have long cherished an affection for that
elemental type of tale which Americans call the 'dime
novel' and which we know as the 'shocker' – the romance
where the incidents defy the probabilities, and march just
inside the borders of the possible. During an illness last
winter I exhausted my store of those aids to cheerfulness,
and was driven to write one for myself. This little volume
is the result, and I should like to put your name on it in
memory of our long friendship, in the days when the wildest
fictions are so much less improbable than the facts.

J.B.

CHAPTER 1

THE MAN WHO DIED

I returned from the City about three o'clock on that May afternoon pretty well disgusted with life. I had been three months in the Old Country and was fed up with it. If any one had told me a year ago that I would have been feeling like that, I should have laughed at him, but there was the fact. The weather made me liverish, the talk of the ordinary Englishman made me sick, I couldn't get enough exercise, and the amusements of London seemed as flat as soda-water that has been standing in the sun. 'Richard Hannay,' I kept telling myself, 'you have got into the wrong ditch, my friend, and you had better climb out.'

It made me bite my lips to think of the plans I had been building up those last years in Bulawayo. I had got my pile – not one of the big ones but good enough for me; and I had figured out all kinds of ways of enjoying myself. My father had brought me out from Scotland at the age of six, and I had never been home since; so England was a sort of *Arabian Nights* to me, and I counted on stopping there for the rest of my days. But from the first I was disappointed with it. In about a week I was tired of seeing sights, and in less than a month I had had enough of restaurants and theatres and race meetings. I had no real pal to go about with, which probably explains things. Plenty of people invited me to their houses, but they didn't seem much interested in me. They would ask me a question or two about South Africa and then get on to their own affairs. A lot of Imperialist ladies asked me to tea to meet schoolmasters from New Zealand and editors from Vancouver, and that was the dismalest business of all. Here was I, thirty-seven years old, sound in wind and limb, with enough money to have a good time, yawning my head off all day. I had just about settled to clear out and get back to the veld, for I was the best bored man in the United Kingdom.

That afternoon I had been worrying my brokers about investments to give my mind something to work on, and on my way home I turned into my club – rather a pot-house, which took in Colonial members. I had a long drink, and read the evening papers. They were full of the row in the Near East, and there was an article about Karolides, the Greek Premier. I rather fancied the chap. From all accounts he seemed the one big man in the show, and he played a straight game, too, which was more than could be said for most of them. I gathered that they hated him pretty blackly in Berlin and Vienna, but that we were going to stick by him, and one paper said that he was the only barrier between Europe and Armageddon. I remember wondering if I could get a job in those parts. It struck me that Albania was the sort of place that might keep a man from yawning.

About six o'clock I went home, dressed, dined at the Café Royal, and turned into a music-hall. It was a silly show, all capering women and monkey-faced men, and I did not stay long. The night was fine and clear as I walked back to the flat I had hired near Portland Place. The crowd surged past me on the pavements, busy and chattering, and I envied the people for having something to do. These shop-girls and clerks and dandies and policemen had some interest in life that kept them going. I gave half a crown to a beggar because I saw him yawn; he was a fellow-sufferer. At Oxford Circus I looked up into the spring sky and I made a vow. I would give the Old Country another day to fit me into something; if nothing happened, I would take the next boat for the Cape.

My flat was the first floor in a new block behind Langham Place. There was a common staircase with a porter and a liftman at the entrance, but there was no restaurant or anything of that sort, and each flat was quite shut off from the others. I hate servants on the premises, so I had a fellow to look after me who came in by the day. He arrived before eight o'clock every morning, and used to depart at seven, for I never dined at home.

I was just fitting my key into the door, when I noticed a man at my elbow. I had not seen him approach, and the sudden appearance made me start. He was a slim man with a short brown beard and small, gimlety blue eyes. I recognized him as the occupant of a flat on the top floor, with whom I had passed the time of day on the stairs.

'Can I speak to you?' he said. 'May I come in for a minute?' He was steadying his voice with an effort, and his hand was pawing my arm.

I got my door open and motioned him in. No sooner was he over the threshold than he made a dash for my back-room, where I used to smoke and write my letters. Then he bolted back.

'Is the door locked?' he asked feverishly, and he fastened the chain with his own hand.

'I'm very sorry,' he said humbly. 'It's a mighty liberty, but you looked the kind of man who would understand. I've had you in my mind all this week when things got troublesome. Say, will you do me a good turn?'

'I'll listen to you,' I said. 'That's all I'll promise.' I was getting worried by the antics of this nervous little chap.

There was a tray of drinks on a table beside him, from which he filled himself a stiff whisky-and-soda. He drank it off in three gulps, and cracked the glass as he set it down.

'Pardon,' he said. 'I'm a bit rattled tonight. You see, I happen at this moment to be dead.'

I sat down in an armchair and lit my pipe. 'What does it feel like?' I asked. I was pretty certain that I had to deal with a madman.

A smile flickered over his drawn face. 'I'm not mad – yet. Say, sir, I've been watching you and I reckon you're a cool customer. I reckon, too, you're an honest man, and not afraid of playing a bold hand. I'm going to confide in you. I need help worse than any man ever needed it, and I want to know if I can count you in.'

'Get on with your yarn,' I said, 'and I'll tell you.'

He seemed to brace himself for a great effort and then started on the queerest rigmarole. I didn't get hold of it at first, and I had to stop and ask him questions. But here is the gist of it.

He was an American, from Kentucky, and after college, being pretty well off, he had started out to see the world. He wrote a bit, and acted as war correspondent for a Chicago paper, and spent a year or two in southeastern Europe. I gathered that he was a fine linguist and had got to know pretty well the society in those parts. He spoke familiarly of many names that I remembered to have seen in the newspapers.

He had played about with politics, he told me, at first for the interest of them, and then because he couldn't help himself. I read him as a sharp, restless fellow, who always wanted to get down to the roots of things. He got a little further down than he wanted.

I am giving you what he told me as well as I could make it out. Away behind all the governments and the armies there was a big subterranean movement going on, engineered by very dangerous people. He had come on it by accident; it fascinated him; he went further, and then got caught. I gathered that most of the people in it were the sort of educated anarchists that make revolutions, but that beside them there were financiers who were playing for money. A clever man can make big profits on a falling market, and it suited the book of both classes to set Europe by the ears.

He told me some queer things that explained a lot that had puzzled me – things that happened in the Balkan War, how one state suddenly came out on top, why alliances were made and broken, why certain men disappeared, and where the sinews of war came from. The aim of the whole conspiracy was to get Russia and Germany at loggerheads.

When I asked why, he said that the anarchist lot thought it would give them their chance. Everything would be in the melting-pot, and they looked to see a new world emerge. The capitalists would rake in the shekels, and make fortunes by buying up wreckage. Capital, he said, had no conscience and no fatherland. Besides, the Jew was behind it, and the Jew hated Russia worse than hell.

'Do you wonder?' he cried. 'For three hundred years they have been persecuted, and this is the return match for the *pogroms*. The Jew is everywhere, but you have to go far down the backstairs to find him.

'Take any big Teutonic business concern. If you have dealings with it the first man you meet is Prince von Und zu Something, an elegant young man who talks Eton-and-Harrow English. But he cuts no ice. If your business is big, you get behind him and find a prognathous Westphalian with a retreating brow and the manners of a hog.

'He is the German business man that gives your English papers the shakes. But if you're on the biggest kind of job and are bound to get to the real boss, ten to one you are brought up against a little, white-faced Jew in a bath-chair, with an eye like a rattlesnake. Yes, sir, he is the man who is ruling the world just now, and he has his knife in the Empire of the Tzar because his aunt was outraged and his father flogged in some one-horse location on the Volga.'

I could not help saying that his Jew-anarchists seemed to have got left behind a little.

'Yes and no,' he said. 'They won up to a point, but they struck a bigger thing than money, a thing that couldn't be bought, the old elemental fighting instincts of man. If you're going to be killed you invent some kind of flag and country to fight for, and if you survive, you get to love the thing. Those foolish devils of soldiers have found something they care for, and that has upset the pretty plan laid in Berlin and Vienna. But my friends haven't played their last card by a long sight. They've gotten the ace up their sleeves, and unless I can keep alive for a month, they are going to play it, and win.'

'But I thought you were dead,' I put in.

'*Mors janua vitae*,' he smiled. (I recognized the quotation: it was about all the Latin I knew.) 'I'm coming to that, but I've got to put you wise about a lot of things first. If you read your newspaper, I guess you know the name of Constantine Karolides?'

I sat up at that, for I had been reading about him that very afternoon.

'He is the man that has wrecked all their games. He is the one big brain in the whole show, and he happens also to be an honest man. Therefore he has been marked down these twelve months past. I found that out – not that it was difficult, for any fool could guess as much. But I found out the way they were going to get him, and that knowledge was deadly. That's why I have had to decease.'

He had another drink and I mixed it for him myself, for I was getting interested in the beggar.

'They can't get him in his own land, for he has a bodyguard of Epirotes that would skin their grandmothers. But on the fifteenth day of June he is coming to this city. The British Foreign Office has taken to having international tea-parties, and the biggest of them is due on that date. Now Karolides is reckoned the principal guest, and if my friends have their way, he will never return to his admiring countrymen.'

'That's simple enough, anyhow,' I said. 'You can warn him and keep him at home.'

'And play their game?' he asked sharply. 'If he does not come they win, for he's the only man that can straighten out the tangle. And if his government is warned he won't come, for he does not know how big the stakes will be on June the 15th.'

'What about the British Government?' I asked. 'They're not going to let their guests be murdered. Tip them the wink, and they'll take extra precautions.'

'No good. They might stuff this city with plain-clothes detectives and double the police, and Constantine would still be a doomed man. My friends are not playing this game for candy. They want a big occasion for the taking off, with the eyes of all Europe on it. He'll be murdered by an Austrian, and there'll be plenty of evidence to show the connivance of the big folk in Vienna and Berlin. It will all be an infernal lie, of course, but the case will look black enough to the world. I'm not talking hot air, my friend. I happen to know every detail of the hellish contrivance, and I can tell you it will be the most finished piece of blackguardism since the Borgias. But it's not going to come off if there's a certain man who knows the wheels of the business alive right here in London on the 15th day of June. And that man is going to be your servant, Franklin P. Scudder.'

I was getting to like the little chap. His jaw had shut like a rat-trap and there was the fire of battle in his gimlety eyes. If he was spinning me a yarn, he could act up to it.

'Where did you find out this story?' I asked.

'I got the first hint in an inn on the Achensee in Tyrol. That set me inquiring, and I collected my other clues in a fur-shop in the Galician quarter of Buda, in a Strangers' Club in Vienna, and in a little book-shop off the Racknitzstrasse in Leipsig. I completed my evidence ten days ago in Paris. I can't tell you the details now, for it's something of a history. When I was quite sure in my own mind, I judged it my business to disappear, and I reached this city by a mighty queer circuit. I left Paris a dandified young French-American, and I sailed from Hamburg a Jew diamond merchant. In Norway I was an English student of Ibsen, collecting materials for lectures, but when I left Bergen I was a cinema-man with special ski films. And I came here from Leith with a lot of pulp-wood propositions in my pocket to put before the London newspapers. Till yesterday I thought I had muddied my trail some, and I was feeling pretty happy. Then…'

The recollection seemed to upset him, and be gulped down some more whisky.

'Then I saw a man standing in the street outside this block. I used to stay close in my room all day, and only slip out after dark for an hour or two. I watched him for a bit from my window, and I thought I recognized him. He came in and spoke to the porter. When I came back from my walk last night I found a card in my letter-box. It bore the name of the man I want least to meet on God's earth.'

I think that the look in my companion's eyes, the sheer naked fright on his face, completed my conviction of his honesty. My own voice sharpened a bit as I asked him what he did next.

'I realized that I was bottled as sure as a pickled herring and that there was only one way out. I had to die. If my pursuers knew I was dead they would go to sleep again.'

'How did you manage it?'

'I told the man that valets me that I was feeling pretty bad, and I got myself up to look like death. That wasn't difficult, for I'm no slouch at disguises. Then I got a corpse – you can always get a body in London if you know where to go for it. I fetched it back in a trunk on the top of a four-wheeler, and I had to be assisted upstairs to my room. You see, I had to pile up some evidence for the inquest. I went to bed and got my man to mix me a sleeping-draught, and then told him to clear out. He wanted to fetch a doctor, but I swore some and said I couldn't abide leeches. When I was left alone I started in to fake up that corpse. He was my size and I judged had perished from too much alcohol, so I put some spirits handy about the place. The jaw was the weak point in the likeness, so I blew it away with a revolver. I dare say there will be somebody tomorrow to swear to having heard a shot, but there are no neighbours on my floor and I guessed I could risk it. So I left the body in bed dressed up in my pyjamas with a revolver lying on the bed-clothes and a considerable mess around. Then I got into a suit of clothes I had kept waiting for emergencies. I didn't dare to shave for fear of leaving tracks, and besides it wasn't any kind of use my trying to get into the streets. I had had you in my mind all day, and there seemed nothing to do but to make an appeal to you. I watched from my window till I saw you come home and then slipped down the stair to meet you... There, sir, I guess you know about as much as me of this business.'

He sat blinking like an owl, fluttering with nerves and yet desperately determined.

By this time I was pretty well convinced that he was going straight with me. It was the wildest sort of narrative, but I had heard in my time many steep tales which had turned out to be true, and I had made a practice of judging the man rather than the story. If he had wanted to get a location in my flat and then cut my throat he would have pitched a milder yarn.

'Hand me your key,' I said, 'and I'll take a look at the corpse. Excuse my caution, but I'm bound to verify a bit if I can.'

He shook his head mournfully. 'I reckoned you'd ask for that, but I haven't got it. It's on my chain on the dressing-table. I had to leave it behind, for I couldn't leave any clues to raise suspicions. The gentry who are after me are pretty bright-eyed citizens. You'll have to take me on trust for the night, and tomorrow you'll get proof of the corpse business right enough.'

I thought for an instant or two.

'Right. I'll trust you for the night. I'll lock you into this room and keep the key. Just one word, Mr Scudder. I believe you're straight, but if so be you are not I should warn you that I'm a handy man with a gun.'

'Sure,' he said, jumping up with some briskness. 'I haven't the privilege of your name, sir, but let me tell you that you're a white man. I'll thank you to lend me a razor.'

I took him into my bedroom and turned him loose. In half an hour's time a figure came out that I scarcely recognized. Only his gimlety, hungry eyes were the same. He was shaved clean, his hair was parted in the middle, and he had cut his eyebrows.

Further, he carried himself as if he had been drilled, and was the very model, even to the brown complexion, of some British officer who had had a long spell in India. He had a monocle, too, which he stuck in his eye, and every trace of the American had gone out of his speech.

'My hat! Mr Scudder—' I stammered.

'Not Mr Scudder,' he corrected, 'Captain Theophilus Digby, of the 40th Gurkhas, presently home on leave. I'll thank you to remember that, sir.'

I made him a bed in my smoking-room and sought my own couch, more cheerful than I had been for the past month. Things did happen occasionally, even in this God-forgotten metropolis!

*   *   *

I woke next morning to hear my man, Paddock, making the deuce of a row at the smoking-room door.

Paddock was a fellow I had done a good turn to out on the Selakwi, and I had in-spanned him as my servant as soon as I got to England. He had about as much gift of the gab as a hippopotamus, and was not a great hand at valeting, but I knew I could count on his loyalty.

'Stop that row, Paddock,' I said. 'There's a friend of mine, Captain – Captain—' (I couldn't remember the name) 'dossing down in there. Get breakfast for two and then come and speak to me.'

I told Paddock a fine story about how my friend was a great swell, with his nerves pretty bad from overwork, who wanted absolute rest and stillness. Nobody had got to know he was here, or he would be besieged by communications from the India office and the Prime Minister and his cure would be ruined.

I am bound to say Scudder played up splendidly when he came to breakfast. He fixed Paddock with his eyeglass, just like a British officer, asked him about the Boer War, and slung out at me a lot of stuff about imaginary pals. Paddock couldn't learn to call me 'sir,' but he 'sirred' Scudder as if his life depended on it.

I left him with the newspaper and a box of cigars, and went down to the city till luncheon. When I got back the porter had a weighty face.

'Nawsty business 'ere this morning, sir. Gent in No. 15 been and shot 'isself. They've just took 'im to the mortuary. The police are up there now.'

I ascended to No. 15 and found a couple of bobbies and an inspector busy making an examination. I asked a few idiotic questions and they soon kicked me out. Then I found the man that had valeted Scudder, and pumped him, but I could see he suspected nothing. He was a whining fellow with a churchyard face, and half a crown went far to console him.

I attended the inquest next day. A partner of some publishing firm gave evidence that the deceased had brought him wood-pulp propositions and had been, he believed, an agent of an American business. The jury found it a case of suicide while of unsound mind, and the few effects were handed over to the American consul to deal with. I gave Scudder a full account of the affair and it interested him greatly. He said he wished he could have attended the inquest for he reckoned it would be about as spicy as to read one's own obituary notice.

The first two days he stayed with me in that back room he was very peaceful. He read and smoked a bit, and made a heap of jottings in a note-book, and every night we had a game of chess, at which he beat me hollow. I think he was nursing his nerves back to health, for he had had a pretty trying time. But on the third day I could see he was beginning to get restless. He fixed up a list of the days till June 15th and ticked each off with a red pencil, making remarks in shorthand against them. I would find him sunk in a brown study, with his sharp eyes abstracted, and after these spells of meditation he was apt to be very despondent.

Then I could see that he began to get edgy again. He listened for little noises, and was always asking me if Paddock could be trusted. Once or twice he got very peevish and apologized for it. I didn't blame him. I made every allowance, for he had taken on a fairly stiff job.

It was not the safety of his own skin that troubled him, but the success of the scheme he had planned. That little man was clean grit all through, without a soft spot in him. One night he was very solemn.

'Say, Hannay,' he said, 'I judge I should let you a bit deeper into this business. I should hate to go out without leaving somebody else to put up a fight.' And he began to tell me in detail what I had only heard from him vaguely.

I did not give him very close attention. The fact is I was more interested in his own adventures than in his high politics. I reckoned that Karolides and his affairs were not my business, leaving all that to him. So a lot that he said slipped clean out of my memory. I remember that he was very clear that the danger to Karolides would not begin till he had got to London, and would come from the very highest quarters, where there would be no thought of suspicion. He mentioned the name of a woman – Julia Czechenyi – as having something to do with the danger. She would be the decoy, I gathered, to get Karolides out of the care of his guards. He talked, too, about a Black Stone and a man that lisped in his speech, and he described very particularly somebody that he never referred to without a shudder – an old man with a young voice who could hood his eyes like a hawk.

He spoke a good deal about death, too. He was mortally anxious about winning through with his job, but he didn't care a rush for his life.

'I reckon it's like going to sleep when you are pretty well tired out, and waking to find a summer day with the scent of hay coming in at the window. I used to thank God for such mornings way back in the blue-grass country and I guess I'll thank Him when I wake up on the other side of Jordan.'

Next day he was much more cheerful and read the life of Stonewall Jackson most of the time. I went out to dinner with a mining engineer I had got to see on business, and came back about half past ten in time for our game of chess before turning in.

I had a cigar in my mouth, I remember, as I pushed open the smoking-room door. The lights were not lit, which struck me as odd.

I wondered if Scudder had turned in already. I snapped the switch, but there was nobody there. Then I saw something in the far corner which made me drop my cigar and fall into a cold sweat.

My guest was lying sprawled on his back. There was a long knife through his heart, which skewered him to the floor.

CHAPTER 2

THE MILKMAN SETS OUT
ON HIS TRAVELS

I sat down in an armchair and felt very sick. That lasted for maybe five minutes, and was succeeded by a fit of the horrors. The poor, staring, white face on the floor was more than I could bear, and I managed to get a table-cloth and cover it. Then I staggered to a cupboard, found the brandy and swallowed several mouthfuls. I had seen men die violently before; indeed, I had killed a few myself in the Matabele War, but this cold-blooded indoor business was different. Still I managed to pull myself together.

I looked at my watch, and saw that it was half past ten. An idea seized me and I went over the flat with a small-tooth comb. There was nobody there, nor any trace of anybody, but I shuttered and bolted all the windows and put the chain on the door.

By this time my wits were coming back to me and I could think again. It took me about an hour to figure the thing out, and I did not hurry, for, unless the murderer came back, I had till about six o'clock in the morning for my cogitations.

I was in the soup – that was pretty clear. Any shadow of a doubt I might have had about the truth of Scudder's tale was now gone. The proof of it was lying under the table-cloth. The men who knew that he knew what he knew had found him, and had taken the best way to make certain of his silence. Yes: but he had been in my rooms four days, and his enemies must have reckoned that he had confided in me. So I would be the next to go. It might be that very night, or next day, or the day after, but my number was up all right.

Then suddenly I thought of another probability. Supposing I went out now and called in the police, or went to bed and let Paddock find the body and call them in the morning.

What kind of a story was I to tell about Scudder? I had lied to Paddock about him, and the whole thing looked desperately fishy. If I made a clean breast of it and told the police everything he had told me, they would simply laugh at me. The odds were a thousand to one that I would be charged with the murder, and the circumstantial evidence was strong enough to hang me. Few people knew me in England; I had no real pal who could come forward and swear to my character. Perhaps that was what those secret enemies were playing for. They were clever enough for anything, and an English prison was as good a way of getting rid of me till after June 15th as a knife in my chest.

Besides, if I told the whole story and by any miracle was believed I would be playing their game. Karolides would stay at home, which was what they wanted. Somehow or other the sight of Scudder's dead face had made me a passionate believer in his scheme. He was gone, but he had taken me into his confidence, and I was pretty well bound to carry on his work. You may think this ridiculous for a man in danger of his life, but that was the way I looked at it. I am an ordinary sort of fellow, not braver than other people, but I hate to see a good man downed, and that long knife would not be the end of Scudder if I could play the game in his place.

It took me an hour or two to think this out, and by that time I had come to a decision. I must vanish somehow, and keep vanished till the end of the second week of June. Then I must somehow find a way to get in touch with the government people and tell them what Scudder had told me. I wished to heaven he had told me more, and that I had listened more carefully to the little he had told me. I knew nothing but the barest facts. There was a big risk that, even if I weathered the other dangers, I would not be believed in the end. I must take my chance of that, and hope that something might happen which would confirm my tale in the eyes of the government.

My first job was to keep going for the next three weeks. It was now the 24th of May, and that meant twenty days of hiding before I could venture to approach the powers that be. I reckoned that two sets of people would be looking for me – Scudder's enemies to put me out of existence, and the police, who would want me for Scudder's murder. It was going to be a giddy hunt, and it was queer how the prospect comforted me. I had been slack so long that almost any chance of activity was welcome. When I had to sit alone with that corpse and wait on Fortune I was no better than a crushed worm, but if my neck's safety was to hang on my own wits I was prepared to be cheerful about it.

My next thought was whether Scudder had any papers about him to give me a better clue to the business. I drew back the table-cloth and searched his pockets, for I had no longer any shrinking from the body. The face was wonderfully calm for a man who had been struck down in a moment. There was nothing in the breast-pocket, and only a few loose coins and a cigar-holder in the waistcoat. The trousers held a little pen-knife and some silver, and the side-pocket of his jacket contained an old crocodile-skin cigar-case. There was no sign of the little black book in which I had seen him making notes. That had, no doubt, been taken by his murderer.

But as I looked up from my task I saw that some drawers had been pulled out in the writing-table. Scudder would never have left them in that state, for he was the tidiest of mortals. Some one must have been searching for something – perhaps for the pocket-book. I went round the flat and found that everything had been ransacked – the inside of books, drawers, cupboards, boxes, even the pockets of the clothes in my wardrobe, and the sideboard in the dining-room. There was no trace of the book. Most likely the enemy had found it, but they had not found it on Scudder's body.

Then I got out an atlas and looked at a big map of the British Isles. My notion was to get off to some wild district, where my veldcraft would be of some use to me, for I would be like a trapped rat in a city. I considered that Scotland would be best, for my people were Scotch and I could pass anywhere as an ordinary Scotsman. I had half an idea at first to be a German tourist, for my father had had German partners and I had been brought up to speak the tongue pretty fluently, not to mention having put in three years prospecting for copper in German Damaraland.

But I calculated that it would be less conspicuous to be a Scot, and less in a line with what the police might know of my past. I fixed on Galloway as the best place to go to. It was the nearest wild part of Scotland, so far as I could figure it out, and from the look of the map was not over-thick with population. A search in Bradshaw informed me that a train left St. Pancras at 7.10, which would land me at any Galloway station in the late afternoon. That was well enough, but a more important matter was how I was to make my way to St Pancras, for

I was pretty certain that Scudder's friends would be watching outside. This puzzled me for a bit; then I had an inspiration, on which I went to bed and slept for two troubled hours.

I got up at four and opened my bedroom shutters. The faint light of a fine summer morning was flooding the skies, and the sparrows had begun to chatter. I had a great revulsion of feeling, and felt a God-forgotten fool. My inclination was to let things slide, and trust to the British police taking a reasonable view of my case. But as I viewed the situation I could find no arguments to bring against my decision of the previous night, so with a wry mouth I resolved to go on with my plan. I was not feeling in any particular funk; only disinclined to go looking for trouble, if you understand me.

I hunted out a well-used tweed suit, a pair of strong nailed boots, and a flannel shirt with a collar. Into my pockets I stuffed a spare shirt, a cloth cap, some handkerchiefs, and a toothbrush. I had drawn a good sum in gold from the bank two days before, in case Scudder should want money, and I took fifty pounds of it in sovereigns in a belt which I had brought back from Rhodesia. That was about all I wanted. Then I had a bath, and cut my moustache, which was long and drooping, into a short stubbly fringe.

Now came the next step. Paddock used to arrive punctually at 7.30 and let himself in with a latch-key. But about twenty minutes to seven, as I knew from bitter experience, the milkman turned up with a great clatter of cans, and deposited my share outside my door. I had seen that milkman sometimes when I had gone out for an early ride. He was a young man about my own height, with a scrubby moustache, dressed in a white overall. On him I staked all my chances.

I went into the darkened smoking-room where the rays of morning light were beginning to creep through the shutters. There I breakfasted off a whisky-and-soda and some biscuits from the cupboard. By this time it was getting on to six o'clock. I put a pipe in my pocket and filled my pouch from the tobacco jar on the table by the fireplace. As I poked into the tobacco my fingers touched something hard, and I drew out Scudder's little black pocket-book.

That seemed to me a good omen. I lifted the cloth from the body and was amazed at the peace and dignity of the dead face.

'Goodbye, old chap,' I said; 'I am going to do my best for you. Wish me well wherever you are.'

Then I hung about in the hall waiting for the milkman. That was the worst part of the business, for I was fairly choking to get out of doors. Six-thirty passed, then six-forty, but still he did not come. The fool had chosen this day of all days to be late.

At one minute after the quarter to seven I heard the rattle of the cans outside. I opened the front door, and there was my man, singling out my cans from a bunch he carried and whistling through his teeth. He jumped a bit at the sight of me.

'Come in here a moment,' I said. 'I want a word with you.' And I led him into the dining-room.

'I reckon you're a bit of a sportsman,' I said, 'and I want you to do me a service. Lend me your cap and overall for ten minutes and here's a sovereign for you.'

His eyes opened at the sight of the gold, and he grinned broadly. 'Wot's the gyme?' he asked.

'A bet,' I said. 'I haven't time to explain, but to win it I've got to be a milkman for the next ten minutes. All you've got to do is to stay here till I come back. You'll be a bit late, but nobody will complain, and you'll have that quid for yourself.'

'Right-o!' he said cheerily, 'I ain't the man to spoil a bit of sport. Here's the rig, guv'nor.'

I stuck on his flat blue hat and his white overall, picked up the cans, banged my door, and went whistling downstairs. The porter at the foot told me to shut my jaw, which sounded as if my make-up was adequate.

At first I thought there was nobody in the street. Then I caught sight of a policeman a hundred yards down, and a loafer shuffling past on the other side. Some impulse made me raise my eyes to the house opposite, and there at a first-floor window was a face. As the loafer passed he looked up and I fancied a signal was exchanged.

I crossed the street, whistling gaily and imitating the jaunty swing of the milkman. Then I took the first side street, and turned up a left-hand turning which led past a bit of vacant ground. There was no one in the little street, so I dropped the milk-cans inside the hoarding and sent the hat and overall after them. I had only just put on my cloth cap, when a postman came round the corner. I gave him good-morning, and he answered me unsuspiciously. At the moment the clock of a neighbouring church struck the hour of seven.

There was not a second to spare. As soon as I got to Euston Road I took to my heels and ran. The clock at Euston Station showed five minutes past the hour. At St. Pancras I had no time to take a ticket, let alone that I had not settled upon my destination. A porter told me the platform, and as I entered it I saw the train already in motion. Two station officials blocked the way, but I dodged them and clambered into the last carriage.

Three minutes later, as we were roaring through the northern tunnels, an irate guard interviewed me. He wrote out for me a ticket to Newtown Stewart, a name which had suddenly come back to my memory, and he conducted me from the first-class compartment where I had ensconced myself to a third-class smoker, occupied by a sailor and a stout woman with a child. He went off grumbling, and as I mopped my brow I observed to my companions in my broadest Scots that it was a sore job catching trains. I had already entered upon my part.

'The impidence o' that guard,' said the lady bitterly. 'He needit a Scotch tongue to pit him in his place. He was complainin' o' this wean no haein' a ticket and her no fower till August twelvemonth, and he was objectin' to this gentleman spittin'.'

The sailor morosely agreed, and I started my new life in an atmosphere of protest against authority. I reminded myself that a week ago I had been finding the world dull.

CHAPTER 3

THE ADVENTURE OF
THE LITERARY INNKEEPER

I had a solemn time travelling north that day. It was fine May weather, with the hawthorn flowering on every hedge, and I asked myself why, when I was still a free man, I had stayed on in London and not got the good of this heavenly country. I didn't dare face the restaurant car, but I got a luncheon basket at Leeds, and shared it with the fat woman. Also I got the morning's papers, with news about starters for the Derby and the beginning of the cricket season, and some paragraphs about how Balkan affairs were settling down and a British squadron was going to Kiel.

When I had done with them I got out Scudder's little black pocket-book and studied it. It was pretty well filled with jottings, chiefly figures, though now and then a name was printed in. For example, I found the words 'Hofgaard', 'Luneville', and 'Avocado' pretty often, and especially the word 'Pavia'.

Now I was certain that Scudder never did anything without a reason, and I was pretty sure that there was a cipher in all this. That is a subject which has always interested me, and I did a bit at it myself once as intelligence officer at Delagoa Bay during the Boer War. I have a head for things like chess and puzzles, and I used to reckon myself pretty good at finding out ciphers. This one looked like the numerical kind where sets of figures correspond to the letters of the alphabet, but any fairly shrewd man can find the clue to that sort after an hour or two's work, and I didn't think Scudder would have been content with anything so easy. So I fastened on the printed words, for you can make a pretty good numerical cipher if you have a key word which gives you the sequence of the letters. I tried for hours, but none of the words answered.

Then I fell asleep and woke at Dumfries just in time to bundle out and get into the slow Galloway train. There was a man on the platform whose looks I didn't like, but he never glanced at me, and when I caught sight of myself in the mirror of an automatic machine, I didn't wonder. With my brown face, my old tweeds and my slouch I was the very model of one of the hill farmers who were crowding into the third-class carriages.

I travelled with half a dozen in an atmosphere of shag and clay pipes. They had come from the weekly market, and their mouths were full of prices. I heard accounts of how the lambing had gone up the Cairn and the Deuch and a dozen other mysterious waters. Above half the men had lunched heavily and were highly flavoured with whisky, but they took no notice of me. We rumbled slowly into a land of little wooded glens and then to a great, wide moorland place, gleaming with lochs, with high, blue hills showing northwards.

About five o'clock the carriage had emptied and I was left alone as I had hoped. I got out at the next station, a little place whose name I scarcely noted, set right in the heart of a bog. It reminded me of one of those forgotten little stations in the Karroo. An old station-master was digging in his garden, and with his spade over his shoulder sauntered to the train, took charge of a parcel and went back to his potatoes. A child of ten received my ticket, and I emerged on a white road that straggled over the brown moor.

It was a gorgeous spring evening, with every hill showing as clear as a cut amethyst. The air had the queer rooty smell of bogs, but it was as fresh as mid-ocean, and it had the strangest effect on my spirits. I actually felt light-hearted. I might have been a boy out for a spring holiday tramp, instead of a man of thirty-seven very much wanted by the police. I felt just as I used to feel when I was starting for a big trek on a frosty morning on the high veld. If you believe me, I swung along that road whistling. There was no plan of campaign in my head, only just to go on and on in this blessed honest-smelling hill country, for every mile put me in better humour with myself.

In a roadside planting I cut a walking stick of hazel, and presently struck off the highway up a by-path which followed the glen of a brawling stream. I reckoned that I was still far ahead of any pursuit, and for that night might please myself. It was some hours since I had tasted food, and I was getting very hungry when I came to a herd's cottage set in a nook beside a waterfall. A brown-faced woman was standing by the door, and greeted me with the kindly shyness of moorland places. When I asked for a night's lodging she said I was welcome to the 'bed in the loft', and very soon she set before me a hearty meal of ham and eggs, scones, and thick sweet milk. At the darkening her man came in from the hills, a lean giant who in one step covered as much ground as three paces of ordinary mortals. They asked no questions, for they had the perfect breeding of all dwellers in the wilds, but I could see they set me down as some kind of dealer, and I took some trouble to confirm their view. I spoke a lot about cattle, of which my host knew little, and I picked up from him a good deal about the local Galloway markets, which I tucked away in my memory for future use. At ten I was nodding in my chair, and the 'bed in the loft' received a weary man, who never opened his eyes till five o'clock set the little homestead a-going once more.

They refused any payment, and by six I had breakfasted and was striding southwards again. My notion was to return to the railway line a station or two further on than the place where I had alighted yesterday and to double back. I reckoned that was the safest way, for the police would naturally assume that I was always making further from London in the direction of some western port. I thought I had still a good bit of a start, for, as I reasoned, it would take some hours to fix the blame on me and several more to identify the fellow who got on board the train at St. Pancras.

It was the same jolly clear spring weather and I simply could not contrive to feel careworn. Indeed, I was in better spirits than I had been for months. Over a long ridge of moorland I took my road, skirting the side of a high hill which the herd had called Cairnsmore of Fleet. Nestling curlews and plovers were crying everywhere and the links of green pasture by the streams were dotted with young lambs. All the slackness of the past months was slipping from my bones and I stepped out like a four-year-old. By and by I came to a swell of moorland which dipped to the vale of a little river, and a mile away in the heather I saw the smoke of a train.

The station, when I reached it, proved to be ideal for my purpose. The moor surged up around it and left room only for the single line, the slender siding, a waiting-room, an office, the station-master's cottage, and a tiny yard of gooseberries and sweet-william. There seemed no road to it from anywhere, and to increase the desolation the waves of a tarn lapped on their grey granite beach half a mile away. I waited in the deep heather till I saw the smoke of an east-going train on the horizon. Then I approached the tiny booking-office and took a ticket for Dumfries.

The only occupants of the carriage were an old shepherd and his dog – a wall-eyed brute that I mistrusted. The man was asleep and on the cushions beside him was that morning's *Scotsman*. Eagerly I seized on it, for I fancied it would tell me something.

There were two columns about the Portland Place murder, as it was called. My man Paddock had given the alarm and had the milkman arrested. Poor devil, it looked as if the latter had earned his sovereign hardly; but for me he had been cheap at the price, for he seemed to have occupied the police the better part of the day. In the stop-press news I found a further instalment of the story. The milkman had been released, I read, and the true criminal, about whose identity the police were reticent, was believed to have got away from London by one of the northern lines. There was a short note about me as the owner of the flat. I guessed the police had stuck that in, as a clumsy contrivance to persuade me that I was unsuspected.

There was nothing else in the paper, nothing about foreign politics or Karolides or the things that had interested Scudder. I laid it down, and found that we were approaching the station at which I had got out yesterday. The potato-digging station-master had been gingered up into some activity, for the west-going train was waiting to let us pass and from it had descended three men who were asking him questions. I supposed that they were the local police who had been stirred up by Scotland Yard and had traced me as far as this one-horse siding. Sitting well back in the shadow I watched them carefully. One of them had a book and took down notes. The old potato-digger seemed to have turned peevish, but the child who had collected my ticket was talking volubly. All the party looked out across the moor where the white road departed. I hoped they were going to take up my tracks there.

As we moved away from that station my companion woke up. He fixed me with a wondering glance, kicked his dog viciously and inquired where he was. Clearly he was very drunk.

'That's what comes o' bein' a teetotaller,' he observed in bitter regret.

I expressed my surprise that in him I should have met a blue-ribbon stalwart.

'Aye, but I'm a strong teetotaller,' he said pugnaciously. 'I took the pledge last Martinmas, and I havena touched a drop o' whisky sinsyne. No even at Hogmanay, though I was sair tempted.'

He swung his heels up on the seat and burrowed a frowsy head into the cushions.

'And that's a' I get,' he moaned. 'A held hetter than hell fire and twae een lookin' different ways for the Sabbath.'

'What did it?' I asked.

'A drink they ca' brandy. Bein' a teetotaller, I keepit off the whisky, but I was nipnippin' a' day yestereen at this brandy, and I doubt I'll no be weel for a fortnicht.'

His voice died away into a stutter, and sleep once more laid its heavy hand on him.

My plan had been to get out at some station down the line, but the train suddenly gave me a better chance, for it came to a standstill at the end of a culvert which spanned a brawling porter-coloured river. I looked out and saw that every carriage window was closed and no human figure appeared in the landscape. So I opened the door, and dropped quickly into the tangle of hazels which edged the line.

It would have been all right but for that infernal dog. Under the impression that I was decamping with its master's belongings, it started to bark and all but got me by the trousers. This woke up the herd who stood bawling at the carriage door in the belief that I had committed suicide. I crawled through the thicket, reached the edge of the stream, and in cover of the bushes put a hundred yards or so behind me. Then from my shelter I peered back, and saw that the guard and several passengers gathered round the open carriage door and stared in my direction. I could not have made a more public departure if I had left with a bugler and a brass band.

Happily the drunken herd provided a diversion. He and his dog, which was attached by a rope to his waist, suddenly cascaded out of the carriage, landed on their heads on the track, and rolled some way down the bank towards the water. In the rescue which followed, the dog bit somebody, for I could hear the sound of hard swearing. Presently they had forgotten me, and when after a quarter of a mile's crawl I ventured to look back, the train had started again and was vanishing in the cutting.

I was in a wide semi-circle of moorland, with the brown river as radius, and the high hills forming the northern circumference. There was not a sign or sound of a human being, only the plashing water and the interminable crying of curlews. Yet, oddly enough, for the first time I felt the terror of the hunted on me. It was not the police that I thought of, but the other folk, who knew that I knew Scudder's secret and dared not let me live. I was certain that they would pursue me with a keenness and vigilance unknown to the British law, and that once their grip closed on me I should find no mercy.

I looked back, but there was nothing in the landscape. The sun glinted on the metals of the line and the wet stones in the stream, and you could not have found a more peaceful sight in the world. Nevertheless, I started to run. Crouching low in the runnels of the bog, I ran till the sweat blinded my eyes. The mood did not leave me till I had reached the rim of mountain and flung myself panting on a ridge high above the young waters of the brown river.

From my vantage ground I could scan the whole moor right away to the railway line and to the south of it where green fields took the place of heather. I have eyes like a hawk, but I could see nothing moving in the whole countryside. Then I looked east beyond the ridge and saw a new kind of landscape – shallow green valleys with plentiful fir plantations and the faint lines of dust which spoke of highroads. Last of all I looked into the blue May sky, and there I saw that which set my pulses racing. Low down in the south a monoplane was climbing into the heavens. I was as certain as if I had been told that that aeroplane was looking for me, and that it did not belong to the police. For an hour or two I watched it from a pit of heather. It flew low along the hilltops and then in narrow circles back over the valley up which I had come. Then it seemed to change its mind, rose to a great height and flew away back to the south.

I did not like this espionage from the air, and I began to think less well of the countryside I had chosen for a refuge. These heather hills were no sort of cover if my enemies were in the sky, and I must find a different kind of sanctuary. I looked with more satisfaction to the green country beyond the ridge, for there I should find woods and stone houses.

About six in the evening I came out of the moorland to a white ribbon of road which wound up the narrow vale of a lowland stream. As I followed it, fields gave place to bent, the glen became a plateau, and presently I had reached a kind of pass, where a solitary house smoked in the twilight. The road swung over a bridge and leaning on the parapet was a young man.

He was smoking a long clay pipe and studying the water with spectacled eyes. In his left hand was a small book with a finger marking the place. Slowly he repeated –

'As when a Gryphon through the wilderness,
With winged step, o'er hill and moory dale
Pursues the Arimaspian.'

He jumped round as my step rung on the keystone, and I saw a pleasant, sunburnt, boyish face.

'Good-evening to you,' he said gravely. 'It's a fine night for the road.'

The smell of peat smoke and of some savoury roast floated to me from the house. 'Is that place an inn?' I asked.

'At your service,' he said politely. 'I am the landlord, sir, and I hope you will stay the night, for to tell you the truth I have had no company for a week.'

I pulled myself up on the parapet of the bridge and filled my pipe. I began to detect an ally.

'You're young to be an innkeeper,' I said.

'My father died a year ago and left me the business. I live there with my grandmother. It's a slow job for a young man, and it wasn't my choice of profession.'

'Which was?'

He actually blushed. 'I want to write books,' he said.

'And what better chance could you ask?' I cried. 'Man, I've often thought that an innkeeper would make the best story-teller in the world.'

'Not now,' he said eagerly. 'Maybe in the old days when you had pilgrims and ballad-makers and highwaymen and mail-coaches on the road; but not now. Nothing comes here but motor-cars full of fat women, who stop for lunch, and a fisherman or two in the spring, and the shooting tenant in August. There is not much material to be got out of that. I want to see life, to travel the world, and write things like Kipling and Conrad. But the most I've done yet is to get some verses printed in *Chambers' Journal.*'

I looked at the inn, standing golden in the sunset against the wine-red hills.

'I've knocked a bit about the world and I wouldn't despise such a hermitage. D'you think that adventure is found only in the tropics or among gentry in red shirts? Maybe you're rubbing shoulders with it at this moment.'

'That's what Kipling says,' he said, his eyes brightening, and he quoted some verse about 'Romance bringing up the 9.15.'

'Here's a true tale for you then,' I cried, 'and a month hence you can make a novel out of it.'

Sitting on the bridge in the soft May gloaming, I pitched him a lovely yarn. It was true in essentials, too, though I altered the minor details. I made out that I was a mining magnate from Kimberley, who had had a lot of trouble with I. D. B. and had shown up a gang. They had pursued me across the ocean and had killed my best friend and were now on my tracks.

I told the story well, though I say it who shouldn't. I pictured a flight across the Kalahari to German Africa, the crackling, parching days, the wonderful blue-velvet nights. I described an attack on my life on the voyage home, and I made a really horrid affair of the Portland Place murder.

'You're looking for adventure,' I cried. 'Well, you've found it here. The devils are after me, and the police are after them. It's a race that I mean to win.'

'By God,' he whispered, drawing his breath in sharply, 'it is all pure Rider Haggard and Conan Doyle.'

'You believe me,' I said gratefully.

'Of course I do,' and he held out his hand. 'I believe everything out of the common. The only thing to distrust is the normal.'

He was very young, but he was the man for my money.

'I think they're off my track for the moment, but I must lie close for a couple of days. Can you take me in?'

He caught my elbow in his eagerness and drew me towards the house. 'You can lie as snug here as if you were in a moss-hole. I'll see that nobody blabs, either. And you'll give me some more material about your adventures?'

As I entered the inn porch I heard from far off the beat of an engine. There silhouetted against the dusky west was my friend, the monoplane.

*   *   *

He gave me a room at the back of the house with a fine outlook over the plateau and he made me free of his own study, which was stacked with cheap editions of his favourite authors. I never saw the grandmother, so I guessed she was bed-ridden. An old woman called Margit brought me my meals, and the innkeeper was around me at all hours. I wanted some time to myself, so I invented a job for him. He had a motor bicycle, and I sent him off next morning for the daily paper, which usually arrived with the post in the late afternoon. I told him to keep his eyes skinned, and make note of any strange figures be saw, keeping a special sharp lookout for motors and aeroplanes. Then I sat down in real earnest to Scudder's note-book.

He came back at midday with the *Scotsman*. There was nothing in it except some further evidence of Paddock and the milkman, and a repetition of yesterday's statement that the murderer had gone north. But there was a long article, reprinted from the *Times*, about Karolides and the state of affairs in the Balkans, though there was no mention of any visit to England. I got rid of the innkeeper for the afternoon, for I was getting very warm in my search for the cipher.

As I told you, it was a numerical cipher, and by an elaborate system of experiments I had pretty well discovered what were the nulls and stops. The trouble was the key word, and when I thought of the odd million words he might have used I felt pretty hopeless. But about three o'clock I had a sudden inspiration.

The name Julia Czechenyi flashed across my memory. Scudder had said it was the key to the Karolides business and it occurred to me to try it on his cipher.

It worked. The five letters of 'Julia' gave me the position of the vowels. A was J, the tenth letter of the alphabet, and so represented by X in the cipher. E was U = XXI and so on. 'Czechenyi' gave me the numerals for the principal consonants. I scribbled that scheme on a bit of paper and sat down to read Scudder's pages.

In half an hour I was reading with a whitish face and fingers that drummed on the table. I glanced out of the window and saw a big touring-car coming up the glen towards the inn. It drew up at the door and there was the sound of people alighting. There seemed to be two of them, men in acquascutums and tweed caps.

Ten minutes later the innkeeper slipped into the room, his eyes bright with excitement.

'There's two chaps below looking for you,' he whispered. 'They're in the dining-room having whiskys and sodas. They asked about you and said they had hoped to meet you here. Oh! and they described you jolly well, down to your boots and shirt. I told them you had been here last night and had gone off on a motor bicycle this morning, and one of the chaps swore like a navvy.'

I made him tell me what they looked like. One was a dark-eyed, thin fellow with bushy eyebrows, the other was always smiling and lisped in his talk. Neither was any kind of foreigner; on this my young friend was positive.

I took a bit of paper and wrote these words in German as if they were part of a letter:

...Black Stone. Scudder had got on to this, but be could not act for a fortnight. I doubt if I can do any good now, especially as Karolides is uncertain about his plans. But if Mr T. advises I will do the best I...

I manufactured it rather neatly, so that it looked like a loose page of a private letter.

'Take this down and say it was found in my bedroom and ask them to return it to me if they overtake me.'

Three minutes later I heard the car begin to move, and peeping from behind the curtain, caught sight of the two figures. One was slim, the other was sleek; that was the most I could make of my reconnaissance.

The innkeeper appeared in great excitement. 'Your paper woke them up,' he said gleefully. 'The dark fellow went as white as death and cursed like blazes, and the fat one whistled and looked ugly. They paid for their drinks with half a sovereign and wouldn't wait for change.'

'Now I'll tell you what I want you to do,' I said. 'Get on your bicycle and go off to Newtown Stewart to the chief constable. Describe the two men, and say you suspect them of having had something to do with the London murder. You can invent reasons. The two will come back, never fear. Not tonight, for they'll follow me forty miles along the road, but first thing tomorrow morning. Tell police to be here bright and early.'

He set off like a docile child, while I worked at Scudder's notes. When he came back we dined together and in common decency I had to let him pump me. I gave him a lot of stuff about lion hunts and the Matabele War, thinking all the while what tame businesses these were compared to this I was now engaged in. When he went to bed I sat up and finished Scudder. I smoked in a chair till daylight, for I could not sleep.

About eight next morning I witnessed the arrival of two constables and a sergeant. They put their car in a coach-house under the innkeeper's instructions and entered the house.

Twenty minutes later I saw from my window a second car come across the plateau from the opposite direction. It did not come up to the inn, but stopped two hundred yards off in the shelter of a patch of wood. I noticed that its occupants carefully reversed it before leaving it. A minute or two later I heard their steps on the gravel outside the window. My plan had been to lie hid in my bedroom and see what happened. I had a notion that, if I could bring the police and my other more dangerous pursuers together, something might work out of it to my advantage. But now I had a better idea. I scribbled a line of thanks to my host, opened the window and dropped quietly into a gooseberry bush. Unobserved I crossed the dyke, crawled down the side of a tributary burn, and won the highroad on the far side of the patch of trees. There stood the car, very spick and span in the morning sunlight, but with the dust on her which told of a long journey. I started her, jumped into the chauffeur's seat, and stole gently out on to the plateau. Almost at once the road dipped so that I lost sight of the inn, but the wind seemed to bring me the sound of angry voices.

CHAPTER 4

THE ADVENTURE OF
THE RADICAL CANDIDATE

You may picture me driving that forty-horse-power car for all she was worth over the crisp moor roads on that shining May morning; glancing back at first over my shoulder and looking anxiously to the next turning; then driving with a vague eye, just wide enough awake to keep on the highway. For I was thinking desperately of what I had found in Scudder's pocket-book.

The little man had told me a pack of lies. All his yarns about the Balkans and the Jew-anarchists and the Foreign Office conference were eye-wash, and so was Karolides. And yet not quite, as you shall hear. I had staked everything on my belief in his story and had been let down; here was his book telling me a different tale, and instead of being once-bit-twice-shy, I believed it absolutely. Why? I don't know.

It rang desperately true, and the first yarn, if you understand me, had been in a queer way true also in spirit. The fifteenth day of June was going to be a day of destiny, a bigger destiny than the killing of a Dago. It was so big that I didn't blame Scudder for keeping me out of the game, and wanting to play a lone hand. That, I was pretty clear, was his intention. He had told me something which sounded big enough, but the real thing was so immortally big that he, the man who had found it out, wanted it all for himself. I didn't blame him. It was risks after all that he was chiefly greedy about.

The whole story was in the notes – with gaps, you understand, which he would have filled up from his memory. He stuck down his authorities too, and had an odd trick of giving them all a numerical value and then striking a balance, which stood for the reliability of each stage in the yarn. The three names he had printed were authorities, and there was a man, Ducrosne, who got five out of a possible five, and another fellow, Ammersfoort, who got three. The bare bones of the tale were all that was in the book – that, and one queer phrase which occurred half a dozen times inside brackets. 'Thirty-nine steps' was the phrase, and at its last time of use it ran – 'Thirty-nine steps, I counted them; high tide 10:17 p.m.' I could make nothing of that.

The first thing I learned was that it was no question of preventing a war. That was coming, as sure as Christmas: had been arranged, said Scudder, ever since February, 1912. Karolides was going to be the occasion. He was booked all right and was to hand in his checks on June 14th, two weeks and four days from that May morning. I gathered from Scudder's notes that nothing on earth could prevent that. His talk of Epirote guards that would skin their own grandmother was all billy-o.

The second thing was that this war was going to come as a mighty surprise to Britain. Karolides' death would set the Balkans by the ears, and then Vienna would chip in with an ultimatum. Russia wouldn't like that, and there would be high words. But Berlin would play the peacemaker and pour oil on the waters, till suddenly she would find a good cause for a quarrel, pick it up, and in five hours let fly at us. That was the idea, and a pretty good one too. Honey and fair speeches and then a stroke in the dark. While we were talking about the good will and good intentions of Germany, our coast would be silently ringed with mines, and submarines would be waiting for every battleship.

But all this depended upon the third thing, which was due to happen on June 15th. I would never have grasped this, if I hadn't once happened to meet a French staff officer, coming back from West Africa, who had told me a lot of things. One was that in spite of all the nonsense talked in Parliament there was a real working alliance between France and Britain, and that the two General Staffs met every now and then and made plans for joint action in time of war. Well, in June, a very great swell was coming over from Paris, and he was going to get nothing less than a statement of the disposition of the British home fleet on mobilization. At least I gathered it was something like that; anyhow, it was something uncommonly important. But on the 15th day of June there were to be others in London – others at whom I could only guess. Scudder was content to call them collectively the 'Black Stone.' They represented not our allies, but our deadly foes, and the information, destined for France, was to be diverted to their pockets. And it was to be used, remember – used a week or two later, with great guns and swift torpedoes, suddenly in the darkness of a summer night.

This was the story I had been deciphering in a back room of a country inn, overlooking a cabbage garden. This was the story that hummed in my brain, as I swung in the big touring-car from glen to glen.

My first impulse had been to write a letter to the Prime Minister, but a little reflection convinced me that that would be useless. Who would believe my tale? I must show a sign, some token in proof, and heaven knew what that could be. Above all I must keep going myself, ready to act when things got riper, and that was going to be no light job with the police of the British Isles in full cry after me, and the watchers of the Black Stone running silently and swiftly on my trail.

I had no very clear purpose in my journey, but I steered east by the sun, for I remembered from the map that if I went north I would come into a region of coal-pits and industrial towns. Presently I was down from the moorlands and traversing the broad haugh of a river. For miles I ran alongside a park wall, and in a break of the trees I saw a great castle. I swung through little old thatched villages, and over peaceful lowland streams, and past gardens blazing with hawthorn and yellow laburnum. The land was so deep in peace that I could scarcely believe that somewhere behind me were those who sought my life; ay, and that in a month's time, unless I had the almightiest of luck, these round, country faces would be pinched and staring, and men would be lying dead in English fields.

About midday I entered a long straggling village, and had a mind to stop and eat. Half way down was the post-office, and on the steps of it stood the post-mistress and a policeman hard at work conning a telegram. When they saw me they wakened up, and the policeman advanced with raised hand and cried on me to stop.

I nearly was fool enough to obey. Then it flashed upon me that the wire had to do with me, that my friends at the inn had come to an understanding and were united in desiring to see more of me, and that it had been easy enough for them to wire the description of me and the car to thirty villages through which I might pass. I released the brakes just in time. As it was the policeman made a claw at the hood and only dropped off when he got my left in his eye.

I saw that main roads were no place for me, and turned into the byways. It wasn't an easy job without a map, for there was the risk of getting onto a farm road and ending in a duck-pond or a stable-yard, and I couldn't afford that kind of delay. I began to see what an ass I had been to steal the car. The big green brute would be the safest kind of clue to me over the breadth of Scotland. If I left it and took to my feet, it would be discovered in an hour or two and I would get no start in the race.

The immediate thing to do was to get to the loneliest roads. These I soon found when I struck up a tributary of the big river, and got into a glen which climbed over a pass. Here I met nobody, but it was taking me too far north, so I slewed east along a bad track and finally struck a big double-line railway. Away below me I saw another broadish valley, and it occurred to me that if I crossed it I might find some remote hostelry to pass the night. The evening was now drawing in, and I was furiously hungry, for I had eaten nothing since breakfast except a couple of buns I had bought from a baker's cart.

Just then I heard a noise in the sky, and lo and behold there was that infernal aeroplane, flying low, about a dozen miles to the south and rapidly coming towards me.

I had the sense to remember that on a bare moor I was at the aeroplane's mercy, and that my only chance was to get to the leafy cover of the valley. Down the hill I went like blue lightning, screwing my head round whenever I dared, to watch that damned flying machine. Soon I was on a road between hedges, and dipping to the deep-cut glen of a stream. Then came a bit of thick wood, where I slackened speed.

Suddenly on my left I heard the hoot of another car and realized to my horror that I was almost upon a couple of gate-posts through which a private road debouched on the highway. My horn gave an agonized roar, but it was too late. I clapped on my brakes, but my impetus was too great, and there before me a car was sliding athwart my course. In a second there would have been the deuce of a wreck. I did the only thing possible, and ran slap into the hedge on the right trusting to find something soft beyond.

But there I was mistaken. My car slithered through the hedge like butter and then gave a sickening plunge forward. I saw what was coming, leaped on the seat and would have jumped out. But a branch of hawthorn got me in the chest, lifted me up and held me, while a ton or two of expensive metal slipped below me, bucked and pitched, and then dropped with an almighty smash fifty feet to the bed of the stream.

*   *   *

Slowly that thorn let me go. I subsided first on the hedge, and then very gently on a bower of nettles. As I scrambled to my feet a hand took me by the arm, and a sympathetic and badly scared voice asked me if I were hurt.

I found myself looking at a tall young man in goggles and a leather ulster who kept on blessing his soul and whinnying apologies. For myself, once I got my wind back, I was rather glad than otherwise. This was one way of getting rid of the car.

'My blame, sir,' I answered him. 'It's lucky that I did not add homicide to my follies. That's the end of my Scotch motor tour, but it might have been the end of my life.'

He plucked out a watch and studied it.

'You're the right sort of fellow,' he said. 'I can spare a quarter of an hour, and my house is two minutes off. I'll see you clothed and fed and snug in bed. Where's your kit, by the way? Is it in the burn along with the car?'

'It's in my pocket,' I said, brandishing a tooth-brush. 'I'm a colonial and travel light.'

'A colonial,' he cried. 'By Gad, you're the very man I've been praying for. Are you by any blessed chance a Free Trader?'

'I am,' said I, without the foggiest notion of what he meant.

He patted my shoulder and hurried me into his car. Three minutes later we drew up before a comfortable-looking shooting-box set among pine trees, and he ushered me indoors. He took me first to a bedroom and flung half a dozen of his suits before me, for my own had been pretty well reduced to rags. I selected a loose blue serge, which differed most conspicuously from my own garments, and borrowed a linen collar. Then he haled me to the dining-room, where the remnants of a meal stood on the table, and announced that I had just five minutes to feed. 'You can take a snack in your pocket, and we'll have supper when we get back. I've got to be at the Masonic Hall at eight o'clock or my agent will comb my hair.'

I had a cup of coffee and some cold ham, while he yarned away on the hearth-rug.

'You find me in the deuce of a mess, Mr —; by the by, you haven't told me your name. Twisden? Any relation of old Tommy Twisden of the Sixtieth? No? Well, you see I'm Liberal candidate for this part of the world, and I had a meeting on tonight at Brattleburn – that's my chief town, and an infernal Tory stronghold. I had got the Colonial ex-Premier fellow, Crumpleton, coming to speak for me tonight, and had the thing tremendously billed and the whole place ground-baited. This afternoon I got a wire from the ruffian saying he has got influenza at Blackpool, and here am I left to do the whole thing myself. I had meant to speak for ten minutes and must now go on for forty, and, though I've been racking my brains for three hours to think of something, I simply cannot last the course. Now you've got to be a good chap and help me. You're a Free Trader and can tell our people what a washout Protection is in the Colonies. All you fellows have the gift of the gab – I wish to heaven I had it. I'll be for evermore in your debt.'

I had very few notions about free trade one way or the other, but I saw no other chance to get what I wanted. My young gentleman was far too absorbed in his own difficulties to think how odd it was to ask a stranger who had just missed death by an ace and had lost a one-thousand-guinea car to address a meeting for him on the spur of the moment. But my necessities did not allow me to contemplate oddnesses or to pick and choose my supports.

'All right,' I said. 'I'm not much good as a speaker, but I'll tell them a bit about Australia.'

At my words the cares of the ages slipped from his shoulders and he was rapturous in his thanks. He lent me a big driving coat – and never troubled to ask why I had started on a motor tour without possessing an ulster – and as we slipped down the dusty roads poured into my ears the simple facts of his history. He was an orphan and his uncle had brought him up – I've forgotten the uncle's name, but he was in the Cabinet and you can read his speeches in the papers. He had gone round the world after leaving Cambridge, and then, being short of a job, his uncle had advised politics. I gathered that he had no preference in parties. 'Good chaps in both,' he said cheerfully, 'and plenty of blighters, too.

I'm Liberal, because my family have always been Whigs.' But if he was lukewarm politically he had strong views on other things. He found out I knew a bit about horses, and jawed away about the Derby entries; and he was full of plans for improving his shooting. Altogether, a very clean, decent, callow young man.

As we passed through a little town two policemen signalled us to stop, and flashed their lanterns on us. 'Beg pardon, Sir Harry,' said one. 'We've got instructions to look out for a car and the description's not unlike yours.'

'Right-o,' said my host, while I thanked Providence for the devious ways I had been brought to safety. After that we spoke no more, for my host's mind began to labour heavily with his coming speech. His lips kept muttering, his eyes wandered, and I began to prepare myself for a second catastrophe. I tried to think of something to say myself, but my mind was dry as a stone. The next thing I knew we had drawn up outside a door in a street and were being welcomed by some noisy gentlemen with rosettes.

The hall had about five hundred in it, women mostly, a lot of bald heads, and a dozen or two young men. The chairman, a weaselly minister with a reddish nose, lamented Crumpleton's absence, soliloquized on his influenza, and gave me a certificate as a 'trusted leader of Australian thought.' There were two policemen at the door and I hoped they took note of that testimonial. Then Sir Harry started.

I never heard anything like it. He didn't begin to know how to talk. He had about a bushel of notes from which he read, and when he let go of them he fell into one prolonged stutter. Every now and then he remembered a phrase he had learned by heart, straightened his back, and gave it off like Henry Irving, and the next moment he was bent double and crooning over his papers. It was the most appalling rot, too. He talked about the 'German menace', and said it was all a Tory invention to cheat the poor of their rights and keep back the great flood of social reform, but that 'organized labour' realized this and laughed the Tories to scorn. He was all for reducing our navy as a proof of our good faith, and then sending Germany an ultimatum telling her to do the same or we would knock her into a cocked hat. He said that but for the Tories, Germany and Britain would be fellow workers in peace and reform.

I thought of the little black book in my pocket! A giddy lot Scudder's friends cared for peace and reform.

Yet in a queer way I liked the speech. You could see the niceness of the chap shining out behind the muck with which he had been spoon-fed. Also it took a load off my mind. I mightn't be much of an orator, but I was a thousand per cent better than Sir Harry.

I didn't get on so badly when it came to my turn. I simply told them all I could remember about Australia, praying there should be no Australian there – all about its labour party and emigration and universal service. I doubt if I remembered to mention free trade, but I said there were no Tories in Australia, only Labour and Liberals. That fetched a cheer, and I woke them up a bit when I started in to tell them the kind of glorious business I thought could be made out of the Empire if we really put our backs into it.

Altogether I fancy I was rather a success. The minister didn't like me, though, and when he proposed a vote of thanks spoke of Sir Harry's speech as 'statesmanlike', and mine as having 'the eloquence of an emigration agent'.

When we were in the car again my host was in wild spirits at having got his job over. 'A ripping speech, Twisden,' he said. 'Now, you're coming home with me. I'm all alone, and if you'll stop a day or two I'll show you some very decent fishing.'

We had a hot supper – and I wanted it pretty badly – and then drank grog in a big, cheery smoking-room with a crackling wood fire. I thought the time had come for me to put my cards on the table. I saw by this man's eye that he was the kind you can trust.

'Listen, Sir Harry,' I said. 'I've something pretty important to say to you. You're a good fellow and I'm going to be frank. Where on earth did you get that poisonous rubbish you talked tonight?'

His face fell. 'Was it as bad as that?' he asked ruefully. 'It did sound rather thin. I got most of it out of the *Progressive Magazine* and pamphlets that agent chap of mine keeps sending me. But you surely don't think Germany would ever go to war with us?'

'Ask that question in six weeks and it won't need an answer,' I said. 'If you'll give me your attention for half an hour I am going to tell you a story.'

I can see yet that bright room with the deers' heads and the old prints on the walls, Sir Harry standing restlessly on the stone curb of the hearth, and myself lying back in an armchair, speaking. I seemed to be another person, standing aside and listening to my own voice, and judging carefully the reliability of my tale. It was the first time I had ever told any one the exact truth, so far as I understood it, and it did me no end of good, for it straightened out the thing in my own mind. I blinked no detail. He heard all about Scudder and the milkman, and the note-book, and my doings in Galloway. Presently he got very excited and walked up and down the hearth-rug.

'So you see,' I concluded, 'you have got here in your house the man that is wanted for the Portland Place murder. Your duty is to send your car for the police and give me up. I don't think I'll get very far. There'll be an accident and I'll have a knife in my ribs an hour or so after arrest. Nevertheless it's your duty, as a law-abiding citizen. Perhaps in a month's time you'll be sorry, but you have no cause to think of that.'

He was looking at me with bright, steady eyes. 'What was your job in Rhodesia, Mr Hannay?' he asked.

'Mining engineer,' I said. 'I've made my pile cleanly and I've had a good time in the making of it.'

'Not a profession that weakens the nerves, is it?'

I laughed. 'Oh, as to that, my nerves are good enough.' I took down a hunting knife from a stand on the wall, and did the old Mashona trick of tossing it and catching it in my lips. That wants a pretty steady heart.

He watched me with a smile. 'I don't want proofs. I may be an ass on a platform, but I can size up a man. You're no murderer and you're no fool, and I believe you are speaking the truth. I'm going to back you up. Now, what can I do?'

'First, I want you to write a letter to your uncle. I've got to get in touch with the government people some time before the 15th of June.'

He pulled his moustache.

'That won't help you. This is Foreign Office business and my uncle would have nothing to do with it. Besides, you'd never convince him. No, I'll go one better. I'll write to the permanent secretary at the Foreign Office. He's my godfather and one of the best going. What do you want?'

He sat down at a table and wrote to my dictation. The gist of it was that if a man called Twisden (I thought I had better stick to that name) turned up before June 15th he was to treat him kindly. He said Twisden would prove his *bona fides* by passing the words 'Black Stone' and whistling 'Annie Laurie'.

'Good,' said Sir Harry. 'That's the proper style. By the way you'll find my godfather – his name's Sir Walter Bullivant – down at his country cottage for Whitsuntide. It's close to Artinswell on the Kennet. That's done. Now, what's the next thing?'

'You're about my height. Lend me the oldest tweed suit you've got. Anything will do, so long as the colour is the opposite of the clothes I destroyed this afternoon. Then show me a map of the neighbourhood and explain to me the lie of the land. Lastly, if the police come asking about me, just show them the car in the glen. If the other lot turn up tell them I caught the south express after your meeting.'

He did, or promised to do, all these things. I shaved off the remnants of my moustache, and got inside an ancient suit of what I believe is called heather mixture. The map gave me some notion of my whereabouts and told me the two things I wanted to know – where the main railway to the south could be joined and what were the wildest districts near at hand.

At two o'clock he wakened me from my slumbers in the smoking-room armchair and led me blinking into the dark, starry night. An old bicycle was found in a tool-shed and handed over to me.

'First turn to the right up by the long fir-wood,' he enjoined. 'By daybreak you'll be well into the hills. Then I should pitch the machine into a bog and take to the moors on foot. You can put in a week among the shepherds, and be as safe as if you were in New Guinea.'

I pedalled diligently up steep roads of hill gravel till the skies grew pale with morning. As the mists cleared before the sun I found myself in a wide green world with glens falling on every side and a faraway blue horizon. Here at any rate I could get early news of my enemies.

CHAPTER 5

THE ADVENTURE OF
THE SPECTACLED ROADMAN

I sat down on the very crest of the pass and took stock of my position.

Behind me was the road climbing through a long cleft in the hills which was the upper glen of some notable river. In front was a flat space of maybe a mile all pitted with bog-holes and rough with tussocks, and then beyond it the road fell steeply down another glen to a plain whose blue dimness melted into the distance. To left and right were round-shouldered, green hills as smooth as pancakes, but to the south – that is the left hand – there was a glimpse of high heathery mountains which I remembered from the map as the big knot of hill which I had chosen for my sanctuary. I was on the central boss of a huge upland country, and could see everything moving for miles. In the meadows below the road, half a mile back, a cottage smoked, but it was the only sign of human life. Otherwise there was only the calling of plovers and the tinkling of little streams.

It was now about seven o'clock, and as I waited I heard once again the ominous beat in the air. Then I realized that my vantage ground might be in reality a trap. There was no cover for a tomtit in those bald green places.

I sat quite still and hopeless while the beat grew louder. Then I saw an aeroplane coming up from the east. It was flying high, but as I looked it dropped several hundred feet and began to circle round the knot of hill in narrowing circles, just as a hawk wheels before it pounces. Now it was flying very low, and now the observer on board caught sight of me. I could see one of the two occupants examining me through glasses. Suddenly it began to rise in swift whorls, and the next I knew it was speeding eastward again till it became a speck in the blue morning.

That made me do some savage thinking. My enemies had located me, and the next thing would be a cordon round me. I didn't know what force they could command, but I was certain it would be sufficient. The aeroplane had seen my bicycle, and would conclude that I would try to escape by the road. In that case there might be a chance on the moors to the right or left. I wheeled the machine a hundred yards from the highway, and plunged it into a moss-hole where it sank among pond-weed and water buttercups. Then I climbed to a knoll which gave me a view of the two valleys. Nothing was stirring on the long white ribbon that threaded them.

I have said there was not cover in the whole place to hide a rat. As the day advanced it was flooded with soft fresh light till it had the fragrant sunniness of the South African veld. At other times I would have liked the place, but now it seemed to suffocate me. The free moorlands were prison walls, and the keen hill-air was the breath of a dungeon.

I tossed a coin – heads right, tails left – and it fell heads, so I turned to the north. In a little I came to the brow of the ridge which was the containing wall of the pass. I saw the highroad for maybe ten miles, and far down it something that was moving and that I took to be a motor-car. Beyond the ridge I looked on a rolling green moor, which fell away into wooded glens. Now my life on the veld has given me the eyes of a kite, and I can see things for which most men need a telescope. Away down the slope, a couple of miles away, several men were advancing like a row of beaters at a shoot.

I dropped out of sight behind the skyline. That way was shut to me, and I must try the bigger hills to the south beyond the highway. The car I had noticed was getting nearer, but it was still a long way off with some very steep gradients before it. I ran hard, crouching low except in the hollows, and as I ran I kept scanning the brow of hill before me. Was it imagination, or did I see figures – one, two, perhaps more – moving in a glen beyond the stream?

If you are hemmed in on all sides in a patch of land there is only one chance of escape. You must stay in the patch, and let your enemies search it and not find you. That was good sense, but how on earth was I to escape notice in that table-cloth of a place? I would have buried myself to the neck in mud or lain below water or climbed the tallest tree. But there was not a stick of wood, the bog-holes were little puddles, the stream was a slender trickle. There was nothing but short heather and bare hill bent and the white highway.

*   *   *

Then in a tiny bight of road, beside a heap of stones, I found the Roadman.

He had just arrived, and was wearily flinging down his hammer. He looked at me with a fishy eye and yawned.

'Confoond the day I ever left the herdin'!' he said as if to the world at large. 'There I was my ain maister. Now I'm a slave to the government, tethered to the roadside, wi' sair een, and a back like a suckle.'

He took up the hammer, struck a stone, dropped the implement with an oath, and put both hands to his ears. 'Mercy on me! My heid's burstin'!' he cried.

He was a wild figure, about my own size, but much bent, with a week's beard on his chin and a pair of big horn spectacles.

'I canna dae't,' he cried again. 'The surveyor maun just report me. I'm for my bed.'

I asked him what was the trouble, though indeed that was clear enough.

'The trouble is that I'm no sober. Last nicht my dochter, Merran, was waddit, and they danced till fower in the byre. Me and some ither chiels sat down to the drinkin' – and here I am. Peety that I ever lookit on the wine when it was red!'

I agreed with him about bed.

'It's easy speakin',' he moaned. 'But I got a post-caird yestereen sayin' that the new road surveyor would be round the day. He'll come and he'll no find me, or else he'll find me fou, and either way I'm a done man. I'll awa back to my bed and say I'm no weel, but I doot that'll no help me, for they ken my kind o' no-weelness.'

Then I had an inspiration. 'Does the new surveyor know you?' I asked.

'No him. He's just been a week at the job. He rins about in a wee motor-car, and wad speir the inside oot o' a whelk.'

'Where's your house?' I asked, and was directed by a wavering finger to the cottage by the stream.

'Well, back to your bed,' I said, 'and sleep in peace. I'll take on your job for a bit and see the surveyor.'

He stared at me blankly; then, as the notion dawned on his fuddled brain, his face broke into the vacant drunkard's smile.

'You're the billy,' he cried. 'It'll be easy eneuch managed. I've finished that bing o' stanes, so you needna chap ony mair this forenoon. Just take the barry, and wheel eneuch metal frae yon quarry doon the road to make anither bing the morn.

'My name's Alexander Turnbull, and I've been seeven year at this trade, and twenty afore that herdin' on Leithen Water. My freends ca' me Ecky, and whiles Specky, for I wear glasses, bein' weak i' the sicht. Just you speak the surveyor fair and ca' him sir, and he'll be fell pleased. I'll be back or midday.'

I borrowed his spectacles and filthy old hat; stripped off coat, waistcoat and collar and gave him them to carry home; borrowed, too, the foul stump of a clay pipe as an extra property. He indicated my simple tasks, and without more ado set off at an amble bedwards. Bed may have been his chief object, but I think there was also something left in the foot of a bottle. I prayed that he might be safe under cover before my friends arrived on the scene.

Then I set to work to dress for the part. I opened the collar of my shirt – it was a vulgar blue-and-white check such as plowmen wear – and revealed a neck as brown as any tinker's. I rolled up my sleeves and there was a forearm which might have been a blacksmith's, sunburnt and rough with old scars. I got my boots and trouser-legs all white from the dust of the road, and hitched up my trousers, tying them with string below the knee. Then I set to work on my face. With a handful of dust I made a water-mark round my neck, the place where Mr Turnbull's Sunday ablutions might be expected to stop. I rubbed a good deal of dirt also into the sunburn of my cheeks. A roadman's eyes would, no doubt, be a little inflamed, so I contrived to get some dust in both of mine, and by dint of vigorous rubbing produced a bleary effect.

The sandwiches Sir Harry had given me had gone off with my coat, but the roadman's lunch, tied up in a red handkerchief, was at my disposal. I ate with great relish several of the thick slabs of scone and cheese and drank a little of the cold tea. In the handkerchief was a local paper tied with string and addressed to Mr Turnbull – obviously meant to solace his midday leisure. I did up the bundle again, and put the paper conspicuously beside it.

My boots did not satisfy me, but by dint of kicking among the stones I reduced them to the granite-like surface which marks a roadman's foot-gear. Then I bit and scraped my fingernails till the edges were all cracked and uneven. The men I was matched against would miss no detail. I broke one of the boot-laces and retied it in a clumsy knot and loosed the other so that my thick grey socks bulged over the uppers. Still no sign of anything on the road. The motor I had observed half an hour ago must have gone home.

My toilet complete, I took up the barrow and began my journeys to and from the quarry a hundred yards off. I remembered an old scout in Rhodesia, who had done many queer things in his day, once telling me that the secret of playing a part was to think yourself into it. You could never keep it up, he said, unless you could manage to convince yourself that you were it. So I shut off all other thoughts and switched them on the road-mending. I thought of the little white cottage as my home, I recalled the years I had spent herding on Leithen Water, I made my mind dwell lovingly on sleep in a box-bed and a bottle of cheap whisky. Still nothing appeared on that long white road.

Now and then a sheep wandered off the heather to stare at me. A heron flopped down to a pool in the stream and started to fish, taking no more notice of me than if I had been a milestone. On I went trundling my loads of stone, with the heavy step of the professional. Soon I grew warm and the dust on my face changed into solid and abiding grit. I was already counting the hours till evening should put a limit to Mr Turnbull's monotonous toil.

Suddenly a crisp voice spoke from the road, and looking up I saw a little Ford two-seater, and a round-faced young man in a bowler hat.

'Are you Alexander Turnbull?' he asked. 'I am the new county road surveyor. You live at Blackhopefoot, and have charge of the section from Laidlawbyres to the Riggs? Good! A fair bit of road, Turnbull, and not badly engineered. A little soft about a mile off, and the edges want cleaning. See you look after that. Good-morning. You'll know me the next time you see me.'

Clearly my get-up was good enough for the dreaded surveyor. I went on with my work, and as the morning grew towards noon I was cheered by a little traffic. A baker's van breasted the hill, and sold me a bag of ginger biscuits which I stowed in my trouser-pockets against emergencies. Then a herd passed with sheep, and disturbed me somewhat by asking loudly, 'What had become o' Specky?'

'In bed wi' the colic,' I replied, and the herd passed on.

Just about midday a big car stole down the hill, glided past and drew up a hundred yards beyond. Its three occupants descended as if to stretch their legs, and sauntered toward me.

Two of the men I had seen before from the window of the Galloway inn – one lean, sharp and dark, the other comfortable and smiling. The third had the look of a countryman – a vet, perhaps, or a small farmer. He was dressed in ill-cut knickerbockers, and the eye in his head was as bright and wary as a hen's.

'Morning,' said the last. 'That's a fine easy job a' yours.'

I had not looked up on their approach, and now, when accosted, I slowly and painfully straightened my back, after the manner of roadmen; spat vigorously, after the manner of the low Scot; and regarded them steadily before replying. I confronted three pairs of eyes that missed nothing.

'There's waur jobs and there's better,' I said sententiously. 'I wad rather hae yours, sittin' a' day on your hinderlands on thae cushions. It's you and your muckle cawrs that wreck my roads! If we a' had oor richts, you sud be made to mend what ye break!'

The bright-eyed man was looking at the newspaper lying beside Turnbull's bundle.

'I see you get your papers in good time,' he said.

I glanced at it casually. 'Aye, in gude time. Seein' that that paper cam out last Setterday, I'm just fower days late.'

He picked it up, glanced at the superscription and laid it down again. One of the others had been looking at my boots, and a word in German called the speaker's attention to them.

'You've a fine taste in boots,' he said. 'These were never made by a country shoemaker.'

'They were not,' I said readily. 'They were made in London. I got them frae the gentleman that was here last year for the shootin'. What was his name now?' And I scratched a forgetful head.

Again the sleek one spoke in German. 'Let us get on,' he said. 'This fellow is all right.'

They asked one last question:

'Did you see any one pass early this morning? He might be on a bicycle or he might be on foot.'

I very nearly fell into the trap and told a story of a bicyclist hurrying past in the grey dawn. But I had the sense to see my danger. I pretended to consider very deeply.

'I wasna up very early,' I said. 'Ye see my dochter was merrit last nicht, and we keepit it up late. I opened the house-door about seeven – and there was naebody on the road then. Since I cam up here there has been just the baker and the Ruchill herd, besides you gentlemen.'

One of them gave me a cigar, which I smelled gingerly and stuck in Turnbull's bundle. They got into their car and were out of sight in three minutes.

My heart leaped with an enormous relief, but I went on wheeling my stones. It was as well, for ten minutes later the car returned, one of the occupants waving a hand to me. These gentry left nothing to chance.

I finished Turnbull's bread and cheese, and pretty soon I had finished the stones. The next step was what puzzled me. I could not keep up this road-making business for long. A merciful Providence had kept Mr Turnbull indoors, but if he appeared on the scene there would be trouble. I had a notion that the cordon was still tight round the glen, and that if I walked in any direction I should meet with questioners. But get out I must. No man's nerve could stand more than a day of being spied on.

I stayed at my post till about five o'clock. By that time I had resolved to go down to Turnbull's cottage at nightfall and take my chance of getting over the hills in the darkness. But suddenly a new car came up the road, and slowed down a yard or two from me. A fresh wind had risen, and the occupant wanted to light a cigarette.

It was a touring-car, with the tonneau full of an assortment of baggage. One man sat in it, and by an amazing chance I knew him. His name was Marmaduke Jopley, and he was an offence to creation. He was a sort of blood stockbroker, who did his business by toadying eldest sons and rich young peers and foolish old ladies.

'Marmie' was a familiar figure, I understood, at balls and polo-weeks and country houses. He was an adroit scandalmonger, and would crawl a mile on his belly to anything that had a title or a million. I had a business introduction to his firm when I came to London, and he was good enough to ask me to dinner at his club.

There he showed off at a great rate, and pattered about his duchesses till the snobbery of the creature turned me sick. I asked a man afterwards why nobody kicked him, and was told that Englishmen reverenced the weaker sex.

Anyhow there he was now, nattily dressed, in a fine new car, obviously on his way to visit some of his fine friends. A sudden daftness took me, and in a second I had jumped into the tonneau and had him by the shoulder.

'Hello, Jopley,' I sang out. 'Well met, my lad!'

He got a horrid fright. His chin dropped as he stared at me. 'Who the devil are you?' he gasped.

'My name's Hannay,' I said, 'from Rhodesia, you remember?'

'Good God, the murderer!' he choked.

'Just so. And there'll be a second murder, my dear, if you don't do as I tell you. Give me that coat of yours. That cap, too.'

He did as he was bid, for he was blind with terror. Over my dirty trousers and vulgar shirt I put on his smart driving-coat, which buttoned high at the top end and thereby hid the deficiencies of my collar. I stuck the cap on my head, and added his gloves to my get-up. The dusty roadman in a minute was transformed into one of the neatest motorists in Scotland. On Mr Jopley's head I clapped Turnbull's unspeakable hat, and told him to keep it there.

Then with some difficulty I turned the car. My plan was to go back the road he had come, for the watchers, having seen it before, would probably let it pass unremarked, and Marmie's figure was in no way like mine.

'Now, my child,' I said, 'sit quite still and be a good boy. I mean you no harm. I'm only borrowing your car for an hour or two. But if you play me any tricks, and above all if you open your mouth, as sure as there's a God above me, I'll wring your neck. *Savez*?'

I enjoyed that evening's ride. We ran eight miles down the valley, through a village or two, and I could not help noticing several strange-looking folk lounging by the roadside. These were the watchers who would have had much to say to me if I had come in other garb or company. As it was, they looked incuriously on. One touched his cap in salute, and I responded graciously.

As the dark fell I turned up a side glen which, as I remembered from the map, led into an unfrequented corner of the hills. Soon the villages were left behind, then the farms, and then even the wayside cottages. Presently we came to a lonely moor where the night was blackening the sunset gleam in the bog-pools. Here we stopped, and I obligingly reversed the car and restored to Mr Jopley his belongings.

'A thousand thanks,' I said. 'There's more use in you than I thought. Now be off and find the police.'

As I sat on the hillside, watching the tail-lights dwindle, I reflected on the various kinds of crime I had now sampled. Contrary to general belief I was not a murderer, but I had become an unholy liar, a shameless impostor, and a highwayman with a marked taste for expensive motor-cars.

CHAPTER 6

THE ADVENTURE OF
THE BALD ARCHAEOLOGIST

I spent the night on a shelf of the hill-side, in the lee of a boulder where the heather grew long and soft. It was a cold business, for I had neither coat nor waistcoat. Those were in Mr Turnbull's keep, as was Scudder's little book, my watch and – worst of all – my pipe and tobacco pouch. Only my money accompanied me in my belt, and about half a pound of ginger biscuits in my trousers pocket.

I supped off half those biscuits, and by worming myself deep into the heather got some kind of warmth. My spirits had risen, and I was beginning to enjoy this crazy game of hide-and-seek. So far I had been miraculously lucky. The milkman, the literary innkeeper, Sir Harry, the roadman, and the idiotic Marmie, were all pieces of undeserved good fortune. Somehow the first success gave me a feeling that I should pull through. My chief trouble was that I was desperately hungry. When a Jew shoots himself in the City and there is an inquest, the newspapers usually report that the deceased was 'well-nourished'. I remember thinking that they would not call me well-nourished if I broke my neck in a bog-hole. I lay and tortured myself – for the ginger biscuits merely emphasized the aching void – with the memory of all the good food I had thought so little of in London. There were Paddock's crisp sausages and fragrant shavings of bacon, and shapely poached eggs – how often I had turned up my nose at them! There were the cutlets they did at the club, and a particular ham that stood on the cold table, for which my soul lusted. My thoughts hovered over all the varieties of mortal edible, and finally settled on a porterhouse steak and a quart of bitter with a Welsh rabbit to follow. In longing hopelessly for these dainties I fell asleep.

I woke very cold and stiff about an hour after dawn. It took me a little while to remember where I was, for I had been very weary and had slept heavily. I saw first the pale blue sky through a net of heather, then a big shoulder of hill, and then my own boots placed neatly in a blackberry-bush. I raised myself on my arms and looked down into the valley, and that one look set me lacing up my boots in mad haste. For there were men below, not more than a quarter of a mile off, spaced out on the hill-side like a fan, and beating the heather. Marmie had not been slow in looking for his revenge.

I crawled out of my shelf into the cover of a boulder, and from it gained a shallow trench which slanted up the mountain face. This led me presently into the narrow gully of a burn, by way of which I scrambled to the top of the ridge. From there I looked back, and saw that I was still undiscovered. My pursuers were patiently quartering the hill-side and moving upwards.

Keeping behind the skyline, I ran for maybe half a mile till I judged I was above the uppermost end of the glen. Then I showed myself, and was instantly noted by one of the flankers who passed the word to the others. I heard cries coming up from below, and saw that the line of search had changed its direction. I pretended to retreat over the skyline, but instead went back the way I had come, and in twenty minutes was behind the ridge overlooking my sleeping place. From that viewpoint I had the satisfaction of seeing the pursuit streaming up the hill at the top of the glen on a hopelessly false scent. I had before me a choice of routes, and I chose a ridge which made an angle with the one I was on, and so would soon put a deep glen between me and my enemies. The exercise had warmed my blood, and I was beginning to enjoy myself amazingly. As I went I breakfasted on the dusty remnants of the ginger biscuits.

I knew very little about the country, and I hadn't a notion what I was going to do. I trusted to the strength of my legs, but I was well aware that those behind me would be familiar with the lie of the land, and that my ignorance would be a heavy handicap. I saw in front of me a sea of hills, rising very high towards the south, but northwards breaking down into broad ridges which separated wide and shallow dales. The ridge I had chosen seemed to sink after a mile or two to a moor which lay like a pocket in the uplands. That seemed as good a direction to take as any other.

My stratagem had given me a fair start – call it twenty minutes – and I had the width of a glen behind me before I saw the first heads of the pursuers. The police had evidently called in local herds or gamekeepers. They hallooed at the sight of me, and I waved my hand. Two dived into the glen and began to climb my ridge, while the others kept their own side of the hill. I felt as if I were taking part in a schoolboy game of hare and hounds.

But very soon it began to seem less of a game. Those fellows behind were hefty men on their native heath. Looking back I saw that only three were following direct and I guessed that the others had fetched a circuit to cut me off. My lack of local knowledge might very well be my undoing, and I resolved to get out of this tangle of glens to the pocket of moor I had seen from the tops. I must so increase my distance as to get clear away from them and I believed I could do this if I could find the right ground for it. If there had been cover I would have tried a bit of stalking, but on these bare slopes you could see a fly a mile off. My hope must be in the length of my legs and the soundness of my wind, but I needed easier ground for that, for I was not bred a mountaineer. How I longed for a good Afrikander pony!

I put on a great spurt and got off my ridge and down into the moor before any figures appeared on the skyline behind me. I crossed a burn, and came out on a highroad which made a pass between two glens. All in front of me was a big field of heather sloping up to a crest which was crowned with an odd feather of trees. In the dyke by the roadside was a gate, from which a grass-grown track led over the first wave of the moor. I jumped the dyke and followed it, and after a few hundred yards – as soon as it was out of sight of the highway – the grass stopped and it became a very respectable road which was evidently kept with some care. Clearly it ran to a house, and I began to think of doing the same. Hitherto my luck had held, and it might be that my best chance would be found in this remote dwelling. Anyhow there were trees there – and that meant cover.

I did not follow the road, but the burn-side which flanked it on the right, where the bracken grew deep and the high banks made a tolerable screen. It was well I did so, for no sooner had I gained the hollow than, looking back, I saw the pursuit topping the ridge from which I had descended.

After that I did not look back; I had no time. I ran up the burn-side, crawling over the open places, and for a large part wading in the shallow stream. I found a deserted cottage with a row of phantom peat-stacks and an overgrown garden. Then I was among young hay, and very soon had come to the edge of a plantation of windblown firs. From there I saw the chimneys of the house smoking a few hundred yards to my left. I forsook the burn-side, crossed another dyke, and almost before I knew was on a rough lawn. A glance back told me that I was well out of sight of the pursuit, which had not yet passed the first lift of the moor.

The lawn was a very rough place, cut with a scythe instead of a mower, and planted with beds of scrubby rhododendrons. A brace of black game, which are not usually garden birds, rose at my approach. The house before me was the ordinary moorland farm, with a more pretentious white-washed wing added. Attached to this wing was a glass verandah, and through the glass I saw the face of an elderly gentleman meekly watching me.

I stalked over the border of coarse hill gravel and entered the verandah door. Within was a pleasant room, glass on one side, and on the other a mass of books. More books showed in an inner room. On the floor, instead of tables, stood cases such as you see in a museum, filled with coins and queer stone implements.

There was a knee-hole desk in the middle, and seated at it, with some papers and open volumes before him, was the benevolent old gentleman. His face was round and shiny, like Mr Pickwick's, big glasses were stuck on the end of his nose, and the top of his head was as bright and bare as a glass bottle. He never moved when I entered, but raised his placid eyebrows and waited on me to speak.

It was not an easy job, with about five minutes to spare, to tell a stranger who I was and what I wanted, and to win his aid. I did not attempt it. There was something about the eye of the man before me, something so keen and knowledgeable, that I could not find a word. I simply stared at him and stuttered.

'You seem in a hurry, my friend,' he said slowly.

I nodded towards the window. It gave a prospect across the moor through a gap in the plantation, and revealed certain figures half a mile off straggling through the heather.

'Ah, I see,' he said, and took up a pair of field glasses, through which he patiently scrutinized the figures.

'A fugitive from justice, eh? Well, we'll go into the matter at our leisure. Meantime, I object to my privacy being broken in upon by the clumsy rural policeman. Go into my study and you will see two doors facing you. Take the one to the left and close it behind you. You will be perfectly safe.'

And this extraordinary man took up his pen again.

I did as I was bid, and found myself in a little dark chamber which smelled of chemicals and was lit only by a tiny window high up in the wall. The door had swung behind me with a click like the door of a safe. Once again I had found an unexpected sanctuary.

All the same I was not comfortable. There was something about the old gentleman which puzzled and rather terrified me. He had been too easy and ready, almost as if he had expected me. And his eyes had been horribly intelligent.

No sound came to me in that dark place. For all I knew the police might be searching the house, and if they did they would want to know what was behind this door. I tried to possess my soul in patience and to forget how hungry I was.

Then I took a more cheerful view. The old gentleman could scarcely refuse me a meal, and I fell to reconstructing my breakfast. Bacon and eggs would content me, but I wanted the better part of a flitch of bacon and half a hundred eggs. And then, while my mouth was watering in anticipation, there was a click and the door stood open.

I emerged into the sunlight to find the master of the house sitting in a deep armchair in the room he called his study, and regarding me with curious eyes.

'Have they gone?' I asked.

'They have gone. I convinced them that you had crossed the hill. I do not choose that the police should come between me and one whom I am delighted to honour. This is a lucky morning for you, Mr Richard Hannay.'

As he spoke his eyelids seemed to tremble and to fall a little over his keen grey eyes. In a flash the phrase of Scudder's came back to me, when he had described the man he most dreaded in the world. He had said that he 'could hood his eyes like a hawk'. Then I saw that I had walked straight into the enemy's headquarters.

My first impulse was to throttle the old ruffian and make for the open air. He seemed to anticipate my intention, for he smiled gently and nodded to the door behind me. I turned and saw two men-servants who had me covered with pistols.

He knew my name, but he had never seen me before. And as the reflection darted across my mind, I saw a slender chance.

'I don't know what you mean,' I said roughly. 'And who are you calling Richard Hannay? My name's Ainslie.'

'So?' he said, still smiling. 'But of course you have others. We won't quarrel about a name.'

I was pulling myself together now and I reflected that my garb, lacking coat and waistcoat and collar, would, at any rate, not betray me. I put on my surliest face and shrugged my shoulders.

'I suppose you're going to give me up after all, and I call it a damned dirty trick. My God, I wish I had never seen that cursed motor-car! Here's the money and be damned to you,' and I flung four sovereigns on the table.

He opened his eyes a little. 'Oh, no, I shall not give you up. My friends and I will have a little private settlement with you, that is all. You know a little too much, Mr Hannay. You are a clever actor, but not quite clever enough.'

He spoke with assurance, but I could see the dawning of a doubt in his mind.

'O, for God's sake stop jawing,' I cried. 'Everything's against me. I haven't had a bit of luck since I came on shore at Leith. What's the harm in a poor devil with an empty stomach picking up some money he finds in a bust-up motor-car? That's all I done, and for that I've been chivvied for two days by those blasted bobbies over those blasted hills. I tell you I'm fair sick of it. You can do what you like, old boy! Ned Ainslie's got no fight left in him.'

I could see that the doubt was gaining.

'Will you oblige me with the story of your recent doings?' he asked.

'I can't, guv'nor,' I said in a real beggar's whine. 'I've not had a bite to eat for two days. Give me a mouthful of food, and then you'll hear God's truth.'

I must have showed my hunger in my face, for he signalled to one of the men in the doorway. A bit of cold pie was brought and a glass of beer, and I wolfed them down like a pig – or rather like Ned Ainslie, for I was keeping up my character. In the middle of my meal he spoke suddenly to me in German, but I turned on him a face as blank as a stone wall.

Then I told him my story – how I had come off an Archangel ship at Leith a week ago, and was making my way overland to my brother at Wigton. I had run short of cash – I hinted vaguely at a spree – and I was pretty well on my uppers when I had come on a hole in a hedge, and, looking through, had seen a big motor-car lying in a burn. I had poked about to see what had happened, and had found three sovereigns lying on the seat and one on the floor. There was nobody there or any sign of an owner, so I had pocketed the cash. But somehow the law had got after me. When I had tried to change a sovereign in a baker's shop the woman had cried on the police, and a little later, when I was washing my face in a burn, I had been nearly gripped, and had only got away by leaving my coat and waistcoat behind me.

'They can have the money back,' I cried, 'for a fat lot of good it's done me. Those perishers are all down on a poor man. Now if it had been you, guv'nor, that had found the quids, nobody would have troubled you.'

'You're a good liar, Hannay,' he said.

I flew into a rage. 'Stop fooling, damn you! I tell you my name's Ainslie, and I never heard of any one called Hannay in my born days. I'd sooner have the police than you with your Hannays and your monkey-faced pistol tricks. No, guv'nor, I don't mean that. I'm much obliged to you for the grub. I'll thank you to let me go now the coast's clear.'

It was obvious that he was badly puzzled. You see he had never seen me, and my appearance must have altered considerably from my photographs – if he had got one of them. I was pretty smart and well dressed in London, and now I was a regular tramp.

'I do not propose to let you go. If you are what you say you are, you will soon have a chance of clearing yourself. If you are what I believe you are, I do not think you will see the light much longer.'

He rang a bell and a third servant appeared from the verandah.

'I want the Lanchester in five minutes,' he said. 'There will be three to luncheon.'

Then he looked steadily at me, and that was the hardest ordeal of all. There was something weird and devilish in those eyes, cold, malignant, unearthly, and most hellishly clever. They fascinated me like the bright eyes of a snake. I had a strong impulse to throw myself on his mercy and offer to join his side, and if you consider the way I felt about the whole thing, you will see that that impulse must have been purely physical, the weakness of a brain mesmerized and mastered by a stronger spirit. But I managed to stick it out and even to grin. 'You'll know me next time, guv'nor,' I said.

'Karl,' he said in German to one of the men in the doorway. 'You will put this fellow in the store-room till I return, and you will be answerable to me for his keeping.'

I was marched out of the room with a pistol at each ear.

* * *

The store-room was a damp chamber in what had been the old farmhouse. There was no carpet on the uneven floor and nothing to sit down on but a school form. It was black as pitch, for the windows were heavily shuttered. I made out by groping that the walls were lined with boxes and barrels and sacks of some heavy stuff. The whole place smelled of mould and disuse. My jailers turned the key in the door, and I could hear them shifting their feet as they stood on guard outside.

I sat down in the chilly darkness in a very miserable frame of mind. The old boy had gone off in a motor to collect the two ruffians who had interviewed me yesterday. Now, they had seen me as the roadman, and they would remember me, for I was in the same rig. What was a roadman doing twenty miles from his beat, pursued by the police? A question or two would put them on the track. Probably they had seen Mr Turnbull, probably Marmie too; most likely they could link me up with Sir Harry, and then the whole thing would be crystal clear. What chance had I in this moorland house with three desperadoes and their armed servants?

I began to think wistfully of the police, now plodding over the hills after my wraith. They at any rate were fellow countrymen and honest men, and their tender mercies would be kinder than these ghoulish aliens. But they wouldn't have listened to me. That old devil with the eyelids had not taken long to get rid of them. I thought he probably had some kind of graft with the constabulary. Most likely he had letters from Cabinet Ministers saying he was to be given every facility for plotting against Britain. That's the sort of owlish way we run our politics in the Old Country.

The three would be back for lunch, so I hadn't more than a couple of hours to wait. It was simply waiting on destruction, for I could see no way out of this mess. I wished that I had Scudder's courage, for I am free to confess I didn't feel any great fortitude. The only thing that kept me going was that I was pretty furious. It made me boil with rage to think of those three spies getting the pull on me like this. I hoped that at any rate I might be able to twist one of their necks before they downed me.

The more I thought of it the angrier I grew, and I had to get up and move about the room. I tried the shutters, but they were the kind that lock with a key and I couldn't move them. From the outside came the faint clucking of hens in the warm sun. Then I groped among the sacks and boxes. I couldn't open the latter and the sacks seemed to be full of things like dog-biscuits that smelled of cinnamon. But, as I circumnavigated the room, I found a handle in the wall which seemed worth investigating.

It was the door of a wall cupboard – what they call a 'press' in Scotland – and it was locked. I shook it and it seemed rather flimsy. For want of something better to do I put out my strength on that door, getting some purchase on the handle by looping my braces round it. Presently the thing gave with a crash which I thought would bring in my warders to inquire. I waited for a bit and started to explore the cupboard shelves. There was a multitude of queer things there. I found an odd vesta or two in my trouser pockets and struck a light. It went out in a second, but it showed me one thing. There was a little stock of electric torches on one shelf. I picked up one and found it was in working order.

With the torch to help me I investigated further. There were bottles and cases of queer smelling stuffs, chemicals no doubt for experiments, and there were coils of fine copper wire and yanks and yanks of a thin oiled silk. There was a box of detonators, and a lot of cord for fuses. Then away at the back of a shelf I found a stout brown cardboard box, and inside it a wooden case. I managed to wrench it open, and within lay half a dozen little grey bricks, each a couple of inches square.

I took up one and found that it crumbled easily in my hand. Then I smelled it and put my tongue to it. After that I sat down to think. I hadn't been a mining engineer for nothing, and I knew lentonite when I saw it. With one of these bricks I could blow the house to smithereens. I had used the stuff in Rhodesia and knew its power. But the trouble was that my knowledge wasn't exact. I had forgotten the proper charge and the right way of preparing it, and I wasn't sure about the timing. I had only a vague notion, too, as to its power, for though I had used it I had not handled it with my own fingers.

But it was a chance, the only possible chance. It was a mighty risk, but against it was an absolute black certainty. If I used it the odds were, as I reckoned, about five to one in favour of my blowing myself into the treetops; but if I didn't I should very likely be occupying a six-foot hole in the garden by the evening. That was the way I had to look at it. The prospect was pretty dark either way, but anyhow there was a chance, both for myself and for my country.

The remembrance of little Scudder decided me. It was about the beastliest moment of my life, for I'm no good at these cold-blooded resolutions. Still I managed to rake up the pluck to set my teeth and choke back the horrid doubts that flooded in on me. I simply shut off my mind and pretended I was doing an experiment as simple as Guy Fawkes fireworks.

I got a detonator, and fixed it to a couple of feet of fuse. Then I took a quarter of a lentonite brick, and buried it near the door, below one of the sacks in a crack of the floor, fixing the detonator in it. For all I knew half those boxes might be dynamite. If the cupboard held such deadly explosives, why not the boxes? In that case there would be a glorious skyward journey for me and the German servants and about an acre of the surrounding country. There was also the risk that the detonation might set off the other bricks in the cupboard, for I had forgotten most that I knew about lentonite. But it didn't do to begin thinking about the possibilities. The odds were horrible, but I had to take them.

I ensconced myself just below the sill of the window and lit the fuse. Then I waited for a moment or two. There was dead silence – only a shuffle of heavy boots in the passage, and the peaceful cluck of hens from the warm out-of-doors. I commended my soul to my Maker, and wondered where I would be in five seconds.

A great wave of heat seemed to surge upwards from the floor, and hang for a blistering instant in the air. Then the wall opposite me flashed into a golden yellow and dissolved with a rending thunder that hammered my brain into a pulp. Something dropped on me, catching the point of my left shoulder.

And then I became unconscious.

My stupor can scarcely have lasted beyond a few seconds. I felt myself being choked by thick yellow fumes, and struggled out of the debris to my feet. Somewhere behind me I felt fresh air. The jambs of the window had fallen, and through the ragged rent the smoke was pouring out to the summer noon. I stepped over the broken lintel, and found myself standing in a yard in a dense and acrid fog. I felt very sick and ill, but I could move my limbs, and I staggered blindly forward away from the house.

A small mill lade ran in a wooden aqueduct at the other side of the yard, and into this I fell. The cool water revived me, and I had just enough wits left to think of escape. I squirmed up the lade among the slippery green slime till I reached the mill-wheel. Then I wriggled through the axle hole into the old mill and tumbled onto a bed of chaff. A nail caught the seat of my trousers, and I left a wisp of heather-mixture behind me.

The mill had been long out of use. The ladders were rotten with age, and in the loft the rats had gnawed great holes in the floor. Nausea shook me, and a wheel in my head kept turning, while my left shoulder and arm seemed to be stricken with the palsy. I looked out of the window and saw a fog still hanging over the house and smoke escaping from an upper window. Please God I had set the place on fire, for I could hear confused cries coming from the other side.

But I had no time to linger, since this mill was obviously a bad hiding-place. Any one looking for me would naturally follow the lade, and I made certain the search would begin as soon as they found that my body was not in the store-room. From another window I saw that on the far side of the mill stood an old stone dovecot. If I could get there without leaving tracks I might find a hiding-place, for I argued that my enemies, if they thought I could move, would conclude I had made for open country, and would go seeking me on the moor.

I crawled down the broken ladder, scattering chaff behind me to cover my footsteps. I did the same on the mill floor, and on the threshold where the door hung on broken hinges. Peeping out I saw that between me and the dovecot was a piece of bare cobbled ground, where no footmarks would show. Also it was mercifully hid by the mill buildings from any view from the house. I slipped across the space, got to the back of the dovecot and prospected a way of ascent.

That was one of the hardest jobs I ever took on. My shoulder and arm ached like hell, and I was so sick and giddy that I was always on the verge of falling. But I managed it somehow. By the use of out-jutting stones and gaps in the masonry and a tough ivy root I got to the top in the end. There was a little parapet, behind which I found space to lie down. Then I proceeded to go into an old-fashioned swoon.

I woke with a burning head and the sun glaring in my face. For a long time I lay motionless, for those horrible fumes seemed to have loosened my joints and dulled my brain. Sounds came to me from the house – men speaking throatily and the throbbing of a stationary car. There was a little gap in the parapet to which I wriggled, and from which I had some sort of prospect of the yard. I saw figures come out – a servant with his head bound up, and then a younger man in knickerbockers. They were looking for something, and moved towards the mill. Then one of them caught sight of the wisp of cloth on the nail, and cried out to the other. They both went back to the house, and brought two more to look at it. I saw the rotund figure of my late captor, and I thought I made out the man with the lisp. I noticed that all had pistols.

For half an hour they ransacked the mill. I could hear them kicking over the barrels and pulling up the rotten planking. Then they came outside, and stood just below the dovecot, arguing fiercely. The servant with the bandage was being soundly rated. I heard them fiddling with the door of the dovecot, and for one horrid moment I thought they were coming up. Then they thought better of it, and went back to the house.

All that long blistering afternoon I lay baking on the roof-top. Thirst was my chief torment. My tongue was like a stick, and to make it worse, I could hear the cool drip of water from the mill-lade. I watched the course of the little stream as it came in from the moor, and my fancy followed it to the top of the glen, where it must issue from an icy fountain fringed with cool ferns and mosses. I would have given a thousand pounds to plunge my face into that.

I had a fine prospect of the whole ring of moorland. I saw the car speed away with two occupants, and a man on a hill pony riding east. I judged they were looking for me, and I wished them joy of their quest. But I saw something else more interesting. The house stood almost on the summit of a swell of moorland which crowned a sort of plateau, and there was no higher point nearer than the big hills six miles off. The actual summit, as I have mentioned, was a biggish clump of trees – firs mostly, with a few ashes and beeches. On the dovecot I was almost on a level with the tree-tops, and could see what lay beyond. The wood was not solid, but only a ring, and inside was an oval of green turf, for all the world like a big cricket field. I didn't take long to guess what it was. It was an aerodrome, and a secret one. The place had been most cunningly chosen. For suppose any one were watching an aeroplane descending here, he would think it had gone over the hill beyond the trees. As the place was on the top of a rise in the midst of a big amphitheatre any observer from any direction would conclude it had passed out of view behind the hill. Only a man very close at hand would realize that the aeroplane had not gone over but had descended in the midst of the wood. An observer with a telescope on one of the higher hills might have discovered the truth, but only herds went there, and herds do not carry spy-glasses. When I looked from the dovecot I could see far away a blue line which I knew was the sea, and I grew furious to think that our enemies had this secret conning-tower to rake our waterways.

Then I reflected that if that aeroplane came back the chances were ten to one that I would be discovered. So through the afternoon I lay and prayed for the coming of darkness, and glad I was when the sun went down over the big western hills and the twilight haze crept over the moor. The aeroplane was late. The gloaming was far advanced when I heard the beat of wings, and saw it volplaning downward to its home in the wood. Lights twinkled for a bit and there was much coming and going from the house. Then the dark fell and silence.

Thank God it was a black night. The moon was well on in its last quarter and would not rise till late. My thirst was too great to allow me to tarry, so about nine o'clock, so far as I could judge, I started to descend. It wasn't easy, and half-way down I heard the back door of the house open, and saw the gleam of a lantern against the mill wall. For some agonizing minutes I hung by the ivy and prayed that whoever it was would not come round by the dovecot. Then the light disappeared, and I dropped as softly as I could onto the hard soil of the yard.

I crawled on my belly in the lee of a stone dyke till I reached the fringe of trees which surrounded the house. If I had known how to do it I would have tried to put that aeroplane out of action, but I realized that any attempt would probably be futile. I was pretty certain that there would be some kind of defence round the house, so I went through the wood on hands and knees, feeling carefully every inch before me. It was as well, for presently I came on a wire about two feet from the ground. If I had tripped over that, it would doubtless have rung some bell in the house and I would have been captured.

A hundred yards further on I found another wire cunningly placed on the edge of a small stream. Beyond that lay the moor, and in five minutes I was deep in bracken and heather. Soon I was round the shoulder of the rise, in the little glen from which the mill-lade flowed. Ten minutes later my face was deep in the spring, and I was soaking down pints of the blessed water. But I did not stop till I had put half a dozen miles between me and that accursed dwelling.

CHAPTER 7

THE DRY-FLY FISHERMAN

I sat down on a hill-top and took stock of my position. I wasn't feeling very happy, for my natural thankfulness at my escape was clouded by my severe bodily discomfort. Those lentonite fumes had fairly poisoned me, and the baking hours on the dovecot hadn't helped matters. I had a crushing headache, and felt as sick as a cat. Also my shoulder was in a bad way. At first I thought it was only a bruise, but it seemed to be swelling and I had no use of my left arm.

My plan was to seek Mr Turnbull's cottage, recover my garments and especially Scudder's note-book, and then make for the main line and get back to the south. It seemed to me that the sooner I got in touch with the Foreign Office man, Sir Walter Bullivant, the better. I didn't see how I could get more proof than I had got already. He must just take or leave my story, and anyway with him I would be in better hands than those devilish Germans. I had begun to feel quite kindly towards the British police.

It was a wonderful starry night and I had not much difficulty about the road. Sir Harry's map had given me the lie of the land, and all I had to do was to steer a point or two west of southwest to come to the stream where I had met the roadman. In all these travels I never knew the names of the places, but I believe this stream was no less than the upper waters of the river Tweed. I calculated I must be about eighteen miles distant, and that meant I could not get there before morning. So I must lie up a day somewhere, for I was too outrageous a figure to be seen in the sunlight. I had neither coat, waistcoat, collar nor hat, my trousers were badly torn, and my face and hands were black with the explosion. I dare say I had other beauties, for my eyes felt as if they were furiously bloodshot. Altogether I was no spectacle for God-fearing citizens to see on a highroad.

Very soon after daybreak I made an attempt to clean myself in a hill burn, and then approached a herd's cottage, for I was feeling the need of food. The herd was away from home, and his wife was alone, with no neighbour for five miles. She was a decent old body, and a plucky one, for though she got a fright when she saw me, she had an axe handy, and would have used it on any evildoer. I told her that I had had a fall – I didn't say how – and she saw by my looks that I was pretty sick. Like a true Samaritan she asked no questions, but gave me a bowl of milk with a dash of whisky in it, and let me sit for a little by her kitchen fire. She would have bathed my shoulder, but it ached so badly that I would not let her touch it. I don't know what she took me for – a repentant burglar, perhaps; for when I wanted to pay her for the milk and tendered a sovereign, which was the smallest coin I had, she shook her head and said something about 'giving it to them that had a right to it'. At this I protested so strongly that I think she believed me honest, for she took the money and gave me a warm new plaid for it and an old hat of her man's. She showed me how to wrap the plaid round my shoulders and when I left that cottage I was the living image of the kind of Scotsman you see in the illustrations to Burns's poems. But at any rate I was more or less clad.

It was as well, for the weather changed before midday to a thick drizzle of rain. I found shelter below an overhanging rock in the crook of a burn, where a drift of dead brackens made a tolerable bed. There I managed to sleep till nightfall, waking very cramped and wretched with my shoulder gnawing like a toothache. I ate the oatcake and cheese the old wife had given me, and set out again just before the darkening.

I passed over the miseries of that night among the wet hills. There were no stars to steer by, and I had to do the best I could from my memory of the map. Twice I lost my way, and I had some nasty falls into peat-bogs. I had only about ten miles to go as the crow flies, but my mistakes made it nearer twenty. The last bit was completed with set teeth and a very light and dizzy head. But I managed it, and in the early dawn I was knocking at Mr Turnbull's door. The mist lay close and thick, and from the cottage I could not see the highroad.

Mr Turnbull himself opened to me – sober and something more than sober. He was primly dressed in an ancient but well-tended suit of black; he had been shaved not later than the night before; he wore a linen collar; and in his left hand he carried a pocket Bible. At first he did not recognize me.

'Whae are ye that comes stravaigin' here on the Sabbath mornin'?' he asked.

I had lost all count of the days. So the Sabbath was the reason for his strange decorum.

My head was swimming so wildly that I could not frame a coherent answer. But he recognized me and he saw that I was ill.

'Hae ye got my specs?' he asked.

I fetched them out of my trousers pocket and gave him them.

'Ye'll hae come for your jacket and west-coat,' he said. 'Come in, bye gosh, man, ye're terrible dune i' the legs. Haud up till I get ye to a chair.'

I perceived I was in for a bout of malaria. I had a good deal of fever in my bones, and the wet night had brought it out, while my shoulder and the effects of the fumes combined to make me feel pretty bad. Before I knew, Mr Turnbull was helping me off with my clothes, and putting me to bed in one of the two cupboards that lined the kitchen walls.

He was a true friend in need, that old roadman. His wife was dead years ago, and since his daughter's marriage he lived alone. For the better part of ten days he did all the rough nursing I needed. I simply wanted to be left in peace while the fever took its course, and when my skin was cool again I found that the bout had more or less cured my shoulder. But it was a baddish go, and though I was out of bed in five days, it took me some time to get my legs again.

He went out each morning, leaving me milk for the day, and locking the door behind him; and came in in the evening to sit silent in the chimney corner. Not a soul came near the place. When I was getting better he never bothered me with a question. Several times he fetched me a two-days-old *Scotsman*, and I noticed that the interest in the Portland Place murder seemed to have died down. There was no mention of it, and I could find very little about anything except a thing called the General Assembly – some ecclesiastical spree, I gathered.

One day he produced my belt from a lock-fast drawer. 'There's a terrible heap o' siller in't,' he said. 'Ye'd better coont it to see it's a' there.'

He never even sought my name. I asked him if anybody had been around making inquiries subsequent to my spell at the roadmaking.

'Aye, there was a man in a motor-cawr. He speired whae had ta'en my place that day, and I let on I thocht him daft. But he keepit on at me, and syne I said he maun be thinkin' o' my gude-brither frae the Cleuch that whiles lent me a haun'. He was a wersh-lookin' soul, and I couldna understand the half o' his English tongue.'

I was getting pretty restless those last days, and as soon as I felt myself fit I decided to be off. That was not till the twelfth day of June, and as luck would have it, a drover went past that morning taking some cattle to Moffat. He was a man named Hislop, a friend of Turnbull's, and he came in to his breakfast with us and offered to take me with him.

I made Turnbull accept five pounds for my lodging, and a hard job I had of it. There never was a more independent being. He grew positively rude when I pressed him, and shy and red, and took the money at last without a thank you. When I told him how much I owed him, he grunted something about 'ae guid turn deservin' anither'. You would have thought from our leave-taking that we had parted in disgust.

Hislop was a cheery soul, who chattered all the way over the pass and down the sunny vale of Annan. I talked of Galloway markets and sheep prices, and he made up his mind I was a 'pack-shepherd' from those parts – whatever that may be. My plaid and my old hat, I have said, gave me a fine theatrical Scots look. But driving cattle is a mortally slow job, and we took the better part of the day to cover a dozen miles. If I had not had such an anxious heart I would have enjoyed that time. It was shining blue weather, with a constantly changing prospect of brown hills and far, green meadows, and a continual sound of larks and curlews and falling streams. But I had no mind for the summer, and little for Hislop's conversation, for as the fateful 15th of June grew near I was over-weighted with the hopeless difficulties of my enterprise.

I got some dinner in a humble Moffat public-house, and walked the two miles to the junction on the main line. The night express for the south was not due till near midnight, and to fill up the time I went up on the hill-side and fell asleep, for the walk had tired me. I all but slept too long, and hoped to run to the station and catch the train with two minutes to spare. The feel of the hard third-class cushions and the smell of stale tobacco cheered me up wonderfully. At any rate I felt now that I was getting to grips with my job.

I was decanted at Crewe in the small hours and had to wait till six to get a train for Birmingham. In the afternoon I got to Reading and changed into a local train which journeyed into the deeps of Berkshire. Presently I was in a land of lush water-meadows and slow reedy streams. About eight o'clock in the evening, a weary and travel-stained being – a cross between a farm labourer and a vet – with a checked black-and-white plaid over his arm (for I did not dare to wear it south of the Border) – descended at the little station of Arstinswell. There were several people on the platform, and I thought I had better wait to ask my way till I was clear of the place.

The road led through a wood of great beeches and then into a shallow valley with the green backs of downs peeping over the distant trees. After Scotland the air smelled heavy and flat, but infinitely sweet, for the limes and chestnuts and lilac-bushes were domes of blossom. Presently I came to a bridge, below which a clear, slow stream flowed between snowy beds of water-buttercups. A little above it was a mill; and the lasher made a pleasant cool sound in the scented dusk. Somehow the place soothed me and put me at my ease. I fell to whistling as I looked into the green depths, and the tune which came to my lips was 'Annie Laurie'.

A fisherman came up from the water-side, and as he neared me he, too, began to whistle. The tune was infectious, for he followed my suit. He was a huge man in untidy old flannels and a wide-brimmed hat, with a canvas bag slung on his shoulder. He nodded to me, and I thought I had never seen a shrewder or better-tempered face. He leaned his delicate ten-foot split cane rod against the bridge and looked with me at the water.

'Clear, isn't it?' he said pleasantly. 'I back our Kennet any day against the Test. Look at that big fellow! Four pounds, if he's an ounce! But the evening rise is over and you can't tempt 'em.'

'I don't see him,' said I.

'Look! There! A yard from the reeds, just above that stickle.'

'I've got him now. You might swear he was a black stone.'

'So,' he said, and whistled another bar of 'Annie Laurie'.

'Twisden's the name, isn't it?' he said over his shoulder, his eyes still fixed on the stream.

'No,' I said. 'I mean to say yes.' I had forgotten all about my alias.

'It's a wise conspirator that knows his own name,' he observed, grinning broadly at a moor-hen that emerged from the bridge's shadow.

I stood up and looked at him, at his square cleft jaw and broad, lined brow and the firm folds of cheek, and began to think that here at last was an ally worth having. His whimsical blue eyes seemed to go very deep. Suddenly he frowned. 'I call it disgraceful,' he said, raising his voice. 'Disgraceful that an able-bodied man like you should dare to beg. You can get a meal from my kitchen, but you'll get no money from me.'

A dog-cart was passing, driven by a young man who raised his whip to salute the fisherman. When he had gone, he picked up his rod.

'That's my house,' he said, pointing to a white gate a hundred yards on. 'Wait five minutes and then go round to the back door.' And with that he left me.

I did as I was bidden. I found a pretty cottage with a lawn running down to the stream, and a perfect jungle of guelder-rose and lilac flanking the path. The back door stood open and a grave butler was awaiting me.

'Come this way, sir,' he said, and he led me along a passage and up a back staircase to a pleasant bedroom looking towards the river. There I found a complete outfit laid out for me, dress clothes with all the fixings, a brown flannel suit, shirts, collars, ties, shaving things and hair-brushes, even a pair of patent shoes. 'Sir Walter thought as how Mr Reggie's things would fit you, sir,' said the butler. 'He keeps some clothes 'ere, for he comes regular on the week-ends. There's a bathroom next door, and I've prepared a 'ot bath. Dinner in 'alf an hour, sir. You'll 'ear the gong.'

The grave being withdrew, and I sat down in a chintz-covered easy chair and gaped. It was like a pantomime to come suddenly out of beggardom into this orderly comfort. Obviously Sir Walter believed in me, though why he did I could not guess. I looked at myself in the mirror, and saw a wild, haggard brown fellow with a fortnight's ragged beard and dust in ears and eyes, collarless, vulgarly shirted, with shapeless old tweed clothes and boots that had not been cleaned for the better part of a month. I made a fine tramp and a fair drover; and here I was ushered by a prim butler into this temple of gracious ease. And the best of it was that they did not even know my name.

I resolved not to puzzle my head, but to take the gifts the gods had provided. I shaved and bathed luxuriously, and got into the dress clothes and clean, crackling shirt, which fitted me not so badly. By the time I had finished the looking-glass showed a not unpersonable young man.

Sir Walter awaited me in a dusky dining-room, where a little round table was lit with silver candles. The sight of him – so respectable and established and secure, the embodiment of law and government and all the conventions – took me aback and made me feel an interloper. He couldn't know the truth about me, or he wouldn't treat me like this. I simply could not accept his hospitality on false pretenses.

'I am more obliged to you than I can say, but I'm bound to make things clear,' I said. 'I'm an innocent man, but I'm wanted by the police. I've got to tell you this, and I won't be surprised if you kick me out.'

He smiled. 'That's all right. Don't let that interfere with your appetite. We can talk about these things after dinner.'

I never ate a meal with greater relish, for I had had nothing all day but railway sandwiches. Sir Walter did me proud, for we drank a good champagne and had some uncommon fine port afterwards. It made me almost hysterical to be sitting there, waited on by a footman and a sleek butler, and remember that I had been living for three weeks like a brigand, with every man's hand against me. I told Sir Walter about tiger-fish in the Zambesi that bite off your fingers if you give them a chance, and we discussed sport up and down the globe, for he had hunted a bit in his day.

We went to his study for coffee, a jolly room full of books and trophies and untidiness and comfort. I made up my mind that if ever I got rid of this business and had a house of my own, I would create just such a room.

Then when the coffee-cups were cleared away, and we had got our cigars alight, my host swung his long legs over the side of his chair and bade me get started with my yarn.

'I've obeyed Harry's instructions,' he said, 'and the bribe he offered me was that you would tell me something to wake me up. I'm ready, Mr

Hannay.' I noticed with a start that he called me by my proper name.

I began at the very beginning. I told of my boredom in London, and the night I had come back to find Scudder gibbering on my doorstep. I told him all Scudder had told me about Karolides and the Foreign Office conference, and that made him purse his lips and grin. Then I got to the murder, and he grew solemn again. He heard all about the milkman and my time in Galloway, and my deciphering Scudder's notes at the inn.

'You've got them here?' he asked sharply, and drew a long breath when I whipped the little book from my pocket.

I said nothing of the contents. Then I described my meeting with Sir Harry, and the speeches at the hall. At that he laughed uproariously.

'Harry talked dashed nonsense, did he? I quite believe it. He's as good a chap as ever breathed, but his idiot of an uncle has stuffed his head with maggots. Go on, Mr Hannay.'

My day as a roadman excited him a bit. He made me describe the two fellows in the car very closely, and seemed to be raking back in his memory. He grew merry again when he heard of the fate of that ass, Jopley.

But the old man in the moorland house solemnized him. Again I had to describe every detail of his appearance.

'Bland and bald-headed and hooded his eyes like a bird... He sounds a sinister wild fowl! And you dynamited his hermitage, after he had saved you from the police? Spirited piece of work, that!'

Presently I reached the end of my wanderings. He got up slowly and looked down at me from the hearth-rug.

'You may dismiss the police from your mind,' he said. 'You're in no danger from the law of this land.'

'Great Scott!' I cried. 'Have they got the murderer?'

'No. But for the last fortnight they have dropped you from the list of possibles.'

'Why?' I asked in amazement.

'Principally because I received a letter from Scudder. I knew something of the man, and he did several jobs for me. He was half crank, half genius, but he was wholly honest. The trouble about him was his partiality for playing a lone hand. That made him pretty well useless in any secret service – a pity, for he had uncommon gifts. I think he was the bravest man in the world, for he was always shivering with fright, and yet nothing would choke him off. I had a letter from him on the 31st of May.'

'But he had been dead a week by then.'

'The letter was written and posted on the 23rd. He evidently did not anticipate an immediate decease. His communications usually took a week to reach me, for they were sent under cover to Spain and then to Newcastle. He had a mania, you know, for concealing his tracks.'

'What did he say?' I stammered.

'Nothing. Merely that he was in danger, but had found shelter with a good friend, and that I would hear from him before the 15th of June. He gave me no address, but said he was living near Portland Place. I think his object was to clear you if anything happened. When I got it I went to Scotland Yard, went over the details of the inquest, and concluded that you were the friend. We made inquiries about you, Mr Hannay, and found you were respectable. I thought I knew the motives for your disappearance – not only the police, the other one too – and when I got Harry's scrawl I guessed at the rest. I have been expecting you any time this past week.'

You can imagine what a load this took off my mind. I felt a free man once more, for I was now up against my country's enemies only, and not my country's law.

'Now let us have the little note-book,' said Sir Walter.

It took us a good hour to work through it. I explained the cipher, and he was jolly quick at picking it up. He amended my reading of it on several points, but I had been fairly correct, on the whole. His face was very grave before he had finished, and he sat silent for a while.

'I don't know what to make of it,' he said at last. 'He is right about one thing – what is going to happen the day after tomorrow. How the devil can it have got known? That is ugly enough in itself. But all this about war and the Black Stone – it reads like some wild melodrama. If only I had more confidence in Scudder's judgment. The trouble about him was that he was too romantic. He had the artistic temperament, and wanted a story to be better than God meant it to be. He had a lot of odd biases, too. Jews, for example, made him see red. Jews and the high finance.'

'The Black Stone,' he repeated. '*Der Schwarze stein*. It's like a penny novelette. And all this stuff about Karolides. That is the weak part of the tale, for I happen to know that the virtuous Karolides is likely to outlast us both. There is no state in Europe that wants him gone. Besides, he has just been playing up to Berlin and Vienna and giving my chief some uneasy moments. No! Scudder has gone off the track there. Frankly, Hannay, I don't believe that part of his story. There's some nasty business afoot, and he found out too much and lost his life over it. But I am ready to take my oath that it is ordinary spy work. A certain great European power makes a hobby of her spy system and her methods are not too particular. Since she pays by piece-work her blackguards are not likely to stick at a murder or two. They want our naval dispositions for their collection at the Marineamt; but they will be pigeon-holed – nothing more.'

Just then the butler entered the room.

'There's a trunk-call from London, Sir Walter. It's Mr 'Eath, and he wants to speak to you personally.'

My host went off to the telephone. He returned in five minutes with a whitish face. 'I apologize to the shade of Scudder,' he said. 'Karolides was shot dead this evening at a few minutes after seven.'

CHAPTER 8

THE COMING OF THE BLACK STONE

I came down to breakfast next morning, after eight hours of blessed dreamless sleep, to find Sir Walter decoding a telegram in the midst of muffins and marmalade. His fresh rosiness of yesterday seemed a thought tarnished.

'I had a busy hour on the telephone after you went to bed,' he said. 'I got my chief to speak to the First Lord and the Secretary for War, and they are bringing Royer over a day sooner. This wire clinches it. He will be in London at five. Odd that the code word for a S*ous-chef d'Etat Major Général* should be "Porker".'

He directed me to the hot dishes and went on.

'Not that I think it will do much good. If your friends were clever enough to find out the first arrangement they are clever enough to discover the change. I would give my head to know where the leak is. We believed there were only five men in England who knew about Royer's visit, and you may be certain there were fewer in France, for they manage these things better there.'

While I ate he continued to talk, making me to my surprise a present of his full confidence.

'Can the dispositions not be changed?' I asked.

'They could,' he said. 'But we want to avoid that if possible. They are the result of immense thought, and no alteration would be as good. Besides, on one or two points change is simply impossible. Still, something could be done, if it were absolutely necessary. But you see the difficulty Hannay. Our enemies are not going to be such fools as to pick Royer's pocket or any childish game like that. They know that would mean a row and put us on our guard. Their aim is to get the details without any of us knowing, so that Royer will go back to Paris in the belief that the whole business is still deadly secret. If they can't do that they fail, for once we suspect they know that the whole thing must be altered.'

'Then we must stick by the Frenchman's side till he is home again,' I said. 'If they thought they could get the information in Paris they would try there. It means that they have some deep scheme on foot in London which they reckon is going to win out.'

'Royer dines with my chief, and then comes to my house where four people will see him – Whittaker from the Admiralty, myself, Sir Arthur Drew, and General Winstanley. The First Lord is ill, and has gone to Sheringham. At my house he will get a certain document from Whittaker, and after that he will be motored to Portsmouth where a destroyer will take him to Havre. His journey is too important for the ordinary boat-train. He will never be left unattended for a moment till he is safe on French soil. The same with Whittaker till he meets Royer. That is the best we can do and it's hard to see how there can be any miscarriage. But I don't mind admitting that I'm horribly nervous. This murder of Karolides will play the deuce in the chancellories of Europe.'

After breakfast he asked me if I could drive a car.

'Well, you'll be my chauffeur today and wear Hudson's rig. You're about his size. You have a hand in this business and we are taking no risks. There are desperate men against us, who will not respect the country retreat of an over-worked official.'

When I first came to London I had bought a car and amused myself with running about the south of England, so I knew something of the geography. I took Sir Walter to town by the Bath Road and made good going. It was a soft breathless June morning, with a promise of sultriness later but it was delicious enough swinging through the little towns with their freshly watered streets, and past the summer gardens of the Thames valley. I landed Sir Walter at his house in Queen Anne's Gate punctually by half-past eleven. The butler was coming up by train with the luggage.

The first thing he did was to take me round to Scotland Yard. There we saw a prim gentleman, with a clean-shaven lawyer's face.

'I've brought you the Portland Place murderer,' was Sir Walter's introduction.

The reply was a wry smile. 'It would have been a welcome present, Bullivant. This, I presume, is Mr Richard Hannay, who for some days greatly interested my department.'

'Mr Hannay will interest it again. He has much to tell you, but not today. For certain grave reasons his tale must wait for twenty-four hours. Then, I can promise you, you will be entertained and possibly edified. I want you to assure Mr Hannay that he will suffer no further inconvenience.'

This assurance was promptly given. 'You can take up your life where you left off,' I was told. 'Your flat, which probably you no longer wish to occupy, is waiting for you, and your man is still there. As you were never publicly accused, we considered that there was no need of a public exculpation. But on that, of course, you must please yourself.'

'We may want your assistance later on, MacGillivray,' Sir Walter said as we left.

Then he turned me loose.

'Come and see me tomorrow, Hannay. I needn't tell you to keep deadly quiet. If I were you I would go to bed, for you must have considerable arrears of sleep to overtake. You had better lie low, for if one of your Black Stone friends saw you there might be trouble.'

I felt curiously at a loose end. At first it was very pleasant to be a free man, able to go where I wanted without fearing anything. I had only been a month under the ban of the law and it was quite enough for me. I went to the Savoy and ordered very carefully a very good luncheon, and then smoked the best cigar the house could provide. But I was still feeling nervous. When I saw anybody look at me in the lounge, I grew shy, and wondered if they were thinking about the murder.

After that I took a taxi and drove miles away up into North London. I walked back through the fields and lines of villas and terraces and then slums and mean streets, and it took me pretty nearly two hours. All the while my restlessness was growing worse. I felt that great things, tremendous things, were happening or about to happen, and I, who was the cog-wheel of the whole business, was out of it. Royer would be landing at Dover, Sir Walter would be making plans with the few people in England who were in the secret, and somewhere in the darkness the Black Stone would be working. I felt the sense of danger and impending calamity, and I had the curious feeling, too, that I alone could avert it, alone could grapple with it. But I was out of the game now. How could it be otherwise? It was not likely that Cabinet Ministers and Admiralty Lords and Generals would admit me to their councils.

I actually began to wish that I could run up against one of my three enemies. That would lead to developments. I felt that I wanted enormously to have a vulgar scrap with those gentry, where I could hit out and flatten something. I was rapidly getting into a very bad temper.

I didn't feel like going back to my flat. That had to be faced sometime, but as I still had sufficient money, I thought I would put it off till next morning and go to a hotel for the night.

My irritation lasted through dinner, which I had at a restaurant in Jermyn Street. I was no longer hungry, and let several courses pass untasted. I drank the best part of a bottle of Burgundy, but it did nothing to cheer me. An abominable restlessness had taken possession of me. Here was I, a very ordinary fellow with no particular brains, and yet I was convinced that somehow I was needed to help this business through – that without me it would all go to blazes. I told myself it was sheer, silly conceit, that four or five of the cleverest people living, with all the might of the British Empire at their back, had the job in hand. Yet I couldn't be convinced. It seemed as if a voice kept speaking in my ear, telling me to be up and doing or I would never sleep again.

The upshot was that about half-past nine I made up my mind to go to Queen Anne's Gate. Very likely I would not be admitted, but it would ease my conscience to try.

I walked down Jermyn Street and at the corner of Duke Street passed a group of young men. They were in evening dress, had been dining somewhere, and were going on to a music-hall. One of them was Mr Marmaduke Jopley.

He saw me and stopped short.

'By God, the murderer!' he cried. 'Here, you fellows, hold him! That's Hannay, the man who did the Portland Place murder!' He gripped me by the arm and the others crowded around; I wasn't looking for any trouble, but my ill temper made me play the fool. A policeman came up, and I should have told him the truth and, if he didn't believe it, demanded to be taken to Scotland Yard or, for that matter, to the nearest police station. But a delay at that moment seemed to me unendurable, and the sight of Marmie's imbecile face was more than I could bear. I let out with my left, and had the satisfaction of seeing him measure his length in the gutter.

Then began an unholy row. They were all on me at once, and the policeman took me in the rear. I got in one or two good blows, for I think with fair play I could have licked the lot of them, but the policeman pinned me behind, and one of them got his fingers on my throat.

Through a black cloud of rage I heard the officer of the law asking what was the matter, and Marmie, between his broken teeth, declaring that I was Hannay, the murderer.

'Oh, damn it all,' I cried, 'make the fellow shut up. I advise you to leave me alone, constable. Scotland Yard knows all about me, and you'll get a proper wigging if you interfere with me.'

'You've got to come along of me, young man,' said the policeman. 'I saw you strike that gentleman crool 'ard. You began it, too, for he wasn't doing nothing. I seen you. Best go quietly or I'll have to fix you up.'

Exasperation and an overwhelming sense that at no cost must I delay gave me the strength of a bull elephant. I fairly wrenched the constable off his feet, floored the man who was gripping my collar, and set off at my best pace down Duke Street. I heard a whistle being blown, and the rush of men behind me.

I have a very fair turn of speed and that night I had wings. In a jiffy I was in Pall Mall and had turned down towards St. James's Park. I dodged the policeman at the Palace Gates, dived through a press of carriages at the entrance to the Mall, and was making for the bridge before my pursuers had crossed the roadway. In the open ways of the park I put on a spurt. Happily there were few people about and no one tried to stop me. I was staking all on getting to Queen Anne's Gate.

When I entered that quiet thoroughfare it seemed deserted. Sir Walter's house was in the narrow part and outside it three or four motor-cars were drawn up. I slackened speed some yards off and walked briskly up to the door. If the butler refused me admission, or if he even delayed to open the door, I was done.

He didn't delay. I had scarcely rung before the door opened.

'I must see Sir Walter,' I panted. 'My business is desperately important.'

That butler was a great man. Without moving a muscle he held the door open, and then shut it behind me. 'Sir Walter is engaged, sir, and I have orders to admit no one. Perhaps you will wait.'

The house was of the old-fashioned kind, with a wide hall and rooms on both sides of it. At the far end was an alcove with a telephone and a couple of chairs, and there the butler offered me a seat.

'See here,' I whispered. 'There's trouble about and I'm in it. But Sir Walter knows and I'm working for him. If any one comes and asks if I am here, tell him a lie.'

He nodded, and presently there was a noise of voices in the street and a furious ringing at the bell. I never admired a man more than that butler. He opened the door and with a face like a graven image waited to be questioned.

Then he gave them it. He told them whose house it was and what his orders were and simply froze them off the doorstep. I could see it all from my alcove, and it was better than any play.

*　　*　　*

I hadn't waited long till there came another ring at the bell. The butler made no bones about admitting this new visitor.

While he was taking off his coat I saw who it was. You couldn't open a newspaper or a magazine without seeing that face – the grey beard cut like a spade, the firm fighting mouth, the blunt square nose, and the keen blue eyes. I recognized the First Sea Lord, the man, they say, that made the new British Navy.

He passed my alcove and was ushered into a room at the back of the hall. As the door opened I could hear the sound of low voices. It shut, and I was left alone again.

For twenty minutes I sat there, wondering what I was to do next. I was still perfectly convinced that I was wanted, but when or how I had no notion. I kept looking at my watch, and as the time crept on to half-past ten I began to think that the conference must soon end. In a quarter of an hour Royer should be speeding along the road to Portsmouth.

Then I heard a bell ring and the butler appeared. The door of the back room opened, and the First Sea Lord came out. He walked past me, and in passing he glanced in my direction, and for a second we looked each other in the face. Only for a second, but it was enough to make my heart jump. I had never seen the great man before, and he had never seen me.

But in that fraction of time something sprang into his eyes, and that something was recognition. You can't mistake it. It is a flicker, a spark of light, a minute shade of difference, which means one thing and one thing only. It came involuntarily, for in a moment it died, and he passed on. In a maze of wild fancies I heard the street door close behind him.

I picked up the telephone-book and looked up the number of his house. We were connected at once and I heard a servant's voice.

'Is his Lordship at home?' I asked.

'His Lordship returned half an hour ago,' said the voice, 'and has gone to bed. He is not very well tonight. Will you leave a message, sir?'

I rang off and almost tumbled into in a chair. My part in this business was not yet ended. It had been a close shave, but I had been in time.

Not a moment could be lost, so I marched boldly to the door of that back room and entered without knocking. Five surprised faces looked up from a round table. There was Sir Walter, and Drew, the war minister, whom I knew from his photographs. There was a slim, elderly man, who was probably Whittaker, the Admiralty official, and there was General Winstanley, conspicuous from the long scar on his forehead. Lastly there was a short stout man with an iron-grey moustache and bushy eyebrows, who had been arrested in the middle of a sentence.

Sir Walter's face showed surprise and annoyance.

'This is Mr Hannay, of whom I have spoken to you,' he said apologetically to the company. 'I'm afraid, Hannay, this visit is ill-timed.'

I was getting back my coolness. 'That remains to be seen, sir,' I said, 'but I think it may be in the nick of time. For God's sake, gentlemen, tell me who went out a minute ago?'

'Lord Alloa,' Sir Walter said, reddening with anger.

'It was not,' I cried. 'It was his living image, but it was not Lord Alloa. It was some one who recognized me, some one I have seen in the last month. He had scarcely left the doorstep when I rang up Lord Alloa's house and was told he had come in half an hour before and had gone to bed.'

'Who – who—' some one stammered.

'The Black Stone,' I cried, and I sat down in the chair so recently vacated and looked round at five badly scared gentlemen.

CHAPTER 9

THE THIRTY-NINE STEPS

'NONSENSE!' said the official from the Admiralty.

Sir Walter got up and left the room, while we looked blankly at the table. He came back in ten minutes with a long face. 'I have spoken to Alloa,' he said. 'Had him out of bed – very grumpy. He went straight home after Mulross's dinner.'

'But it's madness,' broke in General Winstanley. 'Do you mean to tell me that that man came here and sat beside me for the best part of half an hour, and that I didn't detect the imposture? Alloa must be out of his mind.'

'Don't you see the cleverness of it?' I said. 'You were too interested in other things to have the use of your eyes. You took Lord Alloa for granted. If it had been anybody else you might have looked more closely, but it was natural for him to be here, and that put you all to sleep.'

Then the Frenchman spoke, very slowly and in good English.

'The young man is right. His psychology is good. Our enemies have not been foolish!'

He bent his wise brows on the assembly.

'I will tell you a tale,' he said. 'It happened many years ago in Senegal. I was quartered in a remote station, and to pass the time used to go fishing for big barbel in the river. A little Arab mare used to carry my luncheon basket – one of the salted dun breed you got at Timbuctoo in the old days. Well, one morning I had good sport, and the mare was unaccountably restless. I could hear her whinnying and squealing and stamping her feet, and I kept soothing her with my voice while my mind was intent on fish. I could see her all the time, as I thought, out of a corner of my eye, tethered to a tree twenty yards away. After a couple of hours I began to think of food. I collected my fish in a tarpaulin bag, and moved down to the stream towards the mare, trolling my line. When I got up to her I flung the tarpaulin on her back...'

He paused and looked round.

'It was the smell that gave me warning. I turned my head and found myself looking at a lion three feet off... An old man-eater, that was the terror of the village... What was left of the mare, a mass of blood and bones and hide, was behind him.'

'What happened?' I asked. I was enough of a hunter to know a true yarn when I heard it.

'I stuffed my fishing-rod into his jaws, and I had a pistol. Also my servants came presently with rifles. But he left his mark on me.' He held up a hand which lacked three fingers.

'Consider,' he said. 'The mare had been dead more than an hour, and the brute had been patiently watching me ever since. I never saw the kill, for I was accustomed to the mare's fretting, and I never marked her absence, for my consciousness of her was only of something tawny, and the lion filled that part. If I could blunder thus, gentlemen, in a land where men's senses are keen, why should we busy preoccupied urban folk not err also?'

Sir Walter nodded. No one was ready to gainsay him.

'But I don't see,' went on Winstanley. 'Their object was to get these dispositions without our knowing it. Now it only required one of us to mention to Alloa our meeting tonight for the whole fraud to be exposed.'

Sir Walter laughed drily. 'The selection of Alloa shows their acumen. Which of us was likely to speak to him about tonight? Or was he likely to open the subject?' I remembered the First Sea Lord's reputation for taciturnity and shortness of temper.

'The one thing that puzzles me,' said the General, 'is what good his visit here would do that spy fellow? He could not carry away several pages of figures and strange names in his head.'

'That is not difficult,' the Frenchman replied. 'A good spy is trained to have a photographic memory. Like your own Macaulay. You noticed he said nothing, but went through these papers again and again. I think we may assume that he has every detail stamped on his mind. When I was younger I could do the same trick.'

'Well, I suppose there is nothing for it but to change the plans,' said Sir Walter ruefully.

Whittaker was looking very glum. 'Did you tell Lord Alloa what had happened?' he asked. 'No? I can't speak with absolute assurance, but

I'm nearly certain we can't make any serious change unless we alter the geography of England.'

'Another thing must be said.' It was Royer who spoke. 'I talked freely when that man was here. I told something of the military plans of my Government. I was permitted to say so much. But that information would be worth many millions to our enemies. No, my friends, I see no other way. The man who came here and his confederates must be taken and taken at once.'

'Good God,' I cried, 'and we have not a rag of a clue.'

'Besides,' said Whittaker, 'there is the post. By this time the news will be on its way.'

'No,' said the Frenchman. 'You do not understand the habits of the spy. He receives personally his reward, and he delivers personally his intelligence. We in France know something of the breed. There is still a chance, *mes amis*. These men must cross the sea, and there are ships to be searched and ports to be watched. Believe me, the need is desperate for both France and Britain.'

Royer's grave good sense seemed to pull us together. He was the man of action among fumblers. But I saw no hope in any face, and I felt none. Where among the fifty millions of these islands and within a dozen hours were we to lay hands on the three cleverest rogues in Europe?

* * *

Then suddenly I had an inspiration.

'Where is Scudder's book?' I asked Sir Walter. 'Quick, man, I remember something in it.'

He unlocked the drawer of a bureau and gave it to me.

I found the place. 'Thirty-nine steps,' I read, and again, 'thirty-nine steps! I counted them – High tide 10.17 p.m.'

The Admiralty man was looking at me as if he thought I had gone mad.

'Don't you see it's a clue,' I cried. 'Scudder knew where these fellows laired – he knew where they were going to leave the country; though he kept the name to himself. Tomorrow was the day, and it was some place where high tide was at 10.17.'

'They may have gone tonight,' some one said.

'Not them. They have their own snug secret way, and they won't be hurried. I know Germans, and they are mad about working to a plan. Where the devil can I get a book of Tide Tables?'

Whittaker brightened up. 'It's a chance,' be said. 'Let's go over to the Admiralty.'

We got into two of the waiting motor-cars – all but Sir Walter, who went off to Scotland Yard – to 'mobilize MacGillivray', so he said.

We marched through empty corridors and big bare chambers where the charwomen were busy, till we reached a little room lined with books and maps. A resident clerk was unearthed, who presently fetched from the library the Admiralty Tide Tables. I sat at the desk and the others stood round, for somehow or other I had got charge of this outfit.

It was no good. There were hundreds of entries, and as far as I could see 10.17 might cover fifty places. We had to find some way of narrowing the possibilities.

I took my head in my hands and thought. There must be some way of reading this riddle. What did Scudder mean by steps? I thought of dock steps, but if he had meant that I didn't think he would have mentioned the number. It must be some place where there were several staircases and one marked out from the others by having thirty-nine steps.

Then I had a sudden thought and hunted up all the steamer sailings. There was no boat which left for the Continent at 10.17 p.m.

Why was high tide important? If it was a harbour it must be some little place where the tide mattered, or else it was a heavy-draught boat. But there was no regular steamer sailing at that hour, and somehow I didn't think they would travel by a big boat from a regular harbour. So it must be some little harbour where the tide was important, or perhaps no harbour at all.

But if it was a little port I couldn't see what the steps signified. There were no sets of staircases at any harbour that I had ever seen. It must be some place which a particular staircase identified, and where the tide was full at 10.17. On the whole it seemed to me that the place must be a bit of open coast. But the staircases kept puzzling me.

Then I went back to wider considerations. Whereabouts would a man be likely to leave for Germany, a man in a hurry who wanted a speedy and a secret passage? Not from any of the big harbours. And not from the Channel or the west coast or the north or Scotland, for, remember, he was starting from London. I measured the distance on the map, and tried to put myself in the enemy's shoes. I should try for Ostend or Antwerp or Rotterdam and I should sail from somewhere on the east coast between Cromer and Dover.

All this was very loose guessing and I don't pretend it was ingenious or scientific. I wasn't any kind of Sherlock Holmes. But I have always fancied I had a kind of instinct about questions like this. I don't know if I can explain myself, but I used to use my brains as far as they went, and after they came to a blank wall I guessed, and I usually found my guesses pretty right.

So I set out all my conclusions on a bit of Admiralty paper. They ran like this:

FAIRLY CERTAIN.

(1) Place where there are several sets of stairs: one that matters distinguished by having thirty-nine steps.
(2) Full tide at 10.17 p.m. Leaving shore only possible at full tide.
(3) Steps not dock-steps and so place probably not harbour.
(4) No regular night steamer at 10.17. Means of transport must be tramp (unlikely), yacht or fishing-boat.

There my reasoning stopped. I made another list, which I headed 'Guessed', but I was just as sure of the one as the other.

GUESSED.

(1) Place not harbour but open coast.
(2) Boat small – trawler, yacht or launch.
(3) Place somewhere on east coast between Cromer and Dover.

It struck me as odd that I should be sitting at that desk with a Cabinet Minister, a Field Marshal, two high Government officials, and a French General watching me, while from the scribble of a dead man I was trying to drag a secret which meant life or death for us.

Sir Walter had joined us, and presently MacGillivray arrived. He had sent out instructions to watch the ports and railway stations for the three gentlemen whom I had described to Sir Walter. Not that he or anybody else thought that that would do much good.

'Here's the most I can make of it,' I said. 'We have got to find a place where there are several staircases down to the beach, one of which has thirty-nine steps. I think it's a piece of open coast with biggish cliffs somewhere between the Wash and the Channel. Also it's a place where full tide is at 10.17 tomorrow night.'

Then an idea struck me. 'Is there no Inspector of Coastguards or some fellow like that who knows the east coast?'

Whittaker said there was and that he lived in Clapham. He went off in a car to fetch him, and the rest of us sat about the little room and talked of anything that came into our heads. I lit a pipe and went over the whole thing again till my brain grew weary.

About one in the morning the coastguard man arrived. He was a fine old fellow with the look of a naval officer, and was desperately respectful to the company. I left the War Minister to cross-examine him, for I felt he would think it cheek in me to talk.

'We want you to tell us the places you know on the east coast where there are cliffs, and where several sets of steps run down to the beach.'

He thought for a bit. 'What kind of steps do you mean, sir? There are plenty of places with roads cut down through the cliffs, and most roads have a step or two in them. Or do you mean regular staircases – all steps, so to speak?'

Sir Arthur looked towards me. 'We mean regular staircases,' I said.

He reflected a minute or two. 'I don't know that I can think of any. Wait a second. There's a place in Norfolk – Brattlesham – beside a golf course, where there are a couple of staircases to let the gentlemen get a lost ball.'

'That's not it,' I said.

'Then there are plenty of Marine Parades, if that's what you mean. Every seaside resort has them.'

I shook my head.

'It's got to be more retired than that,' I said.

'Well, gentlemen, I can't think of anywhere else. Of course, there's the Ruff —'

'What's that?' I asked.

'The big chalk headland in Kent, close to Bradgate. It's got a lot of villas on the top, and some of the houses have staircases down to a private beach. It's a very high-toned sort of place, and the residents there like to keep by themselves.'

I tore open the Tide Tables and found Bradgate. High tide there was at 10.27 p.m. on the 15th of June.

'We're on the scent at last!' I cried excitedly. 'How can I find out what is the tide at the Ruff?'

'I can tell you that, sir,' said the coastguard man. 'I once was lent a house there in this very month, and I used to go out at night to the deep-sea fishing. The tide's ten minutes before Bradgate.'

I closed the book and looked round at the company.

'If one of those staircases has thirty-nine steps we have solved the mystery, gentlemen,' I said. 'I want the loan of your car, Sir Walter, and a map of the roads. If Mr MacGillivray will spare me ten minutes I think we can prepare something for tomorrow.'

It was ridiculous in me to take charge of the business like this, but they didn't seem to mind, and after all I had been in the show from the start. Besides, I was used to rough jobs, and these eminent gentlemen were too clever not to see it.

It was General Royer who gave me my commission.

'I for one,' he said, 'am content to leave the matter in Mr Hannay's hands.'

By half-past three I was tearing past the moonlit hedgerows of Kent with MacGillivray's best man on the seat beside me.

CHAPTER 10

VARIOUS PARTIES CONVERGING ON THE SEA

A pink and blue June morning found me at Bradgate looking from the Griffin Hotel over a smooth sea to the lightship on the Cock sands which seemed the size of a bell-buoy. A couple of miles further south and much nearer the shore a small destroyer was anchored. Scaife, MacGillivray's man, who had been in the navy, knew the boat and told me her name and her commander's, so I sent off a wire to Sir Walter.

After breakfast Scaife got from a house-agent a key for the gates of the staircases on the Ruff. I walked with him along the sands, and sat down in a nook of the cliffs while he investigated the half dozen of them. I didn't want to be seen, but the place at this hour was quite deserted, and all the time I was on that beach I saw nothing but the seagulls.

It took him more than an hour to do the job, and when I saw him coming towards me, conning a bit of paper, I can tell you my heart was in my mouth. Everything depended, you see, on my guess proving right.

He read aloud the number of steps in the different stairs. 'Thirty-four, thirty-five, thirty-nine, forty-two, forty-seven,' and 'twenty-one' where the cliffs grew lower. I almost got up and shouted.

We hurried back to the town and sent a wire to MacGillivray. I wanted half a dozen men and I directed them to divide themselves among different specified hotels. Then Scaife set out to prospect the house at the head of the thirty-nine steps.

He came back with news that both puzzled and reassured me. The house was called Trafalgar Lodge, and belonged to an old gentleman called Appleton – a retired stockbroker, the house-agent said. Mr Appleton was there a good deal in the summer time, and was in residence now – had been for the better part of a week. Scaife could pick up very little information about him, except that he was a decent old fellow, who paid his bills regularly and was always good for a fiver for a local charity. Then Scaife seems to have penetrated to the back door of the house, pretending he was an agent for sewing machines. Only three servants were kept, a cook, a parlour-maid, and a housemaid, and they were just the sort that you would find in a respectable middle-class household. The cook was not the gossiping kind, and had pretty soon shut the door in his face, but Scaife said he was positive she knew nothing. Next door there was a new house building which would give good cover for observation, and the villa on the other side was to let, and its garden was rough and shrubby.

I borrowed Scaife's telescope, and before lunch went for a walk along the Ruff. I kept well behind the rows of villas, and found a good observation point on the edge of the golf course. There I had a view of the line of turf along the cliff top, with seats placed at intervals and the little square plots, railed in and planted with bushes, whence the staircases descended to the beach. I saw Trafalgar Lodge very plainly, a red-brick villa with a verandah, a tennis lawn behind, and in front the ordinary seaside flower-garden full of marguerites and scraggy geraniums. There was a flagstaff from which an enormous Union Jack hung limply in the still air.

Presently I observed some one leave the house and saunter along the cliff. When I got my glasses on him I saw it was an old man, wearing white flannel trousers, a blue serge jacket and a straw hat. He carried field-glasses and a newspaper, and sat down on one of the iron seats and began to read. Sometimes he would lay down the paper and turn his glasses on the sea. He looked for a long time at the destroyer. I watched him for half an hour, till he got up and went back to the house for his luncheon, when I returned to the hotel for mine.

I wasn't feeling very confident. This decent commonplace dwelling was not what I had expected. The man might be the bald archæologist of that horrible moorland farm, or he might not. He was exactly the kind of satisfied old bird you will find in every suburb and every holiday place. If you wanted a type of the perfectly harmless person you would probably pitch on that.

But after lunch as I sat in the hotel porch I perked up, for I saw the thing I had hoped for and dreaded to miss. A yacht came up from the south and dropped anchor pretty well opposite the Ruff. She seemed about a hundred and fifty tons and I saw she belonged to the Squadron from the white ensign. So Scaife and I went down to the harbour and hired a boatman for an afternoon's fishing.

I spent a warm and peaceful afternoon. We caught between us about twenty pounds of cod and lythe, and out in that dancing blue sea I took a cheerier view of things. Above the white cliffs of the Ruff I saw the green and red of the villas, and especially the great flagstaff of Trafalgar Lodge. About four o'clock when we had fished enough I made the boatman row us round the yacht, which lay like a delicate white bird, ready at a moment to flee. Scaife said she must be a fast boat from her build, and that she was pretty heavily engined.

Her name was the *Ariadne*, as I discovered from the cap of one of the men who was polishing brass-work. I spoke to him and got an answer in the soft dialect of Essex. Another hand that came along passed me the time of day in an unmistakable English tongue. Our boatman had an argument with one of them about the weather, and for a few minutes we lay on our oars close to the starboard bow.

Then the men suddenly disregarded us and bent their heads to their work as an officer came along the deck. He was a pleasant, clean-looking young fellow, and he put a question to us about our fishing in very good English. But there could be no doubt about him. His close-cropped head and the cut of his collar and tie never came out of England.

That did something to reassure me, but as we rowed back to Bradgate my obstinate doubts would not be dismissed. The thing that worried me was the reflection that my enemies knew that I had got my knowledge from Scudder, and it was Scudder who had given me the clue to this place. If they knew that Scudder had this clue would they not be certain to change their plans? Too much depended on their success for them to take any risks. The whole question was how much they understood about Scudder's knowledge. I had talked confidently last night about Germans always sticking to a scheme, but if they had any suspicions that I was on their track they would be fools not to cover it. I wondered if the man last night had seen that I recognized him. Somehow I did not think he had, and to that I clung. But the whole business had never seemed so difficult as that afternoon when by all calculations I should have been rejoicing in assured success.

In the hotel I met the commander of the destroyer, to whom Scaife introduced me and with whom I had a few words. Then I thought I would put in an hour or two watching Trafalgar Lodge.

I found a place further up the hill in the garden of an empty house. From there I had a full view of the court, on which two figures were having a game of tennis. One was the old man, whom I had already seen; the other was a younger fellow, wearing some club colours in the scarf round his middle. They played with tremendous zest, like two city gents who wanted hard exercise to open their pores. You couldn't conceive a more innocent spectacle. They shouted and laughed and stopped for drinks, when a maid brought out two tankards on a salver. I rubbed my eyes and asked myself if I was not the most immortal fool on earth. Mystery and darkness had hung about the men who hunted me over the Scotch moors in aeroplane and motor-car, and notably about that infernal antiquarian. It was easy enough to connect these folk with the knife that pinned Scudder to the floor, and with fell designs on the world's peace. But here were two guileless citizens, taking their innocuous exercise, and soon about to go indoors to a humdrum dinner, where they would talk of market prices and the last cricket scores and the gossip of their native Surbiton. I had been making a net to catch vultures and falcons, and lo and behold! two plump thrushes had blundered into it.

Presently a third figure arrived, a young man on a bicycle, with a bag of golf-clubs slung on his back. He strolled round to the tennis lawn and was welcomed riotously by the players. Evidently they were chaffing him, and their chaff sounded horribly English. Then the plump man, mopping his brow with a silk handkerchief, announced that he must have a tub. I heard his very words – 'I've got into a proper lather,' he said. 'This will bring down my weight and my handicap, Bob. I'll take you on tomorrow and give you a stroke a hole.' You couldn't find anything much more English than that.

They all went into the house, and left me feeling a precious idiot. I had been barking up the wrong tree this time. These men might be acting; but if they were where was their audience? They didn't know I was sitting thirty yards off in a rhododendron. It was simply impossible to believe that these three hearty fellows were anything but what they seemed – three ordinary, game-playing, suburban Englishmen, wearisome, if you like, but sordidly innocent.

*   *   *

And yet there were three of them; and one was old, and one was plump, and one was lean and dark; and their house chimed in with Scudder's notes; and half a mile off was lying a steam yacht with at least one German officer. I thought of Karolides lying dead and all Europe trembling on the edge of an earthquake, and the men I had left behind me in London, who were waiting anxiously on the events of the next hours. There was no doubt that hell was afoot somewhere. The Black Stone had won, and if it survived this June night would bank its winnings.

There seemed only one thing to do – go forward as if I had no doubts, and if I was going to make a fool of myself to do it handsomely. Never in my life have I faced a job with greater disinclination. I would rather in my then mind have walked into a den of anarchists, each with his Browning handy, or faced a charging lion with a popgun, than enter the happy home of three cheerful Englishmen, and tell them that their game was up. How they would laugh at me!

But suddenly I remembered a thing I once heard in Rhodesia from old Peter Pienaar. I have quoted Peter already in this narrative. He was the best scout I ever knew, and before he had turned respectable he had been pretty often on the windy side of the law, when he had been wanted badly by the authorities. Peter once discussed with me the question of disguises, and he had a theory which struck me at the time. He said, barring absolute certainties like finger-prints, mere physical traits were very little use for identification if the fugitive really knew his business. He laughed at things like dyed hair and false beards and such childish follies.

The only thing that mattered was what Peter called 'atmosphere'. If a man could get into perfectly different surroundings from those in which he had been first observed, and – this is the important part – really play up to these surroundings and behave as if he had never been out of them, he would puzzle the cleverest detectives on earth. And he used to tell a story of how he once borrowed a black coat and went to church and shared the same hymn-book with the man that was looking for him. If that man had seen him in decent company before he would have recognized him; but he had only seen him snuffing the lights in a public-house with a revolver.

The recollection of Peter's talk gave me the first real comfort I had had that day. Peter had been a wise old bird, and these fellows I was after were about the pick of the aviary. What if they were playing Peter's game? A fool tries to look different; a clever man looks the same and is different.

Again, there was that other maxim of Peter's, which had helped me when I had been a roadman. 'If you are playing a part, you will never keep it up unless you convince yourself that you are it.' That would explain the game of tennis. Those chaps didn't need to act, they just turned a handle and passed into another life, which came as naturally to them as the first. It sounds a platitude, but Peter used to say that it was the big secret of all the famous criminals.

It was now getting on for eight o'clock, and I went back and saw Scaife to give him his instructions. I arranged with him how to place his men, and then I went for a walk, for I didn't feel up to any dinner. I went round the deserted golf course, and then to a point on the cliffs further north, beyond the line of the villas. On the little, trim, newly-made roads I met people in flannels coming back from tennis and the beach, and a coastguard from the wireless station, and donkeys and pierrots padding homewards. Out at sea in the blue dusk I saw lights appear on the *Ariadne* and on the destroyer away to the south, and beyond the Cock sands the bigger lights of steamers making for the Thames. The whole scene was so peaceful and ordinary that I got more dashed in spirits every second. It took all my resolution to stroll towards Trafalgar Lodge about half-past nine.

On the way I got a piece of solid comfort from the sight of a greyhound that was swinging along at a nursemaid's heels. He reminded me of a dog I used to have in Rhodesia, and of the time when I took him hunting with me in the Pali hills. We were after rhebok, the dun kind, and I recollected how we had followed one beast, and both he and I had clean lost it. A greyhound works by sight, and my eyes are good enough, but that buck simply leaked out of the landscape. Afterwards I found out how it managed it. Against the grey rock of the kopjes it showed no more than a crow against a thundercloud. It didn't need to run away; all it had to do was to stand still and melt into the background.

Suddenly as these memories chased across my brain I thought of my present case and applied the moral. The Black Stone didn't need to bolt.

They were quietly absorbed into the landscape. I was on the right track, and I jammed that down in my mind and vowed never to forget it. The last word was with Peter Pienaar.

Scaife's men would be posted now, but there was no sign of a soul. The house stood as open as a market-place for anybody to observe. A three-foot railing separated it from the cliff road; the low sound of voices revealed where the occupants were finishing dinner. Everything was as public and above-board as a charity bazaar. Feeling the greatest fool on earth, I opened the gate and rang the bell.

*   *   *

A man of my sort, who has travelled about the world in rough places, gets on perfectly well with two classes, what you may call the upper and the lower. He understands them and they understand him. I was at home with herds and tramps and roadmen, and I was sufficiently at my ease with people like Sir Walter and the men I had met the night before. I can't explain why, but it is a fact. But what fellows like me don't understand is the great comfortable, satisfied middle-class world, the folk that live in villas and suburbs. He doesn't know how they look at things, he doesn't understand their conventions, and he is as shy of them as of a black mamba. When a trim parlour-maid opened the door, I could hardly find my voice.

I asked for Mr Appleton and was ushered in. My plan had been to walk straight into the dining-room and by a sudden appearance wake in the men that start of recognition which would confirm my theory. But when I found myself in that neat hall the place mastered me. There were the golf-clubs and tennis-rackets, the straw hats and caps, the rows of gloves, the sheaf of walking-sticks which you will find in ten thousand British homes. A stack of neatly folded coats and waterproofs covered the top of an old oak chest; there was a grandfather clock ticking; and some polished brass warming-pans on the walls, and a barometer, and a print of Chiltern winning the St. Leger. The place was as orthodox as an Anglican church. When the maid asked me for my name I gave it automatically, and was shown into the smoking-room on the right side of the hall. That room was even worse. I hadn't time to examine it, but I could see some framed group photographs above the mantelpiece and I could have sworn they were English public school or college. I had only one glance, for I managed to pull myself together, and go after the maid. But I was too late. She had already entered the dining-room and given my name to her master, and I had missed the chance of seeing how the three took it.

When I walked into the room the old man at the head of the table had risen and turned round to meet me. He was in evening dress – a short coat and black tie, as was the other whom I called in my own mind the plump one. The third, the dark fellow, wore a blue serge suit and a soft white collar and the colours of some club or school.

The old man's manner was perfect. 'Mr Hannay?' he said hesitatingly. 'Did you wish to see me? One moment, you fellows, and I'll rejoin you. We had better go to the smoking-room.'

Though I hadn't an ounce of confidence in me I forced myself to play the game. I pulled up a chair and sat down on it.

'I think we have met before,' I said, 'and I guess you know my business.'

The light in the room was dim, but so far as I could see their faces they played the part of mystification very well.

'Maybe, maybe,' said the old man. 'I haven't a very good memory, but I'm afraid you must tell me your errand, for I really don't know it.'

'Well, then,' I said and all the time I seemed to myself to be talking pure foolishness – 'I have come to tell you that the game's up. I have here a warrant for the arrest of you three gentlemen.'

'Arrest,' said the old man, and he looked really shocked. 'Arrest! Good God, what for?'

'For the murder of Franklin Scudder, in London, on the 23rd day of last month.'

'I never heard the name before,' said the old man in a dazed voice.

One of the others spoke up. 'That was the Portland Place murder. I read about it. Good Heavens, you must be mad, sir! Where do you come from?'

'Scotland Yard,' I said.

After that, for a minute there was utter silence. The old man was staring at his plate and fumbling with a nut, the very model of innocent bewilderment.

Then the plump one spoke up. He stammered a little, like a man picking his words.

'Don't get flustered, uncle,' he said. 'It is all a ridiculous mistake, but these things happen sometimes, and we can easily set it right. It won't be hard to prove our innocence. I can show that I was out of the country on the 23rd of May, and Bob was in a nursing-home. You were in London, but you can explain what you were doing.'

'Right, Percy! Of course that's easy enough. The 23rd! That was the day after Agatha's wedding. Let me see. What was I doing? I came up in the morning from Woking, and lunched at the club with Charlie Symons. Then – Oh, yes, I dined with the Fishmongers. I remember, for the punch didn't agree with me, and I was seedy next morning. Hang it all, there's the cigar-box I brought back from the dinner.'

He pointed to an object on the table, and laughed nervously.

'I think, sir,' said the young man, addressing me respectfully, 'you will see you are mistaken. We want to assist the law like all Englishmen, and we don't want Scotland Yard to be making fools of themselves. That's so, uncle?'

'Certainly, Bob.' The old fellow seemed to be recovering his voice. 'Certainly, we'll do anything in our power to assist the authorities. But – but this is a bit too much. I can't get over it.'

'How Nellie will chuckle,' said the plump man. 'She always said that you would die of boredom because nothing ever happened to you. And now you've got it thick and strong,' and he began to laugh very pleasantly.

'By Jove, yes. Just think of it! What a story to tell at the club. Really, Mr Hannay, I suppose I should be angry, to show my innocence, but it's too funny! I almost forgive you the fright you gave me! You looked so glum I thought I might have been walking in my sleep and killing people.'

It couldn't be acting, it was too confoundedly genuine. My heart went into my boots, and my first impulse was to apologize and clear out. But I told myself I must see it through, even though I was to be the laughing-stock of Britain. The light from the dinner-table candlesticks was not very good, and to cover my confusion I got up, walked to the door and switched on the electric light. The sudden glare made them blink, and I stood scanning the three faces.

Well, I made nothing of it. One was old and bald, one was stout, one was dark and thin. There was nothing in their appearance to prevent them being the three who had hunted me in Scotland, but there was nothing to identify them. I simply can't explain why I, who, as a roadman, had looked into two pairs of eyes, and as Ned Ainslie into another pair, why I, who have a good memory and reasonable powers of observation, could find no satisfaction. They seemed exactly what they professed to be, and I could not have sworn to one of them. There in that pleasant dining-room, with etchings on the walls, and a picture of an old lady in a bib above the mantelpiece, I could see nothing to connect them with the moorland desperadoes. There was a silver cigarette-box beside me and I saw that it had been won by Percival Appleton, Esq., of the St Bede's Club, in a golf tournament. I had to keep firm hold of Peter Pienaar to prevent myself bolting out of that house.

'Well,' said the old man politely, 'are you reassured by your scrutiny, sir? I hope you'll find it consistent with your duty to drop this ridiculous business. I make no complaint, but you see how annoying it must be to respectable people.'

I shook my head.

'Oh, Lord,' said the young man, 'this is a bit too thick!'

'Do you propose to march us off to the police station?' asked the plump one. 'That might be the best way out of it, but I suppose you won't be content with the local branch. I have the right to ask to see your warrant, but I don't wish to cast any aspersions upon you. You are only doing your duty. But you'll admit it's horribly awkward. What do you propose to do?'

There was nothing to do except to call in my men and have them arrested or to confess my blunder and clear out. I felt mesmerized by the whole place, by the air of obvious innocence – not innocence merely, but frank, honest bewilderment and concern in the three faces.

'Oh, Peter Pienaar,' I groaned inwardly, and for a moment I was very near damning myself for a fool and asking their pardon.

'Meantime I vote we have a game of bridge,' said the plump one. 'It will give Mr Hannay time to think over things, and you know we have been wanting a fourth player. Do you play, sir?'

I accepted as if it had been an ordinary invitation at the club. The whole business had mesmerized me. We went into the smoking-room, where a card-table was set out, and I was offered things to smoke and drink. I took my place at the table in a kind of dream. The window was open and the moon was flooding the cliffs and sea with a great tide of yellow light. There was moonshine, too, in my head. The three had recovered their composure, and were talking easily – just the kind of slangy talk you will hear in any golf club-house. I must have cut a rum figure, sitting there knitting my brows with my eyes wandering.

My partner was the young, dark one. I play a fair hand at bridge but I must have been rank bad that night. They saw that they had got me puzzled, and that put them more than ever at their ease. I kept looking at their faces, but they conveyed nothing to me.

It was not that they looked different; they were different. I clung desperately to the words of Peter Pienaar.

* * *

Then something awoke me. The old man laid down his hand to light a cigar. He didn't pick it up at once, but sat back for a moment in his chair, with his fingers tapping on his knees.

It was the movement I remembered when I had stood before him in the moorland farm with the pistols of his servants behind me.

A little thing, lasting only a second, and the odds were a thousand to one that I might have had my eyes on my cards at the time and missed it. But I didn't and, in a flash, the air seemed to clear. Some shadow lifted from my brain and I was looking at the three men with full and absolute recognition.

The clock on the mantelpiece struck ten o'clock.

The three faces seemed to change before my eyes and reveal their secrets. The young one was the murderer. Now I saw cruelty and ruthlessness where before I had only seen good-humour. His knife I made certain had skewered Scudder to the floor. His kind had put the bullet in Karolides.

The plump man's features seemed to dislimn and form again, as I looked at them. He hadn't a face, only a hundred masks that he could assume when he pleased. That chap must have been a superb actor. Perhaps he had been Lord Alloa of the night before; perhaps not; it didn't matter. I wondered if he was the fellow who had first tracked Scudder and left his card on him. Scudder had said he lisped, and I could imagine how the adoption of a lisp might add terror.

But the old man was the pick of the lot. He was sheer brain, icy, cool, calculating, as ruthless as a steam hammer. Now that my eyes were opened I wondered where I had seen the benevolence. His jaw was like chilled steel, and his eyes had the inhuman luminosity of a bird's. I went on playing, and every second a greater hate welled up in my heart. It almost choked me, and I couldn't answer when my partner spoke. Only a little longer could I endure their company.

'Whew! Bob! Look at the time,' said the old man. 'You'd better think about catching your train. Bob's got to go to town tonight,' he added, turning to me. The voice rang now as false as hell.

I looked at the clock and it was nearly half-past ten.

'I am afraid you must put off your journey,' I said.

'O damn!' said the young man. 'I thought you had dropped that rot. I've simply got to go. You can have my address and I'll give any security you like.'

'No,' I said, 'you must stay.'

At that I think they must have realized that the game was desperate. Their only chance had been to convince me that I was playing the fool, and that had failed. But the old man spoke again.

'I'll go bail for my nephew. That ought to content you, Mr Hannay.' Was it fancy, or did I detect some halt in the smoothness of that voice?

There must have been, for, as I glanced at him, his eyelids fell in that hawk-like hood which fear had stamped on my memory.

I blew my whistle.

In an instant the lights were out. A pair of strong arms gripped me round the waist, covering the pockets in which a man might be expected to carry a pistol.

'*Schnell, Franz,*' cried a voice, '*das Boot, das Boot!*' As it spoke I saw two of my fellows emerge on the moonlit lawn.

The young dark man leaped for the window, was through it, and over the low fence before a hand could touch him. I grappled the old chap, and the room seemed to fill with figures. I saw the plump one collared, but my eyes were all for the out-of-doors, where Franz sped on over the road towards the railed entrance to the beach stairs. One man followed him but he had no chance. The gate locked behind the fugitive, and I stood staring, with my hands on the old boy's throat, for such a time as a man might take to descend those steps to the sea.

Suddenly my prisoner broke from me and flung himself on the wall. There was a click as if a lever had been pulled. Then came a low rumbling far, far below the ground, and through the window I saw a cloud of chalky dust pouring out of the shaft of the stairway.

Some one switched on the light.

The old man was looking at me with blazing eyes.

'He is safe!' he cried. 'You cannot follow him in time. He is gone. He has triumphed! *Der Schwarzestein ist in der Siegeskrone.*'

There was more in those eyes than any common triumph. They had been hooded like a bird of prey, and now they flamed with a hawk's pride. A white fanatic heat burned in them, and I realized for the first time the terrible thing I had been up against. This man was more than a spy; in his foul way he had been a patriot.

As the handcuffs clinked on his wrists I said my last word to him.

'I hope Franz will bear his triumph well. I ought to tell you that the *Ariadne* for the last hour has been in our hands.'

* * *

Three weeks later, as all the world knows, we went to war. I joined the New Army the first week, and owing to my Matabele experience got a captain's commission straight off. But I had done my best service, I think, before I put on khaki.

THE POWER-HOUSE

PREFACE BY THE EDITOR

We were at Glenaicill – six of us – for the duck-shooting, when Leithen told us this story. Since five in the morning we had been out on the skerries, and had been blown home by a wind which threatened to root the house and its wind-blown woods from their precarious lodgment on the hill. A vast nondescript meal, luncheon and dinner in one, had occupied us till the last daylight departed, and we settled ourselves in the smoking-room for a sleepy evening of talk and tobacco.

Conversation, I remember, turned on some of Jim's trophies which grinned at us from the firelit walls, and we began to spin hunting yarns. Then Hoppy Bynge, who was killed next year on the Bramaputra, told us some queer things about his doings in New Guinea, where he tried to climb Carstensz, and lived for six months in mud. Jim said he couldn't abide mud – anything was better than a country where your boots rotted. (He was to get enough of it last winter in the Ypres Salient.) You know how one tale begets another, and soon the whole place hummed with odd recollections, for five of us had been a good deal about the world.

All except Leithen, the man who was afterwards Solicitor-General, and, they say, will get to the Woolsack in time. I don't suppose he had ever been farther from home than Monte Carlo, but he liked hearing about the ends of the earth.

Jim had just finished a fairly steep yarn about his experiences on a Boundary Commission near Lake Chad, and Leithen got up to find a drink.

'Lucky devils,' he said. 'You've had all the fun out of life. I've had my nose to the grindstone ever since I left school.'

I said something about his having all the honour and glory.

'All the same,' he went on, 'I once played the chief part in a rather exciting business without ever once budging from London. And the joke of it was that the man who went out to look for adventure only saw a bit of the game, and I who sat in my chambers saw it all and pulled the strings. "They also serve who only stand and wait", you know.'

Then he told us this story. The version I give is one he afterwards wrote down, when he had looked up his diary for some of the details.

CHAPTER 1

BEGINNING OF
THE WILD-GOOSE CHASE

It all started one afternoon early in May when I came out of the House of Commons with Tommy Deloraine. I had got in by an accident at a by-election, when I was supposed to be fighting a forlorn hope, and as I was just beginning to be busy at the Bar I found my hands pretty full. It was before Tommy succeeded, in the days when he sat for the family seat in Yorkshire, and that afternoon he was in a powerful bad temper. Out of doors it was jolly spring weather; there was greenery in Parliament Square and bits of gay colour, and a light wind was blowing up from the river. Inside a dull debate was winding on, and an advertising member had been trying to get up a row with the Speaker. The contrast between the frowsy place and the cheerful world outside would have impressed even the soul of a Government Whip.

Tommy sniffed the spring breeze like a supercilious stag.

'This about finishes me,' he groaned. 'What a juggins I am to be mouldering here! Joggleberry is the celestial limit, what they call in happier lands the pink penultimate. And the frowst on those back benches! Was there ever such a moth-eaten old museum?'

'It is the Mother of Parliaments,' I observed.

'Damned monkey-house,' said Tommy. 'I must get off for a bit or I'll bonnet Joggleberry or get up and propose a national monument to Guy Fawkes or something silly.'

I did not see him for a day or two, and then one morning he rang me up and peremptorily summoned me to dine with him. I went, knowing very well what I should find. Tommy was off next day to shoot lions on the Equator, or something equally unconscientious. He was a bad acquaintance for a placid, sedentary soul like me, for though he could work like a Trojan when the fit took him, he was never at the same job very long. In the same week he would harass an Under-Secretary about horses for the Army, write voluminously to the press about a gun he had invented for potting aeroplanes, give a fancy-dress ball which he forgot to attend, and get into the semi-final of the racquets championship. I waited daily to see him start a new religion.

That night, I recollect, he had an odd assortment of guests. A Cabinet Minister was there, a gentle being for whom Tommy professed public scorn and private affection; a sailor; an Indian cavalry fellow; Chapman, the Labour member, whom Tommy called Chipmunk; myself, and old Milson of the Treasury. Our host was in tremendous form, chaffing everybody, and sending Chipmunk into great rolling gusts of merriment. The two lived adjacent in Yorkshire, and on platforms abused each other like pick-pockets.

Tommy enlarged on the misfits of civilized life. He maintained that none of us, except perhaps the sailor and the cavalryman, were at our proper jobs. He would have had Wytham – that was the Minister – a cardinal of the Roman Church, and he said that Milson should have been the Warden of a college full of port and prejudice. Me he was kind enough to allocate to some reconstructed Imperial General Staff, merely because I had a craze for military history. Tommy's perception did not go very deep. He told Chapman he should have been a lumberman in California. 'You'd have made an uncommon good logger, Chipmunk, and you know you're a dashed bad politician.'

When questioned about himself he became reticent, as the newspapers say. 'I doubt if I'm much good at any job,' he confessed, 'except to ginger up my friends. Anyhow I'm getting out of this hole. Paired for the rest of the session with a chap who has lockjaw. I'm off to stretch my legs and get back my sense of proportion.'

Someone asked him where he was going, and was told 'Venezuela, to buy Government bonds and look for birds' nests.'

Nobody took Tommy seriously, so his guests did not trouble to bid him the kind of farewell a prolonged journey would demand. But when the others had gone, and we were sitting in the little back smoking-room on the first floor, he became solemn. Portentously solemn, for he wrinkled up his brows and dropped his jaw in the way he had when he fancied he was in earnest.

'I've taken on a queer job, Leithen,' he said, 'and I want you to hear about it. None of my family know, and I would like to leave someone behind me who could get on to my tracks if things got troublesome.'

I braced myself for some preposterous confidence, for I was experienced in Tommy's vagaries. But I own to being surprised when he asked me if I remembered Pitt-Heron.

I remembered Pitt-Heron very well. He had been at Oxford with me, but he was no great friend of mine, though for about two years Tommy and he had been inseparable. He had had a prodigious reputation for cleverness with everybody but the college authorities, and used to spend his vacations doing mad things in the Alps and the Balkans, and writing about them in the halfpenny press. He was enormously rich – cotton-mills and Liverpool ground-rents – and being without a father, did pretty much what his fantastic taste dictated. He was rather a hero for a bit after he came down, for he had made some wild journey in the neighbourhood of Afghanistan, and written an exciting book about it.

Then he married a pretty cousin of Tommy's, who happened to be the only person that ever captured my stony heart, and settled down in London. I did not go to their house, and soon I found that very few of his friends saw much of him either. His travels and magazine articles suddenly stopped, and I put it down to the common course of successful domesticity. Apparently I was wrong.

'Charles Pitt-Heron,' said Tommy, 'is blowing up for a most thundering mess.'

I asked what kind of mess, and Tommy said he didn't know. 'That's the mischief of it. You remember the wild beggar he used to be, always off on the spree to the Mountains of the Moon or somewhere. Well, he has been damping down his fires lately, and trying to behave like a respectable citizen, but God knows what he has been thinking! I go a good deal to Portman Square, and all last year he has been getting queerer.'

Questions as to the nature of the queerness only elicited the fact that Pitt-Heron had taken to science with some enthusiasm.

'He has got a laboratory at the back of the house – used to be the billiard-room – where he works away half the night. And Lord! The crew you meet there! Every kind of heathen – Chinese and Turks, and long-haired chaps from Russia, and fat Germans. I've several times blundered into the push. They've all got an odd secretive air about them, and Charlie is becoming like them. He won't answer a plain question or look you straight in the face. Ethel sees it too, and she has often talked to me about it.'

I said I saw no harm in such a hobby.

'I do,' said Tommy grimly. 'Anyhow, the fellow has bolted.'

'What on earth—' I began, but was cut short.

'Bolted without a word to a mortal soul. He told Ethel he would be home for luncheon yesterday, and never came. His man knew nothing about him, hadn't packed for him or anything; but he found he had stuffed some things into a kit-bag and gone out by the back through the mews. Ethel was in terrible straits and sent for me, and I ranged all yesterday afternoon like a wolf on the scent. I found he had drawn a biggish sum in gold from the bank, but I couldn't find any trace of where he had gone.

'I was just setting out for Scotland Yard this morning when Tomlin, the valet, rang me up and said he had found a card in the waistcoat of the dress clothes that Charles had worn the night before he left. It had a name on it like Konalevsky, and it struck me that they might know something about the business at the Russian Embassy. Well, I went round there, and the long and short of it was that I found there was a fellow of that name among the clerks. I saw him, and he said he had gone to see Mr Pitt-Heron two days before with a letter from some Embassy chap. Unfortunately the man in question had gone off to New York next day, but Konalevsky told me one thing which helped to clear up matters. It seemed that the letter had been one of those passports that Embassies give to their friends – a higher-powered sort than the ordinary make – and Konalevsky gathered from something he had heard that Charles was aiming at Moscow.'

Tommy paused to let his news sink in.

'Well, that was good enough for me. I'm off tomorrow to run him to ground.'

'But why shouldn't a man go to Moscow if he wants?' I said feebly.

'You don't understand,' said the sage Tommy. 'You don't know old Charles as I know him. He's got into a queer set, and there's no knowing what mischief he's up to. He's perfectly capable of starting a revolution in Armenia or somewhere merely to see how it feels like to be a revolutionary. That's the damned thing about the artistic temperament.

Anyhow, he's got to chuck it. I won't have Ethel scared to death by his whims. I am going to hale him back from Moscow, even if I have to pretend he's an escaped lunatic. He's probably enough like one by this time if he has taken no clothes.'

I have forgotten what I said, but it was some plea for caution. I could not see the reason for these heroics. Pitt-Heron did not interest me greatly, and the notion of Tommy as a defender of the hearth amused me. I thought that he was working on very slight evidence, and would probably make a fool of himself.

'It's only another of the man's fads,' I said. 'He never could do things like an ordinary mortal. What possible trouble could there be? Money?'

'Rich as Crœsus,' said Tommy.

'A woman?'

'Blind as a bat to female beauty.'

'The wrong side of the law?'

'Don't think so. He could settle any ordinary scrape with a cheque.'

'Then I give it up. Whatever it is, it looks as if Pitt-Heron would have a companion in misfortune before you are done with the business. I'm all for you taking a holiday, for at present you are a nuisance to your friends and a disgrace to your country's legislature. But for goodness' sake curb your passion for romance. They don't like it in Russia.'

Next morning Tommy turned up to see me in Chambers. The prospect of travel always went to his head like wine. He was in wild spirits, and had forgotten his anger at the defaulting Pitt-Heron in gratitude for his provision of an occupation. He talked of carrying him off to the Caucasus when he had found him, to investigate the habits of the Caucasian stag.

I remember the scene as if it were yesterday. It was a hot May morning, and the sun which came through the dirty window in Fountain Court lit up the dust and squalor of my working chambers. I was pretty busy at the time, and my table was well nourished with briefs. Tommy picked up one and began to read it. It was about a new drainage scheme in West Ham. He tossed it down and looked at me pityingly.

'Poor old beggar!' he said. 'To spend your days on such work when the world is chock-full of amusing things. Life goes roaring by and you only hear the echo in your stuffy rooms. You can hardly see the sun for the cobwebs on these windows of yours. Charles is a fool, but I'm blessed if he isn't wiser than you. Don't you wish you were coming with me?'

The queer thing was that I did. I remember the occasion, as I have said, for it was one of the few on which I have had a pang of dissatisfaction with the calling I had chosen. As Tommy's footsteps grew faint on the stairs I suddenly felt as if I were missing something, as if somehow I were out of it. It is an unpleasant feeling even when you know that the thing you are out of is foolishness.

Tommy went off at 11 from Victoria, and my work was pretty well ruined for the day. I felt oddly restless, and the cause was not merely Tommy's departure. My thoughts kept turning to the Pitt-Herons – chiefly to Ethel, that adorable child unequally yoked to a perverse egoist, but a good deal to the egoist himself. I have never suffered much from whimsies, but I suddenly began to feel a curious interest in the business – an unwilling interest, for I found it in my heart to regret my robust scepticism of the night before. And it was more than interest. I had a sort of presentiment that I was going to be mixed up in the affair more than I wanted. I told myself angrily that the life of an industrious common-law barrister could have little to do with the wanderings of two maniacs in Muscovy. But, try as I might, I could not get rid of the obsession. That night it followed me into my dreams, and I saw myself with a knout coercing Tommy and Pitt-Heron in a Russian fortress which faded away into the Carlton Hotel.

Next morning I found my steps wending in the direction of Portman Square. I lived at the time in Down Street, and I told myself I would be none the worse of a walk in the Park before dinner. I had a fancy to see Mrs Pitt-Heron, for, though I had only met her twice since her marriage, there had been a day when we were the closest of friends.

I found her alone, a perplexed and saddened lady with imploring eyes. Those eyes questioned me as to how much I knew. I told her presently that I had seen Tommy and was aware of his errand. I was moved to add that she might count on me if there were anything she wished done on this side of the Channel.

She was very little changed. There was still the old exquisite slimness, the old shy courtesy. But she told me nothing. Charles was full of business and becoming very forgetful. She was sure the Russian journey was all a stupid mistake. He probably thought he had told her of his departure. He would write; she expected a letter by every post.

But her haggard eyes belied her optimism. I could see that there had been odd happenings of late in the Pitt-Heron household. She either knew or feared something; – the latter, I thought, for her air was more of apprehension than of painful enlightenment.

I did not stay long, and, as I walked home, I had an awkward feeling that I had intruded. Also I was increasingly certain that there was trouble brewing, and that Tommy had more warrant for his journey than I had given him credit for. I cast my mind back to gather recollections of Pitt-Heron, but all I could find was an impression of a brilliant, uncomfortable being, who had been too fond of the byways of life for my sober tastes. There was nothing crooked in him in the wrong sense, but there might be a good deal that was perverse. I remember consoling myself with the thought that, though he might shatter his wife's nerves by his vagaries, he would scarcely break her heart.

To be watchful, I decided, was my business. And I could not get rid of the feeling that I might soon have cause for all my vigilance.

CHAPTER 2

I FIRST HEAR OF
MR ANDREW LUMLEY

A fortnight later – to be accurate, on the 21st of May – I did a thing I rarely do, and went down to South London on a County Court case. It was an ordinary taxi-cab accident, and, as the solicitors for the company were good clients of mine and the regular County Court junior was ill in bed, I took the case to oblige them. There was the usual dull conflict of evidence. An empty taxi-cab, proceeding slowly on the right side of the road and hooting decorously at the corners, had been run into by a private motor-car which had darted down a side street. The taxi had been swung round and its bonnet considerably damaged, while its driver had suffered a dislocated shoulder. The bad feature in the case was that the motor-car had not halted to investigate the damage, but had proceeded unconscientiously on its way, and the assistance of the London police had been called in to trace it. It turned out to be the property of a Mr Julius Pavia, a retired East India merchant, who lived in a large villa in the neighbourhood of Blackheath, and at the time of the accident it had been occupied by his butler. The company brought an action for damages against its owner.

The butler, Tuke by name, was the only witness for the defence. He was a tall man, with a very long, thin face, and a jaw, the two parts of which seemed scarcely to fit. He was profuse in his apologies on behalf of his master, who was abroad. It seemed that on the morning in question – it was the 8th of May – he had received instructions from Mr Pavia to convey a message to a passenger by the Continental express from Victoria, and had been hot on this errand when he met the taxi. He was not aware that there had been any damage, thought it only a slight grazing of the two cars, and on his master's behalf consented to the judgment of the court.

It was a commonplace business, but Tuke was by no means a commonplace witness. He was very unlike the conventional butler, much liker one of those successful financiers whose portraits you see in the picture papers. His little eyes were quick with intelligence, and there were lines of ruthlessness around his mouth, like those of a man often called to decisive action. His story was simplicity itself, and he answered my questions with an air of serious candour. The train he had to meet was the 11 a.m. from Victoria, the train by which Tommy had travelled. The passenger he had to see was an American gentleman, Mr Wright Davies. His master, Mr Pavia, was in Italy, but would shortly be home again.

The case was over in twenty minutes, but it was something unique in my professional experience. For I took a most intense and unreasoning dislike to that bland butler. I cross-examined with some rudeness, was answered with steady courtesy, and hopelessly snubbed. The upshot was that I lost my temper, to the surprise of the County Court judge. All the way back I was both angry and ashamed of myself. Half-way home I realized that the accident had happened on the very day that Tommy left London. The coincidence merely flickered across my mind, for there could be no earthly connection between the two events.

That afternoon I wasted some time in looking up Pavia in the Directory. He was there sure enough as the occupier of a suburban mansion called the White Lodge. He had no city address, so it was clear that he was out of business. My irritation with the man had made me inquisitive about the master. It was a curious name he bore, possibly Italian, possibly Goanese. I wondered how he got on with his highly competent butler. If Tuke had been my servant I would have wrung his neck or bolted before a week was out.

Have you ever noticed that, when you hear a name that strikes you, you seem to be constantly hearing it for a bit? Once I had a case in which one of the parties was called Jubber, a name I had never met before, but I ran across two other Jubbers before the case was over. Anyhow, the day after the Blackheath visit I was briefed in a big Stock Exchange case, which turned on the true ownership of certain bearer bonds. It was a complicated business, which I need not trouble you with, and it involved a number of consultations with my lay clients, a famous firm of brokers. They produced their books, and my chambers were filled with glossy gentlemen talking a strange jargon.

I had to examine my clients closely on their practice in treating a certain class of bearer security, and they were very frank in expounding their business. I was not surprised to hear that Pitt-Heron was one of the most valued names on their lists. With his wealth he was bound to be a good deal in the city. Now I had no desire to pry into Pitt-Heron's private affairs, especially his financial arrangements, but his name was in my thoughts at the time, and I could not help looking curiously at what was put before me. He seemed to have been buying these bonds on a big scale. I had the indiscretion to ask if Mr Pitt-Heron had long followed this course, and was told that he had begun to purchase some six months before.

'Mr Pitt-Heron,' volunteered the stockbroker, 'is very closely connected in his financial operations with another esteemed client of ours, Mr Julius Pavia. They are both attracted by this class of security.'

At the moment I scarcely noted the name, but after dinner that night I began to speculate about the connection. I had found out the name of one of Charles's mysterious new friends.

It was not a very promising discovery. A retired East India merchant did not suggest anything wildly speculative, but I began to wonder if Charles's preoccupation, to which Tommy had been witness, might not be connected with financial worries. I could not believe that the huge Pitt-Heron fortunes had been seriously affected, or that his flight was that of a defaulter, but he might have got entangled in some shady city business which preyed on his sensitive soul. Somehow or other I could not believe that Mr Pavia was a wholly innocent old gentleman; his butler looked too formidable. It was possible that he was blackmailing Pitt-Heron, and that the latter had departed to get out of his clutches.

But on what ground? I had no notion as to the blackmailable thing that might lurk in Charles's past, and the guesses which flitted through my brain were too fantastic to consider seriously. After all, I had only the flimsiest basis for conjecture. Pavia and Pitt-Heron were friends; Tommy had gone off in quest of Pitt-Heron; Pavia's butler had broken the law of the land in order, for some reason or other, to see the departure of the train by which Tommy had travelled. I remember laughing at myself for my suspicions, and reflecting that, if Tommy could see into my head, he would turn a deaf ear in the future to my complaints of his lack of balance.

But the thing stuck in my mind, and I called again that week on Mrs. Pitt-Heron. She had had no word from her husband, and only a bare line from Tommy, giving his Moscow address. Poor child, it was a wretched business for her. She had to keep a smiling face to the world, invent credible tales to account for her husband's absence, and all the while anxiety and dread were gnawing at her heart. I asked her if she had ever met a Mr Pavia, but the name was unknown to her. She knew nothing of Charles's business dealings, but at my request she interviewed his bankers, and I heard from her next day that his affairs were in perfect order. It was no financial crisis which had precipitated him abroad.

A few days later I stumbled by the merest accident upon what sailors call a 'cross-bearing'. At the time I used to 'devil' a little for the Solicitor-General, and 'note' cases sent to him from the different Government offices. It was thankless work, but it was supposed to be good for an ambitious lawyer. By this prosaic channel I received the first hint of another of Charles's friends.

I had sent me one day the papers dealing with the arrest of a German spy at Plymouth, for at the time there was a sort of epidemic of roving Teutons, who got themselves into compromising situations, and gravely troubled the souls of the Admiralty and the War Office. This case was distinguished from the common ruck by the higher social standing of the accused. Generally the spy is a photographer or bagman who attempts to win the bibulous confidence of minor officials. But this specimen was no less than a professor of a famous German university, a man of excellent manners, wide culture, and attractive presence, who had dined with Port officers and danced with Admirals' daughters.

I have forgotten the evidence, or what was the legal point submitted for the Law Officers' opinion; in any case it matters little, for he was acquitted. What interested me at the time were the testimonials as to character which he carried with him. He had many letters of introduction. One was from Pitt-Heron to his wife's sailor uncle; and when he was arrested one Englishman went so far as to wire that he took upon himself the whole costs of the defence. This gentleman was a Mr Andrew Lumley, stated in the papers sent me to be a rich bachelor, a member of the Athenæum and Carlton Clubs, and a dweller in the Albany.

Remember that, till a few weeks before, I had known nothing of Pitt-Heron's circle, and here were three bits of information dropping in on me unsolicited, just when my interest had been awakened. I began to get really keen, for every man at the bottom of his heart believes that he is a born detective. I was on the look-out for Charles's infrequent friends, and I argued that if he knew the spy and the spy knew Mr Lumley, the odds were that Pitt-Heron and Lumley were acquaintances. I hunted up the latter in the Red Book. Sure enough he lived in the Albany, belonged to half a dozen clubs, and had a country house in Hampshire.

I tucked the name away in a pigeon-hole of my memory, and for some days asked everyone I met if he knew the philanthropist of the Albany. I had no luck till the Saturday, when, lunching at the club, I ran against Jenkinson, the art critic.

I forget if you know that I have always been a bit of a connoisseur in a mild way. I used to dabble in prints and miniatures, but at that time my interest lay chiefly in Old Wedgwood, of which I had collected some good pieces. Old Wedgwood is a thing which few people collect seriously, but the few who do are apt to be monomaniacs. Whenever a big collection comes into the market it fetches high prices but it generally finds its way into not more than half a dozen hands. Wedgwoodites all know each other, and they are less cut-throat in their methods than most collectors. Of all I have ever met Jenkinson was the keenest, and he would discourse for hours on the 'feel' of good jasper, and the respective merits of blue and sage-green grounds.

That day he was full of excitement. He babbled through luncheon about the Wentworth sale, which he had attended the week before. There had been a pair of magnificent plaques, with a unique Flaxman design, which had roused his enthusiasm. Urns and medallions and what not had gone to this or that connoisseur, and Jenkinson could quote their prices, but the plaques dominated his fancy, and he was furious that the nation had not acquired them. It seemed that he had been to South Kensington and the British Museum, and all sorts of dignitaries, and he thought he might yet persuade the authorities to offer for them if the purchaser would re-sell. They had been bought by Lutrin for a well-known private collector, by name Andrew Lumley.

I pricked up my ears and asked about Mr Lumley.

Jenkinson said he was a rich old buffer who locked up his things in cupboards and never let the public get a look at them. He suspected that a lot of the best things at recent sales had found their way to him, and that meant that they were put in cold storage for good.

I asked if he knew him.

No, he told me, but he had once or twice been allowed to look at his things for books he had been writing. He had never seen the man, for he always bought through agents, but he had heard of people who knew him. 'It is the old silly game,' he said. 'He will fill half a dozen houses with priceless treasures, and then die, and the whole show will be sold at auction and the best things carried off to America. It's enough to make a patriot swear.'

There was balm in Gilead, however. Mr Lumley apparently might be willing to re-sell the Wedgwood plaques if he got a fair offer. So Jenkinson had been informed by Lutrin, and that very afternoon he was going to look at them. He asked me to come with him, and, having nothing to do, I accepted.

Jenkinson's car was waiting for us at the club door. It was closed, for the afternoon was wet. I did not hear his directions to the chauffeur, and we had been on the road ten minutes or so before I discovered that we had crossed the river and were traversing South London. I had expected to find the things in Lutrin's shop, but to my delight I was told that Lumley had taken delivery of them at once.

'He keeps very few of his things in the Albany except his books,' I was told. 'But he has a house at Blackheath which is stuffed from cellar to garret.'

'What is the name of it?' I asked with a sudden suspicion.

'The White Lodge,' said Jenkinson.

'But that belongs to a man called Pavia,' I said.

'I can't help that. The things in it belong to old Lumley, all right. I know, for I've been three times there with his permission.'

Jenkinson got little out of me for the rest of the ride. Here was excellent corroborative evidence of what I had allowed myself to suspect. Pavia was a friend of Pitt-Heron; Lumley was a friend of Pitt-Heron; Lumley was obviously a friend of Pavia, and he might be Pavia himself, for the retired East India merchant, as I figured him, would not be above an innocent impersonation. Anyhow, if I could find one or the other, I might learn something about Charles's recent doings. I sincerely hoped that the owner might be at home that afternoon when we inspected his treasures, for so far I had found no one who could procure me an introduction to that mysterious old bachelor of artistic and philo-Teutonic tastes.

We reached the White Lodge about half-past three. It was one of those small, square, late-Georgian mansions which you see all around London – once a country house among fields, now only a villa in a pretentious garden. I looked to see my super-butler Tuke, but the door was opened by a female servant who inspected Jenkinson's card of admission, and somewhat unwillingly allowed us to enter.

My companion had not exaggerated when he described the place as full of treasures. It was far more like the shop of a Bond Street art-dealer than a civilized dwelling. The hall was crowded with Japanese armour and lacquer cabinets. One room was lined from floor to ceiling with good pictures, mostly seventeenth-century Dutch, and had enough Chippendale chairs to accommodate a public meeting. Jenkinson would fain have prowled round, but we were moved on by the inexorable servant to the little back room where lay the objects of our visit. The plaques had been only half-unpacked, and in a moment Jenkinson was busy on them with a magnifying glass, purring to himself like a contented cat.

The housekeeper stood on guard by the door, Jenkinson was absorbed, and after the first inspection of the treasures I had leisure to look about me. It was an untidy little room, full of fine Chinese porcelain in dusty glass cabinets, and in a corner stood piles of old Persian rugs.

Pavia, I reflected, must be an easy-going soul, entirely oblivious of comfort, if he allowed his friend to turn his dwelling into such a pantechnicon. Less and less did I believe in the existence of the retired East India merchant. The house was Lumley's, who chose to pass under another name during his occasional visits. His motive might be innocent enough, but somehow I did not think so. His butler had looked too infernally intelligent.

With my foot I turned over the lid of one of the packing-cases that had held the Wedgwoods. It was covered with a litter of cotton-wool and shavings, and below it lay a crumpled piece of paper. I looked again, and saw that it was a telegraph form. Clearly somebody, with the telegram in his hand, had opened the cases, and had left it on the top of one, whence it had dropped to the floor, and been covered by the lid when it was flung off.

I hope and believe that I am as scrupulous as other people, but then and there came on me the conviction that I must read that telegram. I felt the gimlet eye of the housekeeper on me, so I had recourse to craft. I took out my cigarette-case as if to smoke, and clumsily upset its contents amongst the shavings. Then on my knees I began to pick them up, turning over the litter till the telegram was exposed.

It was in French, and I read it quite clearly. It had been sent from Vienna, but the address was in some code. '*Suivez a Bokhare Saronov*' – these were the words. I finished my collection of the cigarettes, and turned the lid over again on the telegram, so that its owner, if he chose to look for it diligently, might find it.

When we sat in the car going home, Jenkinson absorbed in meditation on the plaques, I was coming to something like a decision. A curious feeling of inevitability possessed me. I had collected by accident a few odd, disjointed pieces of information, and here by the most amazing accident of all was the connecting link. I knew I had no evidence to go upon which would have convinced the most credulous common jury. Pavia knew Pitt-Heron; so probably did Lumley. Lumley knew Pavia, possibly was identical with him. Somebody in Pavia's house got a telegram in which a trip to Bokhara was indicated. It didn't sound much. Yet I was absolutely convinced, with the queer subconscious certitude of the human brain, that Pitt-Heron was or was about to be in Bokhara, and that Pavia-Lumley knew of his being there and was deeply concerned in his journey.

That night after dinner I rang up Mrs Pitt-Heron.

She had had a letter from Tommy, a very dispirited letter, for he had had no luck. Nobody in Moscow had seen or heard of any wandering Englishman remotely like Charles; and Tommy, after playing the private detective for three weeks, was nearly at the end of his tether and spoke of returning home.

I told her to send him the following wire in her own name: 'Go on to Bokhara. Have information you will meet him there.'

She promised to send the message next day, and asked no further questions. She was a pearl among women.

CHAPTER 3

TELLS OF A MIDSUMMER NIGHT

Hitherto I had been the looker-on; now I was to become a person of the drama. That telegram was the beginning of my active part in this curious affair. They say that everybody turns up in time at the corner of Piccadilly Circus if you wait long enough. I was to find myself like a citizen of Baghdad in the days of the great Caliph, and yet never stir from my routine of flat, chambers, club, flat.

I am wrong: there was one episode out of London, and that perhaps was the true beginning of my story.

Whitsuntide that year came very late, and I was glad of the fortnight's rest, for Parliament and the Law Courts had given me a busy time. I had recently acquired a car and a chauffeur called Stagg, and I looked forward to trying it in a tour in the West Country. But before I left London I went again to Portman Square.

I found Ethel Pitt-Heron in grave distress. You must remember that Tommy and I had always gone on the hypothesis that Charles's departure had been in pursuance of some mad scheme of his own which might get him into trouble. We thought that he had become mixed up with highly undesirable friends, and was probably embarking in some venture which might not be criminal but was certain to be foolish. I had long rejected the idea of blackmail, and convinced myself that Lumley and Pavia were his colleagues. The same general notion, I fancy, had been in his wife's mind. But now she had found something which altered the case.

She had ransacked his papers in the hope of finding a clue to the affair which had taken him abroad, but there was nothing but business letters, notes of investments, and such-like. He seemed to have burned most of his papers in the queer laboratory at the back of the house. But, stuffed into the pocket of a blotter on a bureau in the drawing-room where he scarcely ever wrote, she had found a document. It seemed to be the rough draft of a letter, and it was addressed to her. I give it as it was written; the blank spaces were left blank in the manuscript.

'You must have thought me mad, or worse, to treat you as I have done. But there was a terrible reason, which some day I hope to tell you. I want you as soon as you get this to make ready to come out to me at… You will travel by… and arrive at… I enclose a letter which I want you to hand in deepest confidence to Knowles, the solicitor. He will make all arrangements about your journey and about sending me the supplies of money I want. Darling, you must leave as secretly as I did, and tell nobody anything, not even that I am alive – that least of all. I would not frighten you for worlds, but I am on the edge of a horrible danger, which I hope with God's help and yours to escape…'

That was all – obviously the draft of a letter which he intended to post to her from some foreign place. But can you conceive a missive more calculated to shatter a woman's nerves? It filled me, I am bound to say, with heavy disquiet. Pitt-Heron was no coward, and he was not the man to make too much of a risk. Yet it was clear that he had fled that day in May under the pressure of some mortal fear.

The affair in my eyes began to look very bad. Ethel wanted me to go to Scotland Yard, but I dissuaded her. I have the utmost esteem for Scotland Yard, but I shrank from publicity at this stage. There might be something in the case too delicate for the police to handle, and I thought it better to wait.

I reflected a great deal about the Pitt-Heron business the first day or two of my trip, but the air and the swift motion helped me to forget it. We had a fortnight of superb weather, and sailed all day through a glistening green country under the hazy blue heavens of June. Soon I fell into the blissful state of physical and mental ease which such a life induces. Hard toil, such as deer-stalking, keeps the nerves on the alert and the mind active, but swimming in a smooth car through a heavenly landscape mesmerizes brain and body.

We ran up the Thames valley, explored the Cotswolds, and turned south through Somerset till we reached the fringes of Exmoor. I stayed a day or two at a little inn high up in the moor, and spent the time tramping the endless ridges of hill or scrambling in the arbutus thickets where the moor falls in steeps to the sea. We returned by Dartmoor and the south coast, meeting with our first rain in Dorset, and sweeping into sunlight again on Salisbury Plain. The time came when only two days remained to me. The car had behaved beyond all my hopes, and Stagg, a sombre and silent man, was lyrical in its praise.

I wanted to be in London by the Monday afternoon, and to ensure this I made a long day of it on the Sunday. It was the long day which brought our pride to a fall. The car had run so well that I resolved to push on and sleep in a friend's house near Farnham. It was about half-past eight, and we were traversing the somewhat confused and narrow roads in the neighbourhood of Wolmer Forest, when, as we turned a sharp corner, we ran full into the tail of a heavy carrier's cart. Stagg clapped on the brakes, but the collision, though it did no harm to the cart, was sufficient to send the butt-end of something through our glass screen, damage the tyre of the near front wheel, and derange the steering gear. Neither of us suffered much hurt, but Stagg got a long scratch on his cheek from broken glass, and I had a bruised shoulder.

The carrier was friendly but useless, and there was nothing for it but to arrange for horses to take the car to Farnham. This meant a job of some hours, and I found on inquiry at a neighbouring cottage that there was no inn where I could stay within eight miles. Stagg borrowed a bicycle somehow and went off to collect horses, while I morosely reviewed the alternatives before me.

I did not like the prospect of spending the June night beside my derelict car, and the thought of my friend's house near Farnham beckoned me seductively. I might have walked there, but I did not know the road, and I found that my shoulder was paining me, so I resolved to try to find some gentleman's house in the neighbourhood where I could borrow a conveyance. The south of England is now so densely peopled by Londoners that even in a wild district, where there are no inns and few farms, there are certain to be several week-end cottages.

I walked along the white ribbon of road in the scented June dusk. At first it was bounded by high gorse, then came patches of open heath, and then woods. Beyond the woods I found a park railing, and presently an entrance gate with a lodge. It seemed to be the place I was looking for, and I woke the lodge-keeper, who thus early had retired to bed. I asked the name of the owner, but was told the name of the place instead – it was High Ashes. I asked if the owner was at home, and got a sleepy nod for answer.

The house, as seen in the half-light, was a long white-washed cottage, rising to two storeys in the centre. It was plentifully covered with creepers and roses, and the odour of flowers was mingled with the faintest savour of wood-smoke, pleasant to a hungry traveller in the late hours. I pulled an old-fashioned bell, and the door was opened by a stolid young parlour-maid.

I explained my errand, and offered my card. I was, I said, a Member of Parliament and of the Bar, who had suffered a motor accident. Would it be possible for the master of the house to assist me to get to my destination near Farnham? I was bidden enter, and wearily seated myself on a settle in the hall.

In a few minutes an ancient house-keeper appeared, a grim dame whom at other times I should have shunned. She bore, however, a hospitable message. There was no conveyance in the place, as the car had gone that day to London for repairs. But if I cared to avail myself of the accommodation of the house for the night it was at my service. Meantime my servant could be looking after the car, and a message would go to him to pick me up in the morning.

I gratefully accepted, for my shoulder was growing troublesome, and was conducted up a shallow oak staircase to a very pleasant bedroom with a bathroom adjoining. I had a bath, and afterwards found a variety of comforts put at my service from slippers to razors. There was also some Elliman for my wounded shoulder. Clean and refreshed I made my way downstairs and entered a room from which I caught a glow of light.

It was a library, the most attractive I think I have ever seen. The room was long, as libraries should be, and entirely lined with books, save over the fireplace, where hung a fine picture which I took to be a Raeburn. The books were in glass cases, which showed the beautiful shallow mouldings of a more artistic age. A table was laid for dinner in a corner, for the room was immense, and the shaded candlesticks on it, along with the late June dusk, gave such light as there was. At first I thought the place was empty, but as I crossed the floor a figure rose from a deep chair by the hearth.

'Good evening, Mr Leithen,' a voice said. 'It is a kindly mischance which gives a lonely old man the pleasure of your company.'

He switched on an electric lamp, and I saw before me – what

I had not guessed from the voice – an old man. I was thirty-four at the time, and counted anything over fifty old, but I judged my host to be well on in the sixties. He was about my own size, but a good deal bent in the shoulders, as if from study. His face was clean-shaven and extraordinarily fine, with every feature delicately chiselled. He had a sort of Hapsburg mouth and chin, very long and pointed, but modelled with a grace which made the full lower lip seem entirely right. His hair was silver, brushed so low on the forehead as to give him a slightly foreign air, and he wore tinted glasses, as if for reading.

Altogether it was a very dignified and agreeable figure who greeted me in a voice so full and soft that it belied his obvious age.

Dinner was a light meal, but perfect in its way. There were soles, I remember, an exceedingly well-cooked chicken, fresh strawberries, and a savoury. We drank a '95 Perrier-Jouet and some excellent Madeira. The stolid parlour-maid waited on us, and, as we talked of the weather and the Hampshire roads, I kept trying to guess my host's profession. He was not a lawyer, for he had not the inevitable lines on the cheek. I thought that he might be a retired Oxford don, or one of the higher civil servants, or perhaps some official of the British Museum. His library proclaimed him a scholar, and his voice a gentleman.

Afterwards we settled ourselves in arm-chairs, and he gave me a good cigar. We talked about many things – books, the right furnishing of a library, a little politics, in deference to my M.P.-ship. My host was apathetic about party questions, but curious about defence matters, and in his way an amateur strategist. I could fancy his inditing letters to *The Times* on national service.

Then we wandered into foreign affairs, where I found his interest acute, and his knowledge immense. Indeed he was so well informed that I began to suspect that my guesses had been wrong, and that he was a retired diplomat. At that time there was some difficulty between France and Italy over customs duties, and he sketched for me with remarkable clearness the weak points in the French tariff administration. I had been recently engaged in a big South American railway case, and I asked him a question about the property of my clients. He gave me a much better account than I had ever got from the solicitors who briefed me.

The fire had been lit before we finished dinner, and presently it began to burn up and light the figure of my host, who sat in a deep arm-chair. He had taken off his tinted glasses, and as I rose to get a match I saw his eyes looking abstractedly before him.

Somehow they reminded me of Pitt-Heron. Charles had always a sort of dancing light in his, a restless intelligence which was at once attractive and disquieting. My host had this and more. His eyes were paler than I had ever seen in a human head – pale, bright, and curiously wild. But, whereas Pitt-Heron's had only given the impression of reckless youth, this man's spoke of wisdom and power as well as of endless vitality.

All my theories vanished, for I could not believe that my host had ever followed any profession. If he had, he would have been at the head of it, and the world would have been familiar with his features. I began to wonder if my recollection was not playing me false, and I was in the presence of some great man whom I ought to recognize.

As I dived into the recesses of my memory I heard his voice asking if I were not a lawyer.

I told him, Yes. A barrister with a fair common-law practice and some work in Privy Council appeals.

He asked me why I chose the profession.

'It came handiest,' I said. 'I am a dry creature, who loves facts and logic. I am not a flier, I have no new ideas, I don't want to lead men, and I like work. I am the ordinary educated Englishman, and my sort gravitates to the Bar. We like feeling that, if we are not the builders, at any rate we are the cement of civilization.'

He repeated the words 'cement of civilization' in his soft voice.

'In a sense you are right. But civilization needs more than the law to hold it together. You see, all mankind are not equally willing to accept as divine justice what is called human law.'

'Of course there are further sanctions,' I said. 'Police and armies and the goodwill of civilization.'

He caught me up quickly. 'The last is your true cement. Did you ever reflect, Mr Leithen, how precarious is the tenure of the civilization we boast about?'

'I should have thought it fairly substantial,' I said, 'and the foundations grow daily firmer.'

He laughed. 'That is the lawyer's view, but, believe me, you are wrong.

Reflect, and you will find that the foundations are sand. You think that a wall as solid as the earth separates civilization from barbarism. I tell you the division is a thread, a sheet of glass. A touch here, a push there, and you bring back the reign of Saturn.'

It was the kind of paradoxical, undergraduate speculation which grown men indulge in sometimes after dinner. I looked at my host to discover his mood, and at the moment a log flared up again.

His face was perfectly serious. His light wild eyes were intently watching me.

'Take one little instance,' he said. 'We are a commercial world, and have built up a great system of credit. Without our cheques and bills of exchange and currency the whole of our life would stop. But credit only exists because behind it we have a standard of value. My Bank of England notes are worthless paper unless I can get sovereigns for them if I choose. Forgive this elementary disquisition, but the point is important. We have fixed a gold standard, because gold is sufficiently rare, and because it allows itself to be coined into a portable form. I am aware that there are economists who say that the world could be run equally well on a pure credit basis, with no metal currency at the back of it; but, however sound their argument may be in the abstract, the thing is practically impossible. You would have to convert the whole of the world's stupidity to their economic faith before it would work.

'Now, suppose something happened to make our standard of value useless. Suppose the dream of the alchemists came true, and all metals were readily transmutable. We have got very near it in recent years, as you will know if you interest yourself in chemical science. Once gold and silver lost their intrinsic value, the whole edifice of our commerce would collapse. Credit would become meaningless, because it would be untranslatable. We should be back at a bound in the age of barter, for it is hard to see what other standard of value could take the place of the precious metals. All our civilization, with its industries and commerce, would come toppling down. Once more, like primitive man, I would plant cabbages for a living, and exchange them for services in kind from the cobbler and the butcher. We should have the simple life with a vengeance – not the self-conscious simplicity of the civilized man, but the compulsory simplicity of the savage.'

I was not greatly impressed by the illustration. 'Of course there are many key-points in civilization,' I said, 'and the loss of them would bring ruin. But those keys are strongly held.'

'Not so strongly as you think. Consider how delicate the machine is growing. As life grows more complex, the machinery grows more intricate, and therefore more vulnerable. Your so-called sanctions become so infinitely numerous that each in itself is frail. In the Dark Ages you had one great power – the terror of God and His Church. Now you have a multiplicity of small things, all delicate and fragile, and strong only by our tacit agreement not to question them.'

'You forget one thing,' I said – 'the fact that men really are agreed to keep the machine going. That is what I called the "goodwill of civilization".'

He got up from his chair and walked up and down the floor, a curious dusky figure lit by the rare spurts of flame from the hearth.

'You have put your finger on the one thing that matters. Civilization is a conspiracy. What value would your police be if every criminal could find a sanctuary across the Channel, or your law courts, if no other tribunal recognized their decisions? Modern life is the silent compact of comfortable folk to keep up pretences. And it will succeed till the day comes when there is another compact to strip them bare.'

I do not think that I have ever listened to a stranger conversation. It was not so much what he said – you will hear the same thing from any group of half-baked young men – as the air with which he said it. The room was almost dark, but the man's personality seemed to take shape and bulk in the gloom. Though I could scarcely see him, I knew that those pale strange eyes were looking at me. I wanted more light, but did not know where to look for a switch. It was all so eerie and odd that I began to wonder if my host were not a little mad. In any case, I was tired of his speculations.

'We won't dispute on the indisputable,' I said. 'But I should have thought that it was the interest of all the best brains of the world to keep up what you call the conspiracy.'

He dropped into his chair again.

'I wonder,' he said slowly. 'Do we really get the best brains working on the side of the compact? Take the business of Government. When all is said, we are ruled by the amateurs and the second-rate. The methods of our departments would bring any private firm to bankruptcy. The methods of Parliament – pardon me – would disgrace any board of directors. Our rulers pretend to buy expert knowledge, but they never pay the price for it that a business man would pay, and if they get it they have not the courage to use it. Where is the inducement for a man of genius to sell his brains to our insipid governors?

'And yet knowledge is the only power – now as ever. A little mechanical device will wreck your navies. A new chemical combination will upset every rule of war. It is the same with our commerce. One or two minute changes might sink Britain to the level of Ecuador, or give China the key of the world's wealth. And yet we never dream that these things are possible. We think our castles of sand are the ramparts of the universe.'

I have never had the gift of the gab, but I admire it in others. There is a morbid charm in such talk, a kind of exhilaration, of which one is half ashamed. I found myself interested, and more than a little impressed.

'But surely,' I said, 'the first thing a discoverer does is to make his discovery public. He wants the honour and glory, and he wants money for it. It becomes part of the world's knowledge, and everything is readjusted to meet it. That was what happened with electricity. You call our civilization a machine, but it is something far more flexible. It has the power of adaptation of a living organism.'

'That might be true if the new knowledge really became the world's property. But does it? I read now and then in the papers that some eminent scientist has made a great discovery. He reads a paper before some Academy of Science, and there are leading articles on it, and his photograph adorns the magazines. That kind of man is not the danger. He is a bit of the machine, a party to the compact. It is the men who stand outside it that are to be reckoned with, the artists in discovery who will never use their knowledge till they can use it with full effect. Believe me, the biggest brains are without the ring which we call civilization.'

Then his voice seemed to hesitate. 'You may hear people say that submarines have done away with the battleship, and that aircraft have annulled the mastery of the sea. That is what our pessimists say. But do you imagine that the clumsy submarine or the fragile aeroplane is really the last word of science?'

'No doubt they will develop,' I said, 'but by that time the power of the defence will have advanced also.'

He shook his head. 'It is not so. Even now the knowledge which makes possible great engines of destruction is far beyond the capacity of any defence. You see only the productions of second-rate folk who are in a hurry to get wealth and fame. The true knowledge, the deadly knowledge, is still kept secret. But, believe me, my friend, it is there.'

He paused for a second, and I saw the faint outline of the smoke from his cigar against the background of the dark. Then he quoted me one or two cases, slowly, as if in some doubt about the wisdom of his words.

It was these cases that startled me. They were of different kinds – a great calamity, a sudden breach between two nations, a blight on a vital crop, a war, a pestilence. I will not repeat them. I do not think I believed in them then, and now I believe less. But they were horribly impressive, as told in that quiet voice in that sombre room on that dark June night. If he was right, these things had not been the work of Nature or accident, but of a devilish art. The nameless brains that he spoke of, working silently in the background, now and then showed their power by some cataclysmic revelation. I did not believe him, but, as he put the case, showing with strange clearness the steps in the game, I had no words to protest.

At last I found my voice.

'What you describe is super-anarchy, and yet it makes no headway. What is the motive of those diabolical brains?'

He laughed. 'How should I be able to tell you? I am a humble inquirer, and in my researches I come on curious bits of fact. But I cannot pry into motives. I only know of the existence of great extra-social intelligences. Let us say that they distrust the machine. They may be idealists and desire to make a new world, or they may simply be artists, loving for its own sake the pursuit of truth. If I were to hazard a guess, I should say that it took both types to bring about results, for the second find the knowledge and the first the will to use it.'

A recollection came back to me. It was of a hot upland meadow in Tyrol, where among acres of flowers and beside a leaping stream I was breakfasting after a morning spent in climbing the white crags. I had picked up a German on the way, a small man of the Professor class, who did me the honour to share my sandwiches. He conversed fluently but quaintly in English, and he was, I remember, a Nietzschean and a hot rebel against the established order. 'The pity,' he cried, 'is that the reformers do not know, and those who know are too idle to reform. Some day there will come the marriage of knowledge and will, and then the world will march.'

'You draw an awful picture,' I said. 'But if those extra-social brains are so potent, why after all do they effect so little? A dull police-officer, with the machine behind him, can afford to laugh at most experiments in anarchy.'

'True,' he said, 'and civilization will win until its enemies learn from it the importance of the machine. The compact must endure until there is a counter-compact. Consider the ways of that form of foolishness which today we call nihilism or anarchy. A few illiterate bandits in a Paris slum defy the world, and in a week they are in jail. Half a dozen crazy Russian intellectuals in Geneva conspire to upset the Romanovs, and are hunted down by the police of Europe. All the Governments and their not very intelligent police forces join hands, and hey, presto! there is an end of the conspirators. For civilization knows how to use such powers as it has, while the immense potentiality of the unlicensed is dissipated in vapour. Civilization wins because it is a world-wide league; its enemies fail because they are parochial. But supposing—'

Again he stopped and rose from his chair. He found a switch and flooded the room with light. I glanced up blinking to see my host smiling down on me, a most benevolent and courteous old gentleman. He had resumed his tinted glasses.

'Forgive me,' he said, 'for leaving you in darkness while I bored you with my gloomy prognostications. A recluse is apt to forget what is due to a guest.'

He handed the cigar-box to me, and pointed to a table where whisky and mineral waters had been set out.

'I want to hear the end of your prophecies,' I said. 'You were saying—?'

'I said – supposing anarchy learned from civilization and became international. Oh, I don't mean the bands of advertising donkeys who call themselves International Unions of Workers and such-like rubbish. I mean if the real brain-stuff of the world were internationalized.

Suppose that the links in the cordon of civilization were neutralised by other links in a far more potent chain. The earth is seething with incoherent power and unorganized intelligence. Have you ever reflected on the case of China? There you have millions of quick brains stifled in trumpery crafts. They have no direction, no driving power, so the sum of their efforts is futile, and the world laughs at China. Europe throws her a million or two on loan now and then, and she cynically responds by begging the prayers of Christendom. And yet, I say, supposing—'

'It's a horrible idea,' I said, 'and, thank God, I don't believe it possible. Mere destruction is too barren a creed to inspire a new Napoleon, and you can do with nothing short of one.'

'It would scarcely be destruction,' he replied gently. 'Let us call it iconoclasm, the swallowing of formulas, which has always had its full retinue of idealists. And you do not want a Napoleon. All that is needed is direction, which could be given by men of far lower gifts than a Bonaparte. In a word, you want a Power-House, and then the age of miracles will begin.'

I got up, for the hour was late, and I had had enough of this viewy talk. My host was smiling, and I think that smile was the thing I really disliked about him. It was too – what shall I say? – superior and Olympian.

As he led me into the hall he apologized for indulging his whims. 'But you, as a lawyer, should welcome the idea. If there is an atom of truth in my fancies, your task is far bigger than you thought. You are not defending an easy case, but fighting in a contest where the issues are still doubtful. That should encourage your professional pride…'

By all the rules I should have been sleepy, for it was past midnight, and I had had a long day in the open air. But that wretched talk had unsettled me, and I could not get my mind off it. I have reproduced very crudely the substance of my host's conversation, but no words of mine could do justice to his eerie persuasiveness. There was a kind of magnetism in the man, a sense of vast powers and banked-up fires, which would have given weight to the tritest platitudes. I had a horrible feeling that he was trying to convince me, to fascinate me, to prepare the ground for some proposal. Again and again I told myself it was crazy nonsense, the heated dream of a visionary, but again and again I came back to some detail which had a horrid air of reality. If the man was a romancer he had an uncommon gift of realism.

I flung open my bedroom window and let in the soft air of the June night and the scents from leagues of clover and pines and sweet grasses. It momentarily refreshed me for I could not believe that this homely and gracious world held such dire portents.

But always that phrase of his, the 'Power-House', kept recurring. You know how twisted your thoughts get during a wakeful night, and long before I fell asleep towards morning I had worked myself up into a very complete dislike of that bland and smiling gentleman, my host. Suddenly it occurred to me that I did not know his name, and that set me off on another train of reflection.

I did not wait to be called, but rose about seven, dressed, and went downstairs. I heard the sound of a car on the gravel of the drive, and to my delight saw that Stagg had arrived. I wanted to get away from the house as soon as possible, and I had no desire to meet its master again in this world.

The grim housekeeper, who answered my summons, received my explanation in silence. Breakfast would be ready in twenty minutes: eight was Mr Lumley's hour for it.

'Mr Andrew Lumley?' I asked with a start.

'Mr Andrew Lumley,' she said.

So that was my host's name. I sat down at a bureau in the hall and did a wildly foolish thing.

I wrote a letter, beginning 'Dear Mr Lumley,' thanking him for his kindness and explaining the reason of my early departure. It was imperative, I said, that I should be in London by midday. Then I added: 'I wish I had known who you were last night, for I think you know an old friend of mine, Charles Pitt-Heron.'

Breakfastless I joined Stagg in the car, and soon we were swinging down from the uplands to the shallow vale of the Wey. My thoughts were very little on my new toy or on the midsummer beauties of Surrey. The friend of Pitt-Heron, who knew about his going to Bokhara, was the maniac who dreamed of the 'Power-House'. There were going to be dark scenes in the drama before it was played out.

CHAPTER 4

I FOLLOW THE TRAIL OF
THE SUPER-BUTLER

My first thought, as I journeyed towards London, was that I was horribly alone in this business.

Whatever was to be done I must do it myself, for the truth was I had no evidence which any authority would recognize. Pitt-Heron was the friend of a strange being who collected objects of art, probably passed under an alias in South London, and had absurd visions of the end of civilization. That, in cold black and white, was all my story came to. If I went to the police they would laugh at me, and they would be right.

Now I am a sober and practical person, but, slender though my evidence was, it brought to my mind the most absolute conviction. I seemed to know Pitt-Heron's story as if I had heard it from his own lips – his first meeting with Lumley and their growing friendship; his initiation into secret and forbidden things; the revolt of the decent man, appalled that his freakishness had led him so far; the realization that he could not break so easily with his past and that Lumley held him in his power; and last, the mad flight under the pressure of overwhelming terror.

I could read, too, the purpose of that flight. He knew the Indian frontier as few men know it, and in the wild tangle of the Pamirs he hoped to baffle his enemy. Then from some far refuge he would send for his wife, and spend the rest of his days in exile. It must have been an omnipotent terror to drive such a man, young, brilliant, rich, successful, to the fate of an absconding felon.

But Lumley was on his trail. So I read the telegram I had picked up on the floor of the Blackheath house, and my business was to frustrate the pursuit. Someone must have gone to Bokhara, some creature of Lumley's, perhaps the super-butler I had met in the County Court. The telegram, for I had noted the date, had been received on the 27th day of May. It was now the 15th of June, so if someone had started immediately on its receipt, in all probability he would by now be in Bokhara.

I must find out who had gone, and endeavour to warn Tommy. I calculated that it would have taken him seven or eight days to get from Moscow by the Transcaspian; probably he would find Pitt-Heron gone, but inquiries would set him on the track. I might be able to get in touch with him through the Russian officials. In any case, if Lumley were stalking Pitt-Heron, I, unknown and unsuspected, would be stalking Lumley.

And then in a flash I realized my folly.

The wretched letter I had written that morning had given the whole show away. Lumley knew that I was a friend of Pitt-Heron, and that I knew that he was a friend of Pitt-Heron. If my guess was right, friendship with Lumley was not a thing Charles was likely to confess to, and he would argue that my knowledge of it meant that I was in Charles's confidence. I would therefore know of his disappearance and its cause, and alone in London would connect it with the decorous bachelor of the Albany. My letter was a warning to him that he could not play the game unobserved, and I, too, would be suspect in his eyes.

It was no good crying over spilt milk, and Lumley's suspicions must be accepted. But I confess that the thought gave me the shivers. The man had a curious terror for me, a terror I cannot hope to analyse and reproduce for you. My bald words can give no idea of the magnetic force of his talk, the sense of brooding and unholy craft. I was proposing to match my wits against a master's – one, too, who must have at his command an organization far beyond my puny efforts. I have said that my first feeling was that of loneliness and isolation; my second was one of hopeless insignificance. It was a boy's mechanical toy arrayed against a Power-House with its shining wheels and monstrous dynamos.

My first business was to get into touch with Tommy.

At that time I had a friend in one of the Embassies, whose acquaintance I had made on a dry-fly stream in Hampshire. I will not tell you his name, for he has since become a great figure in the world's diplomacy, and I am by no means certain that the part he played in this tale was strictly in accordance with official etiquette. I had assisted him on the legal side in some of the international worries that beset all Embassies, and we had reached the point of intimacy which is marked by the use of Christian names and by dining frequently together. Let us call him Monsieur Felix. He was a grave young man, slightly my senior, learned, discreet, and ambitious, but with an engaging boyishness cropping up now and then under the official gold lace. It occurred to me that in him I might find an ally.

I reached London about eleven in the morning, and went straight to Belgrave Square. Felix I found in the little library off the big secretaries' room, a sunburnt sportsman fresh from a Norwegian salmon river. I asked him if he had half an hour to spare, and was told that the day was at my service.

'You know Tommy Deloraine?' I asked.

He nodded.

'And Charles Pitt-Heron?'

'I have heard of him.'

'Well, here is my trouble. I have reason to believe that Tommy has joined Pitt-Heron in Bokhara. If he has, my mind will be greatly relieved, for, though I can't tell you the story, I can tell you that Pitt-Heron is in very considerable danger. Can you help me?'

Felix reflected. 'That should be simple enough. I can wire in cipher to the Military Governor. The police there are pretty efficient, as you may imagine, and travellers don't come and go without being remarked. I should be able to give you an answer within twenty-four hours. But I must describe Tommy. How does one do that in telegraphese?'

'I want you to tell me another thing,' I said. 'You remember that Pitt-Heron has some reputation as a Central Asian traveller. Tommy, as you know, is as mad as a hatter. Suppose these two fellows at Bokhara, wanting to make a long trek into wild country – how would they go? You've been there, and know the lie of the land.'

Felix got down a big German atlas, and for half an hour we pored over it. From Bokhara, he said, the only routes for madmen ran to the south. East and north you got into Siberia; west lay the Transcaspian desert; but southward you might go through the Hissar range by Pamirski Post to Gilgit and Kashmir, or you might follow up the Oxus and enter the north of Afghanistan, or you might go by Merv into north-eastern Persia. The first he thought the likeliest route, if a man wanted to travel fast.

I asked him to put in his cable a suggestion about watching the Indian roads, and left him with a promise of early enlightenment.

Then I went down to the Temple, fixed some consultations, and spent a quiet evening in my rooms. I had a heavy sense of impending disaster, not unnatural in the circumstances. I really cannot think what it was that held me to the job, for I don't mind admitting that I felt pretty queasy about it. Partly, no doubt, liking for Tommy and Ethel, partly regret for that unfortunate fellow Pitt-Heron, most of all, I think, dislike of Lumley. That bland superman had fairly stirred my prosaic antipathies.

That night I went carefully over every item in the evidence to try and decide on my next step. I had got to find out more about my enemies. Lumley, I was pretty certain, would baffle me, but I thought I might have a better chance with the super-butler. As it turned out, I hit his trail almost at once.

Next day I was in a case at the Old Bailey. It was an important prosecution for fraud, and I appeared, with two leaders, for the bank concerned. The amazing and almost incredible thing about this story of mine is the way clues kept rolling in unsolicited, and I was to get another from this dull prosecution. I suppose that the explanation is that the world is full of clues to everything, and that if a man's mind is sharp-set on any quest, he happens to notice and take advantage of what otherwise he would miss. My leaders were both absent the first day, and I had to examine our witnesses alone.

Towards the close of the afternoon I put a fellow in the box, an oldish, drink-sodden clerk from a Cannon Street bucket-shop. His evidence was valuable for our case, but I was very doubtful how he would stand a cross-examination as to credit. His name was Routh, and he spoke with a strong north-country accent. But what caught my attention was his face. His jaw looked as if it had been made in two pieces which did not fit, and he had little, bright, protuberant eyes. At my first glance I was conscious of a recollection.

He was still in the box when the Court rose, and I informed the solicitors that before going further I wanted a conference with the witness. I mentioned also that I should like to see him alone. A few minutes later he was brought to my chambers, and I put one or two obvious questions on the case, till the managing clerk who accompanied him announced with many excuses that he must hurry away. Then I shut the door, gave Mr Routh a cigar, and proceeded to conduct a private inquiry.

He was a pathetic being, only too ready to talk. I learned the squalid details of his continuous misfortunes. He had been the son of a dissenting minister in Northumberland, and had drifted through half a dozen occupations till he found his present unsavoury billet. Truth was written large on his statement; he had nothing to conceal, for his foible was folly, not crime, and he had not a rag of pride to give him reticence. He boasted that he was a gentleman and well-educated, too, but he had never had a chance. His brother had advised him badly; his brother was too clever for a prosaic world; always through his reminiscences came this echo of fraternal admiration and complaint.

It was about the brother I wanted to know, and Mr Routh was very willing to speak. Indeed, it was hard to disentangle facts from his copious outpourings. The brother had been an engineer and a highly successful one; had dallied with politics, too, and had been a great inventor. He had put Mr Routh on to a South American speculation, where he had made a little money, but speedily lost it again. Oh, he had been a good brother in his way, and had often helped him, but he was a busy man, and his help never went quite far enough. Besides, he did not like to apply to him too often. I gathered that the brother was not a person to take liberties with.

I asked him what he was doing now.

'Ah,' said Mr Routh, 'that is what I wish I could tell you. I will not conceal from you that for the moment I am in considerable financial straits, and this case, though my hands are clean enough, God knows, will not make life easier for me. My brother is a mysterious man, whose business often takes him abroad. I have never known even his address, for I write always to a London office from which my communications are forwarded. I only know that he is in some big electrical business, for I remember that he once let drop the remark that he was in charge of some power station. No, I do not think it is in London; probably somewhere abroad. I heard from him a fortnight ago, and he told me he was just leaving England for a couple of months. It is very annoying, for I want badly to get into touch with him.'

'Do you know, Mr Routh,' I said, 'I believe I have met your brother. Is he like you in any way?'

'We have a strong family resemblance, but he is taller and slimmer. He has been more prosperous, and has lived a healthier life, you see.'

'Do you happen to know,' I asked, 'if he ever uses another name? I don't think that the man I knew was called Routh.'

The clerk flushed. 'I think it highly unlikely that my brother would use an alias. He has done nothing to disgrace a name of which we are proud.'

I told him that my memory had played me false, and we parted on very good terms. He was an innocent soul, one of those people that clever rascals get to do their dirty work for them. But there was no mistaking the resemblance. There, without the brains and force and virility, went my super-butler of Blackheath, who passed under the name of Tuke.

The clerk had given me the name of the office to whose address he had written to his brother. I was not surprised to find that it was that of the firm of stockbrokers for whom I was still acting in the bearer-bonds case where I had heard Pavia's name.

I rang up the partner whom I knew, and told him a very plausible story of having a message for one of Mr Pavia's servants, and asked him if he were in touch with them and could forward letters. He made me hold the line, and then came back and told me that he had forwarded letters for Tuke, the butler, and one Routh who was a groom or footman. Tuke had gone abroad to join his master and he did not know his address. But he advised me to write to the White Lodge.

I thanked him and rang off. That was settled, anyhow. Tuke's real name was Routh, and it was Tuke who had gone to Bokhara.

My next step was to ring up Macgillivray at Scotland Yard and get an appointment in half an hour's time. Macgillivray had been at the Bar – I had read in his chambers – and was now one of the heads of the Criminal Investigation Department. I was about to ask him for information which he was in no way bound to give me, but I presumed on our old acquaintance.

I asked him first whether he had ever heard of a secret organization which went under the name of the Power-House. He laughed out loud at my question.

'I should think we have several hundreds of such pet names on our records,' he said. 'Everything from the Lodge of the Baldfaced Ravens to

Solomon's Seal No X. Fancy nomenclature is the relaxation of the tired anarchist and matters very little. The dangerous fellows have no names, no numbers even, which we can get hold of. But I'll get a man to look up our records. There may be something filed about your Power-House.'

My second question he answered differently. 'Routh! Routh! Why, yes, there was a Routh we had dealings with a dozen years ago when I used to go the North-Eastern Circuit. He was a Trade Union official who bagged the funds, and they couldn't bring him to justice because of the ridiculous extra-legal status they possess. He knew it, and played their own privileges against them. Oh yes, he was a very complete rogue. I once saw him at a meeting in Sunderland, and I remember his face – sneering eyes, diabolically clever mouth, and with it all as smug as a family butler. He has disappeared from England – at least we haven't heard of him for some years, but I can show you his photograph.'

Macgillivray took from a lettered cabinet a bundle of cards, selected one, and tossed it towards me. It was that of a man of thirty or so, with short side-whiskers and a drooping moustache. The eyes, the ill-fitting jaw, and the brow were those of my friend Mr Tuke, brother and patron of the sorrowful Mr Routh, who had already that afternoon occupied my attention.

Macgillivray promised to make certain inquiries, and I walked home in a state of elation. Now I knew for certain who had gone to Bokhara, and I knew something, too, of the traveller's past. A discredited genius was the very man for Lumley's schemes – one who asked for nothing better than to use his brains outside the ring-fence of convention. Somewhere in the wastes of Turkestan the ex-Trade Union official was in search of Pitt-Heron. I did not fancy that Mr Tuke would be very squeamish.

I dined at the club and left early. Going home, I had an impression that I was being shadowed.

You know the feeling that someone is watching you, a sort of sensation which the mind receives without actual evidence. If the watcher is behind, where you can't see him, you have a cold feeling between your shoulders. I daresay it is a legacy from the days when the cave-man had to look pretty sharp to keep from getting his enemy's knife between the ribs.

It was a bright summer evening, and Piccadilly had its usual crowd of motor-cars and buses and foot passengers. I halted twice, once in St James's Street and once at the corner of Stratton Street, and retraced my steps for a bit; and each time I had the impression that someone a hundred yards or so off had done the same. My instinct was to turn round and face him, whoever he was, but I saw that that was foolishness. Obviously in such a crowd I could get no certainty in the matter, so I put it out of my mind.

I spent the rest of the evening in my rooms, reading cases and trying to keep my thoughts off Central Asia. About ten I was rung up on the telephone by Felix. He had had his answer from Bokhara. Pitt-Heron had left with a small caravan on June 2nd by the main road through the Hissar range. Tommy had arrived on June 10th, and on the 12th had set off with two servants on the same trail. Travelling the lighter of the two, he should have overtaken Pitt-Heron by the 15th at latest.

That was yesterday, and my mind was immensely relieved. Tommy in such a situation was a tower of strength, for, whatever his failings in politics, I knew no one I would rather have with me to go tiger-shooting.

Next day the sense of espionage increased. I was in the habit of walking down to the Temple by way of Pall Mall and the Embankment, but, as I did not happen to be in Court that morning, I resolved to make a detour and test my suspicions. There seemed to be nobody in Down Street as I emerged from my flat, but I had not walked five yards before, turning back, I saw a man enter from the Piccadilly end, while another moved across the Hertford Street opening. It may have been only my imagination, but I was convinced that these were my watchers.

I walked up Park Lane, for it seemed to me that by taking the Tube at the Marble Arch Station I could bring matters to the proof. I have a knack of observing small irrelevant details, and I happened to have noticed that a certain carriage in the train which left Marble Arch about 9.30 stopped exactly opposite the exit at the Chancery Lane Station, and by hurrying up the passage one could just catch the lift which served an earlier train, and so reach the street before any of the other travellers.

I performed this manœuvre with success, caught the early lift, reached the street, and took cover behind a pillar-box, from which I could watch the exit of passengers from the stairs. I judged that my tracker, if he missed me below, would run up the stairs rather than wait on the lift. Sure enough, a breathless gentleman appeared, who scanned the street eagerly, and then turned to the lift to watch the emerging passengers. It was clear that the espionage was no figment of my brain.

I walked slowly to my chambers, and got through the day's work as best I could, for my mind was preoccupied with the unpleasant business in which I found myself entangled. I would have given a year's income to be honestly quit of it, but there seemed to be no way of escape. The maddening thing was that I could do so little. There was no chance of forgetting anxiety in strenuous work. I could only wait with the patience at my command, and hope for the one chance in a thousand which I might seize. I felt miserably that it was no game for me. I had never been brought up to harry wild beasts and risk my neck twice a day at polo like Tommy Deloraine. I was a peaceful sedentary man, a lover of a quiet life, with no appetite for perils and commotions. But I was beginning to realize that I was very obstinate.

At four o'clock I left the Temple and walked to the Embassy. I had resolved to banish the espionage from my mind for that was the least of my difficulties.

Felix gave me an hour of his valuable time. It was something that Tommy had joined Pitt-Heron, but there were other matters to be arranged in that far country. The time had come, in my opinion, to tell him the whole story.

The telling was a huge relief to my mind. He did not laugh at me as I had half feared, but took the whole thing as gravely as possible. In his profession, I fancy, he had found too many certainties behind suspicions to treat anything as trivial. The next step, he said, was to warn the Russian police of the presence of the man called Saronov and the super-butler. Happily we had materials for the description of Tuke or Routh, and I could not believe that such a figure would be hard to trace. Felix cabled again in cipher, asking that the two should be watched, more especially if there was reason to believe that they had followed Tommy's route. Once more we got out the big map and discussed the possible ways. It seemed to me a land created by Providence for surprises, for the roads followed the valleys, and to the man who travelled light there must be many short-cuts through the hills.

I left the Embassy before six o'clock and, crossing the Square engrossed with my own thoughts, ran full into Lumley.

I hope I played my part well, though I could not repress a start of surprise. He wore a grey morning-coat and a white top-hat, and looked the image of benevolent respectability.

'Ah, Mr Leithen,' he said, 'we meet again.'

I murmured something about my regrets at my early departure three days ago, and added the feeble joke that I wished he would hurry on his Twilight of Civilization, for the burden of it was becoming too much for me.

He looked me in the eyes with all the friendliness in the world. 'So you have not forgotten our evening's talk? You owe me something, my friend, for giving you a new interest in your profession.'

'I owe you much,' I said, 'for your hospitality, your advice, and your warnings.'

He was wearing his tinted glasses, and peered quizzically into my face.

'I am going to make a call in Grosvenor Place,' he said, 'and shall beg in return the pleasure of your company. So you know my young friend, Pitt-Heron?'

With an ingenuous countenance I explained that he had been at Oxford with me and that we had common friends.

'A brilliant young man,' said Lumley. 'Like you, he has occasionally cheered an old man's solitude. And he has spoken of me to you?'

'Yes,' I said, lying stoutly. 'He used to tell me about your collections.' (If Lumley knew Charles well he would find me out, for the latter would not have crossed the road for all the treasures of the Louvre.)

'Ah, yes, I have picked up a few things. If ever you should care to see them I should be honoured. You are a connoisseur? Of a sort? You interest me, for I should have thought your taste lay in other directions than the dead things of art. Pitt-Heron is no collector. He loves life better than art, as a young man should. A great traveller, our friend – the Laurence Oliphant or Richard Burton of our day.'

We stopped at a house in Grosvenor Place, and he relinquished my arm. 'Mr Leithen,' he said, 'a word from one who wishes you no ill. You are a friend of Pitt-Heron, but where he goes you cannot follow. Take my advice and keep out of his affairs. You will do no good to him, and you may bring yourself into serious danger. You are a man of sense, a practical man, so I speak to you frankly. But, remember, I do not warn twice.'

He took off his glasses, and his light, wild eyes looked me straight in the face. All benevolence had gone, and something implacable and deadly burned in them. Before I could say a word in reply he shuffled up the steps of the house and was gone...

CHAPTER 5

I TAKE A PARTNER

That meeting with Lumley scared me badly, but it also clinched my resolution. The most pacific fellow on earth can be gingered into pugnacity. I had now more than my friendship for Tommy and my sympathy with Pitt-Heron to urge me on. A man had tried to bully me, and that roused all the worst stubbornness of my soul. I was determined to see the game through at any cost.

But I must have an ally if my nerves were to hold out, and my mind turned at once to Tommy's friend, Chapman. I thought with comfort of the bluff independence of the Labour Member. So that night at the House I hunted him out in the smoking-room.

He had been having a row with the young bloods of my party that afternoon and received me ungraciously.

'I'm about sick of you fellows,' he growled. (I shall not attempt to reproduce Chapman's accent. He spoke rich Yorkshire, with a touch of the drawl of the western dales.) 'They went and spoiled the best speech, though I say it as shouldn't, which this old place has heard for a twelvemonth. I've been workin' for days at it in the Library. I was tellin' them how much more bread cost under Protection, and the Jew Hilderstein started a laugh because I said kilometres for kilograms. It was just a slip o' the tongue, for I had it right in my notes, and besides, these furrin words don't matter a curse. Then that young lord as sits for East Claygate gets up and goes out as I was gettin' into my peroration, and he drops his topper and knocks off old Higgins's spectacles, and all the idiots laughed. After that I gave it them hot and strong, and got called to order. And then Wattles, him as used to be as good a Socialist as me, replied for the Government and his blamed Board, and said that the Board thought this and the Board thought that, and was blessed if the Board would stir its stumps. Well I mind the day when I was hanging on to the Board's coattails in Hyde Park to keep it from talking treason.'

It took me a long time to get Chapman settled down and anchored to a drink.

'I want you,' I said, 'to tell me about Routh – you know the fellow I mean – the ex-Union leader.'

At that he fairly blazed up.

'There you are, you Tories,' he shouted, causing a pale Liberal Member on the next sofa to make a hurried exit. 'You can't fight fair. You hate the Unions, and you rake up any rotten old prejudice to discredit them. You can find out about Routh for yourself, for I'm damned if I help you.'

I saw I could do nothing with Chapman unless I made a clean breast of it, so for the second time that day I told the whole story.

I couldn't have wished for a better audience. He got wildly excited before I was half through with it. No doubt of the correctness of my evidence ever entered his head, for, like most of his party, he hated anarchism worse than capitalism, and the notion of a highly-capitalized, highly-scientific, highly-undemocratic anarchism fairly revolted his soul. Besides, he adored Tommy Deloraine.

Routh, he told me, had been a young engineer of a superior type, with a job in a big shop at Sheffield. He had professed advanced political views, and, although he had strictly no business to be there, had taken a large part in Trade Union work, and was treasurer of one big branch. Chapman had met him often at conferences and on platforms, and had been impressed by the fertility and ingenuity of his mind and the boldness of his purpose. He was the leader of the left wing of the movement, and had that gift of half-scientific, half-philosophic jargon which is dear at all times to the hearts of the half-baked. A seat in Parliament had been repeatedly offered him, but he had always declined; wisely, Chapman thought, for he judged him the type which is more effective behind the scenes.

But with all his ability he had not been popular. 'He was a cold-blooded, sneering devil,' as Chapman put it, 'a sort of Parnell. He tyrannized over his followers, and he was the rudest brute I ever met.'

Then followed the catastrophe, in which it became apparent that he had speculated with the funds of the Union and had lost a large sum. Chapman, however, was suspicious of these losses, and was inclined to suspect that he had the money all the time in a safe place. A year or two earlier the Unions, greatly to the disgust of old-fashioned folk, had been given certain extra-legal privileges, and this man Routh had been one of the chief advocates of the Unions' claims. Now he had the cool effrontery to turn the tables on them, and use those very privileges to justify his action and escape prosecution.

There was nothing to be done. Some of the fellows, said Chapman, swore to wring his neck, but he did not give them the chance. He had disappeared from England, and was generally believed to be living in some foreign capital.

'What I would give to be even with the swine!' cried my friend, clenching and unclenching his big fist. 'But we're up against no small thing in Josiah Routh. There isn't a crime on earth he'd stick at, and he's as clever as the old Devil, his master.'

'If that's how you feel, I can trust you to back me up,' I said. 'And the first thing I want you to do is to come and stay at my flat. God knows what may happen next, and two men are better than one. I tell you frankly, I'm nervous, and I would like to have you with me.'

Chapman had no objection. I accompanied him to his Bloomsbury lodgings, where he packed a bag, and we returned to the Down Street flat. The sight of his burly figure and sagacious face was a relief to me in the mysterious darkness where I now found myself walking.

Thus began my housekeeping with Chapman, one of the queerest episodes in my life. He was the best fellow in the world, but I found that I had misjudged his character. To see him in the House you would have thought him a piece of granite, with his Yorkshire bluntness and hard, downright, north-country sense. He had all that somewhere inside him, but he was also as romantic as a boy. The new situation delighted him. He was quite clear that it was another case of the strife between Capital and Labour – Tommy and I standing for Labour, though he used to refer to Tommy in public as a 'gilded popinjay', and only a month before had described me in the House as a 'viperous lackey of Capitalism'. It was the best kind of strife in which you had not to meet your adversary with long-winded speeches, but might any moment get a chance to pummel him with your fists.

He made me ache with laughter. The spying business used to rouse him to fury. I don't think he was tracked as I was, but he chose to fancy he was, and was guilty of assault and battery on one butcher's boy, two cabbies, and a gentleman who turned out to be a bookmaker's assistant. This side of him got to be an infernal nuisance, and I had many rows with him. Among other things, he chose to suspect my man Waters of treachery – Waters, who was the son of a gardener at home, and hadn't wits enough to put up an umbrella when it rained.

'You're not taking this business rightly,' he maintained one night. 'What's the good of waiting for these devils to down you? Let's go out and down them.' And he announced his intention, from which no words of mine could dissuade him, of keeping watch on Mr Andrew Lumley at the Albany.

His resolution led to a complete disregard of his Parliamentary duties. Deputations of constituents waited for him in vain. Of course he never got a sight of Lumley. All that happened was that he was very nearly given in charge more than once for molesting peaceable citizens in the neighbourhood of Piccadilly and Regent Street.

One night on my way home from the Temple I saw in the bills of the evening papers the announcement of the arrest of a Labour Member. It was Chapman, sure enough. At first I feared that he had got himself into serious trouble, and was much relieved to find him in the flat in a state of blazing anger. It seemed that he had found somebody whom he thought was Lumley, for he only knew him from my descriptions. The man was in a shop in Jermyn Street, with a car waiting outside, and Chapman had – politely, as he swore – asked the chauffeur his master's name. The chauffeur had replied abusively, upon which Chapman had haled him from the driver's seat and shaken him till his teeth rattled. The owner came out, and Chapman was arrested and taken off to the nearest police court. He had been compelled to apologize, and had been fined five pounds and costs.

By the mercy of Heaven the chauffeur's master was a money-lender of evil repute, so the affair did Chapman no harm. But I was forced to talk to him seriously. I knew it was no use explaining that for him to spy on the Power-House was like an elephant stalking a gazelle. The only way was to appeal to his incurable romanticism.

'Don't you see,' I told him, 'that you are playing Lumley's game? He will trap you sooner or later into some escapade which will land you in jail, and where will I be then? That is what he and his friends are out for. We have got to meet cunning with cunning, and lie low till we get our chance.'

He allowed himself to be convinced, and handed over to me the pistol he had bought, which had been the terror of my life.

'All right,' he said, 'I'll keep quiet. But you promise to let me into the big scrap when it comes off.'

I promised. Chapman's notion of the grand finale was a Homeric combat in which he would get his fill of fisticuffs.

He was an anxiety, but all the same he was an enormous comfort. His imperturbable cheerfulness and his racy talk were the tonics I wanted. He had plenty of wisdom, too. My nerves were getting bad those days, and, whereas I had rarely touched the things before, I now found myself smoking cigarettes from morning till night. I am pretty abstemious, as you know, but I discovered to my horror that I was drinking far too many whiskys-and-sodas. Chapman knocked me off all that, and got me back to a pipe and a modest nightcap.

He did more, for he undertook to put me in training. His notion was that we should win in the end by superior muscles. He was a square, thick-set fellow, who had been a good middle-weight boxer. I could box a bit myself, but I improved mightily under his tuition. We got some gloves, and used to hammer each other for half an hour every morning. Then might have been seen the shameful spectacle of a rising barrister with a swollen lip and a black eye arguing in Court and proceeding of an evening to his country's legislature, where he was confronted from the opposite benches by the sight of a Léader of the People in the same vulgar condition.

In those days I wanted all the relief I could get, for it was a beastly time. I knew I was in grave danger, so I made my will and went through the other doleful performances consequent on the expectation of a speedy decease. You see I had nothing to grip on, no clear job to tackle, only to wait on the off-chance, with an atmosphere of suspicion thickening around me. The spying went on – there was no mistake about that – but I soon ceased to mind it, though I did my best to give my watchers little satisfaction. There was a hint of bullying about the spying. It is disconcerting at night to have a man bump against you and look you greedily in the face.

I did not go again to Scotland Yard, but one night I ran across Macgillivray in the club.

He had something of profound interest to tell me. I had asked about the phrase, the 'Power-House'. Well, he had come across it, in the letter of a German friend, a private letter, in which the writer gave the results of his inquiries into a curious affair which a year before had excited Europe.

I have forgotten the details, but it had something to do with the Slav States of Austria and an Italian Students' Union, and it threatened at one time to be dangerous. Macgillivray's correspondent said that in some documents which were seized he found constant allusion to a thing called the *Krafthaus*, evidently the staff headquarters of the plot. And this same word *Krafthaus* had appeared elsewhere – in a sonnet of a poet-anarchist who shot himself in the slums of Antwerp, in the last ravings of more than one criminal, in the extraordinary testament of Professor M— of Jena, who, at the age of thirty-seven, took his life after writing a strange mystical message to his fellow-citizens.

Macgillivray's correspondent concluded by saying that, in his opinion, if this *Krafthaus* could be found, the key would be discovered to the most dangerous secret organization in the world. He added that he had some reason to believe that the motive power of the concern was English.

'Macgillivray,' I said, 'you have known me for some time, and I fancy you think me a sober and discreet person. Well, I believe I am on the edge of discovering the secret of your *Krafthaus*. I want you to promise me that if in the next week I send you an urgent message you will act on it, however fantastic it seems. I can't tell you more. I ask you to take me on trust, and believe that for anything I do I have tremendous reasons.'

He knit his shaggy grey eyebrows and looked curiously at me. 'Yes, I'll go bail for your sanity. It's a good deal to promise, but if you make an appeal to me, I will see that it is met.'

Next day I had news from Felix. Tuke and the man called Saronov had been identified. If you are making inquiries about anybody it is fairly easy to find those who are seeking for the same person, and the Russian police, in tracking Tommy and Pitt-Heron, had easily come on the two gentlemen who were following the same trail. The two had gone by Samarkand, evidently intending to strike into the hills by a shorter route than the main road from Bokhara. The frontier posts had been warned, and the stalkers had become the stalked.

That was one solid achievement, at any rate. I had saved Pitt-Heron from the worst danger, for first I had sent him Tommy, and now I had put the police on guard against his enemies. I had not the slightest doubt that enemies they were. Charles knew too much, and Tuke was the man appointed to reason with him, to bring him back, if possible, or if not – As Chapman had said, the ex-Union leader was not the man to stick at trifles.

It was a broiling June, the London season was at its height, and I had never been so busy in the Courts before. But that crowded and garish world was little more than a dream to me. I went through my daily tasks, dined out, went to the play, had consultations, talked to my fellows, but all the while I had the feeling that I was watching somebody else perform the same functions. I believe I did my work well, and I know I was twice complimented by the Court of Appeal.

But my real interests were far away. Always I saw two men in the hot glens of the Oxus, with the fine dust of the *loess* rising in yellow clouds behind them. One of these men had a drawn and anxious face, and both rode hard. They passed by the closes of apricot and cherry and the green watered gardens, and soon the Oxus ceased to flow wide among rushes and water-lilies and became a turbid hill-stream. By-and-by the roadside changed, and the horses of the travellers trod on mountain turf, crushing the irises and marigolds and thyme. I could feel the free air blowing from the roof of the world, and see far ahead the snowy saddle of the pass which led to India.

Far behind the riders I saw two others, and they chose a different way, now over waterless plateaux, now in rugged *nullahs*. They rode the faster and their route was the shorter. Sooner or later they must catch up the first riders, and I knew, though how I could not tell, that death would attend the meeting.

I, and only I, sitting in London four thousand miles away, could prevent disaster. The dream haunted me at night, and often, walking in the Strand or sitting at a dinner-table, I have found my eyes fixed clearly on the shining upland with the thin white mountains at the back of it, and the four dots, which were men, hurrying fast on their business.

One night I met Lumley. It was at a big political dinner given by the chief of my party in the House of Lords – fifty or sixty guests, and a blaze of stars and decorations. I sat near the bottom of the table, and he was near the top, sitting between a famous General and an ex-Viceroy of India. I asked my right-hand neighbour who he was, but he could not tell me. The same question to my left-hand neighbour brought an answer.

'It's old Lumley. Have you never met him? He doesn't go out much, but he gives a man's dinner now and then, which are the best in London. No. He's not a politician, though he favours our side, and I expect has given a lot to our funds. I can't think why they don't make him a Peer. He's enormously rich and very generous, and the most learned old fellow in Britain. My Chief' – my neighbour was an Under-Secretary – 'knows him, and told me once that if you wanted any out-of-the-way bit of knowledge you could get it by asking Lumley. I expect he pulls the strings more than anybody living. But he scarcely ever goes out, and it's a feather in our host's cap to have got him tonight. You never see his name in the papers, either. He probably pays the Press to keep him out, like some of those millionaire fellows in America.'

I watched him through dinner. He was the centre of the talk at his end of the table. I could see the blue ribbon bulging out on Lord Morecambe's breast as he leaned forward to question him. He was wearing some foreign orders, including the Legion of Honour, and I could hear in the pauses of conversation echoes of his soft rich voice. I could see him beaming through his glasses on his neighbours, and now and then he would take them off and look mildly at a speaker. I wondered why nobody realized, as I did, what was in his light wild eyes.

The dinner, I believe, was excellent, and the company was good, but down at my end I could eat little, and I did not want to talk. Here in this pleasant room, with servants moving softly about, and a mellow light on the silver from the shaded candles, I felt the man was buttressed and defended beyond my reach. A kind of despairing hatred gripped me when I looked his way. For I was always conscious of that other picture – the Asian desert, Pitt-Heron's hunted face, and the grim figure of Tuke on his trail. That, and the great secret wheels of what was too inhuman to be called crime, moving throughout the globe under this man's hand.

There was a party afterwards, but I did not stay. No more did Lumley, and for a second I brushed against him in the hall at the foot of the big staircase.

He smiled on me affectionately.

'Have you been dining here? I did not notice you.'

'You had better things to think of,' I said. 'By the way, you gave me good advice some weeks ago. It may interest you to hear that I have taken it.'

'I am so glad,' he said softly. 'You are a very discreet young man.'

But his eyes told me that he knew I lied.

CHAPTER 6

THE RESTAURANT IN ANTIOCH STREET

I was working late at the Temple next day, and it was nearly seven before I got up to go home. Macgillivray had telephoned to me in the afternoon saying he wanted to see me and suggesting dinner at the club, and I had told him I should come straight there from my chambers. But just after six he had rung me up again and proposed another meeting-place.

'I've got some very important news for you and want to be quiet. There's a little place where I sometimes dine – Rapaccini's, in Antioch Street. I'll meet you there at half-past seven.'

I agreed, and sent a message to Chapman at the flat, telling him I would be out to dinner. It was a Wednesday night, so the House rose early. He asked me where I was dining and I told him, but I did not mention with whom. His voice sounded very cross, for he hated a lonely meal.

It was a hot, still night, and I had had a heavy day in Court, so heavy that my private anxieties had almost slipped from my mind. I walked along the Embankment, and up Regent Street towards Oxford Circus. Antioch Street, as I had learned from the Directory, was in the area between Langham Place and Tottenham Court Road. I wondered vaguely why Macgillivray should have chosen such an out-of-the-way spot, but I knew him for a man of many whims.

The street, when I found it, turned out to be a respectable little place – boarding-houses and architects' offices, with a few antiquity shops, and a picture-cleaner's. The restaurant took some finding, for it was one of those discreet establishments, common enough in France, where no edibles are displayed in the British fashion, and muslin half-curtains deck the windows. Only the door-mat, lettered with the proprietor's name, remained to guide the hungry.

I gave a waiter my hat and stick and was ushered into a garish dining-room, apparently full of people. A single violinist was discoursing music from beside the grill. The occupants were not quite the kind one expects to find in an eating-house in a side street. The men were all in evening dress with white waistcoats, and the women looked either demi-mondaines or those who follow their taste in clothes. Various eyes looked curiously at me as I entered. I guessed that the restaurant had by one of those odd freaks of Londoners become for a moment the fashion.

The proprietor met me half-way up the room. He might call himself Rapaccini, but he was obviously a German.

'Mr Geelvrai,' he nodded. 'He has engaged a private room. Vill you follow, sir?'

A narrow stairway broke into the wall on the left side of the dining-room. I followed the manager up it and along a short corridor to a door which filled its end. He ushered me into a brightly-lit little room where a table was laid for two.

'Mr Geelvrai comes often here,' said the manager. 'He vill be late – sometimes. Everything is ready, sir. I hope you vill be pleased.'

It looked inviting enough, but the air smelt stuffy. Then I saw that, though the night was warm, the window was shut and the curtains drawn. I pulled back the curtains, and to my surprise saw that the shutters were closed.

'You must open these,' I said, 'or we'll stifle.'

The manager glanced at the window. 'I vill send a waiter,' he said, and departed. The door seemed to shut with an odd click.

I flung myself down in one of the arm-chairs, for I was feeling pretty tired. The little table beckoned alluringly, for I was also hungry. I remember there was a mass of pink roses on it. A bottle of champagne, with the cork loose, stood in a wine-cooler on the sideboard, and there was an unopened bottle beside it. It seemed to me that Macgillivray, when he dined here, did himself rather well.

The promised waiter did not arrive, and the stuffiness was making me very thirsty. I looked for a bell, but could not see one. My watch told me it was now a quarter to eight, but there was no sign of Macgillivray. I poured myself out a glass of champagne from the opened bottle, and was just about to drink it, when my eye caught something in a corner of the room.

It was one of those little mid-Victorian corner tables – I believe they call them 'what-nots' – which you will find in any boarding-house littered up with photographs and coral and 'Presents from Brighton'. On this one stood a photograph in a shabby frame, and I thought I recognized it.

I crossed the room and picked it up. It showed a man of thirty, with short side-whiskers, an ill-fitting jaw, and a drooping moustache. The duplicate of it was in Macgillivray's cabinet. It was Mr Routh, the ex-Union leader.

There was nothing very remarkable about that after all, but it gave me a nasty shock. The room now seemed a sinister place, as well as intolerably close. There was still no sign of the waiter to open the window, so I thought I would wait for Macgillivray downstairs.

But the door would not open. The handle would not turn. It did not seem to be locked, but rather to have shut with some kind of patent spring. I noticed that the whole thing was a powerful piece of oak with a heavy framework, very unlike the usual flimsy restaurant doors.

My first instinct was to make a deuce of a row and attract the attention of the diners below. I own I was beginning to feel badly frightened. Clearly I had got into some sort of trap. Macgillivray's invitation might have been a hoax, for it is not difficult to counterfeit a man's voice on the telephone. With an effort I forced myself into calmness. It was preposterous to think that anything could happen to me in a room not thirty feet from where a score or two of ordinary citizens were dining. I had only to raise my voice to bring inquirers.

Yes, but above all things I did not want a row. It would never do for a rising lawyer and a Member of Parliament to be found shouting for help in an upper chamber of a Bloomsbury restaurant. The worst deductions would be drawn from the open bottle of champagne. Besides, it might be all right after all. The door might have got stuck. Macgillivray at that very moment might be on his way up.

So I sat down and waited. Then I remembered my thirst, and stretched out my hand to the glass of champagne.

But at that instant I looked towards the window, and set down the wine untasted.

It was a very odd window. The lower end was almost flush with the floor, and the hinges of the shutters seemed to be only on one side. As I stared I began to wonder whether it was a window at all.

Next moment my doubts were solved. The window swung open like a door, and in the dark cavity stood a man.

Strangely enough I knew him. His figure was not one that is readily forgotten.

'Good evening, Mr Docken,' I said; 'will you have a glass of champagne?'

A year before, on the South-Eastern Circuit, I had appeared for the defence in a burglary case. Criminal law was not my province, but now and then I took a case to keep my hand in, for it is the best training in the world for the handling of witnesses. This case had been peculiar. A certain Bill Docken was the accused, a gentleman who bore a bad reputation in the eyes of the police. The evidence against him was strong, but it was more or less tainted, being chiefly that of two former accomplices – a proof that there is small truth in the proverbial honour among thieves. It was an ugly business, and my sympathies were with the accused, for though he may very well have been guilty, yet he had been the victim of a shabby trick. Anyhow I put my back into the case, and after a hard struggle got a verdict of 'Not Guilty'. Mr Docken had been kind enough to express his appreciation of my efforts, and to ask in a hoarse whisper how I had 'squared the old bird', meaning the Judge. He did not understand the subtleties of the English law of evidence.

He shambled into the room, a huge hulking figure of a man, with the thickness of chest which under happier circumstances might have made him a terror in the prize-ring. His features wore a heavy scowl which slowly cleared to a flicker of recognition.

'By God, it's the lawyer-chap,' he muttered.

I pointed to the glass of champagne.

'I don't mind if I do,' he said. ''Ere's 'ealth!' He swallowed the wine at a gulp and wiped his mouth on his sleeve. ''Ave a drop yourself, guv'nor,' he added. 'A glass of bubbly will cheer you up.'

'Well, Mr Docken,' I said, 'I hope I see you fit.' I was getting wonderfully collected now that the suspense was over.

'Pretty fair, sir. Pretty fair. Able to do my day's work like an honest man.'

'And what brings you here?'

'A little job I'm on. Some friends of mine wants you out of the road for a bit and they've sent me to fetch you. It's a bit of luck for you that you've struck a friend. We needn't 'ave no unpleasantness seein' we're both what you might call men of the world.'

'I appreciate the compliment,' I said. 'But where do you propose to take me?'

'Dunno. It's some lay near the Docks. I've got a motor-car waitin' at the back of the 'ouse.'

'But supposing I don't want to go?'

'My orders admits no excuse,' he said solemnly. 'You're a sensible chap, and can see that in a scrap I could down you easy.'

'Very likely,' I said. 'But, man, you must be mad to talk like that. Downstairs there is a dining-room full of people. I have only to lift my voice to bring the police.'

'You're a kid,' he said scornfully. 'Them geysers downstairs are all in the job. That was a flat-catching rig to get you up here so as you wouldn't suspect nothing. If you was to go down now – which you ain't going to be allowed to do – you wouldn't find a blamed soul in the place. I must say you're a bit softer than I 'oped after the 'andsome way you talked over yon old juggins with the wig at Maidstone.'

Mr Docken took the bottle from the wine-cooler and filled himself another glass.

It sounded horribly convincing. If I was to be kidnapped and smuggled away, Lumley would have scored half a success. Not the whole; for, as I swiftly reflected, I had put Felix on the track of Tuke, and there was every chance that Tommy and Pitt-Heron would be saved. But for myself it looked pretty black. The more my scheme succeeded the more likely the Power-House would be to wreak its vengeance on me once I was spirited from the open-air world into its dark labyrinths.

I made a great effort to keep my voice even and calm.

'Mr Docken,' I said, 'I once did you a good turn. But for me you might be doing time now instead of drinking champagne like a gentleman. Your pals played you a pretty low trick and that was why I stuck out for you. I didn't think you were the kind of man to forget a friend.'

'No more I am,' said he. 'The man who says Bill Docken would go back on a pal is a liar.'

'Well, here's your chance to pay your debts. The men who employ you are my deadly enemies and want to do me in. I'm not a match for you. You're a stronger fellow and can drag me off and hand me over to them. But if you do I'm done with. Make no mistake about that. I put it to you as a decent fellow. Are you going to go back on the man who has been a good friend to you?'

He shifted from one foot to another with his eyes on the ceiling. He was obviously in difficulties. Then he tried another glass of champagne.

'I dursn't, guv'nor. I dursn't let you go. Them I work for would cut my throat as soon as look at me. Besides it ain't no good. If I was to go off and leave you there'd be plenty more in this 'ouse as would do the job. You're up against it, guv'nor. But take a sensible view and come with me. They don't mean you no real 'arm. I'll take my Bible oath on it. Only to keep you quiet for a bit, for you've run across one of their games. They won't do you no 'urt if you speak 'em fair. Be a sport and take it smiling-like—'

'You're afraid of them,' I said.

'Yuss. I'm afraid. Black afraid. So would you be if you knew the gents. I'd rather take on the whole Rat Lane crowd – you know them as I mean – on a Saturday night when they're out for business than go back to my gents and say as 'ow I had shirked the job.'

He shivered. 'Good Lord, they'd freeze the 'eart out of a bull-pup.'

'You're afraid,' I said slowly. 'So you're going to give me up to the men you're afraid of to do as they like with me. I never expected it of you, Bill. I thought you were the kind of lad who would send any gang to the devil before you'd go back on a pal.'

'Don't say that,' he said almost plaintively. 'You don't 'alf know the 'ole I'm in.' His eye seemed to be wandering, and he yawned deeply.

Just then a great noise began below. I heard a voice speaking, a loud peremptory voice. Then my name was shouted: 'Leithen! Leithen! Are you there?'

There could be no mistaking that stout Yorkshire tongue. By some miracle Chapman had followed me and was raising Cain downstairs.

My heart leaped with the sudden revulsion. 'I'm here,' I yelled. 'Upstairs. Come up and let me out!'

Then I turned with a smile of triumph to Bill.

'My friends have come,' I said. 'You're too late for the job. Get back and tell your masters that.'

He was swaying on his feet, and he suddenly lurched towards me. 'You come along. By God, you think you've done me. I'll let you see.'

His voice was growing thick and he stopped short. 'What the 'ell's wrong with me?' he gasped. 'I'm goin' all queer. I…'

He was like a man far gone in liquor, but three glasses of champagne would never have touched a head like Bill's. I saw what was up with him. He was not drunk, but drugged.

'They've doped the wine,' I cried. 'They put it there for me to drink it and go to sleep.'

There is always something which is the last straw to any man. You may insult and outrage him and he will bear it patiently, but touch the quick in his temper and he will turn. Apparently for Bill drugging was the unforgivable sin. His eye lost for a moment its confusion. He squared his shoulders and roared like a bull.

'Doped, by God!' he cried. 'Who done it?'

'The men who shut me in this room. Burst that door and you will find them.'

He turned a blazing face on the locked door and hurled his huge weight on it. It cracked and bent, but the lock and hinges held. I could see that sleep was overwhelming him and that his limbs were stiffening, but his anger was still strong enough for another effort. Again he drew himself together like a big cat and flung himself on the woodwork. The hinges tore from the jambs and the whole outfit fell forward into the passage in a cloud of splinters and dust and broken plaster.

It was Mr Docken's final effort. He lay on the top of the wreckage he had made, like Samson among the ruins of Gaza, a senseless and slumbering hulk.

I picked up the unopened bottle of champagne – it was the only weapon available – and stepped over his body. I was beginning to enjoy myself amazingly.

As I expected, there was a man in the corridor, a little fellow in waiter's clothes with a tweed jacket instead of a dress-coat. If he had a pistol I knew I was done, but I gambled upon the disinclination of the management for the sound of shooting.

He had a knife, but he never had a chance to use it. My champagne bottle descended on his head and he dropped like a log.

There were men coming upstairs – not Chapman, for I still heard his hoarse shouts in the dining-room. If they once got up they could force me back through that hideous room by the door through which Docken had come, and in five minutes I should be in their motor-car.

There was only one thing to do. I jumped from the stair-head right down among them. I think there were three, and my descent toppled them over. We rolled in a wild whirling mass and cascaded into the dining-room, where my head bumped violently on the parquet.

I expected a bit of a grapple, but none came. My wits were pretty woolly, but I managed to scramble to my feet. The heels of my enemies were disappearing up the staircase. Chapman was pawing my ribs to discover if there were any bones broken. There was not another soul in the room except two policemen who were pushing their way in from the street.

Chapman was flushed and breathing heavily: his coat had a big split down the seams at the shoulder, but his face was happy as a child's.

I caught his arm and spoke in his ear. 'We've got to get out of this at once. How can we square these policemen? There must be no inquiry and nothing in the papers. Do you hear?'

'That's all right,' said Chapman. 'These bobbies are friends of mine, two good lads from Wensleydale. On my road here I told them to give me a bit of law and follow me, for I thought they might be wanted. They didn't come too soon to spoil sport, for I've been knocking furriners about for ten minutes. You seem to have been putting up a tidy scrap yourself.'

'Let's get home first,' I said, for I was beginning to think of the bigger thing.

I wrote a chit for Macgillivray which I asked one of the constables to take to Scotland Yard. It was to beg that nothing should be done yet in the business of the restaurant, and above all, that nothing should get into the papers. Then I asked the other to see us home. It was a queer request for two able-bodied men to make on a summer evening in the busiest part of London, but I was taking no chances. The Power-House had declared war on me, and I knew it would be war without quarter.

I was in a fever to get out of that place. My momentary lust of battle had gone, and every stone of that building seemed to me a threat.

Chapman would have liked to spend a happy hour rummaging through the house, but the gravity of my face persuaded him. The truth is, I was bewildered. I could not understand the reason of this sudden attack. Lumley's spies must long ago have told him enough to connect me with the Bokhara business. My visits to the Embassy alone were proof enough. But now he must have found out something new, something which startled him, or else there had been wild doings in Turkestan.

I won't forget that walk home in a hurry. It was a fine June twilight. The streets were full of the usual crowd, shop-girls in thin frocks, promenading clerks, and all the flotsam of a London summer. You would have said it was the safest place on earth. But I was glad we had the policeman with us, who at the end of one beat passed us on to his colleague, and I was glad of Chapman. For I am morally certain I would never have got home alone.

The queer thing is that there was no sign of trouble till we got into Oxford Street. Then I became aware that there were people on these pavements who knew all about me. I first noticed it at the mouth of one of those little dark side-alleys which run up into mews and small dingy courts. I found myself being skilfully edged away from Chapman into the shadow, but I noticed it in time and butted my way back to the pavement. I couldn't make out who the people were who hustled me. They seemed nondescripts of all sorts, but I fancied there were women among them.

This happened twice, and I got wary, but I was nearly caught before we reached Oxford Circus. There was a front of a big shop rebuilding, and the usual wooden barricade with a gate. Just as we passed it there was a special throng on the pavement, and I, being next the wall, got pushed against the gate. Suddenly it gave, and I was pressed inward. I was right inside before I realized my danger, and the gate was closing. There must have been people there, but I could see nothing in the gloom.

It was no time for false pride. I yelled to Chapman, and the next second his burly shoulder was in the gap. The hustlers vanished, and I seemed to hear a polite voice begging my pardon.

After that Chapman and I linked arms and struck across Mayfair. But I did not feel safe till I was in the flat with the door bolted.

We had a long drink, and I stretched myself in an armchair, for I was as tired as if I had come out of a big game of Rugby football.

'I owe you a good deal, old man,' I said. 'I think I'll join the Labour Party. You can tell your fellows to send me their whips. What possessed you to come to look for me?'

The explanation was simple. I had mentioned the restaurant in my telephone message, and the name had awakened a recollection in Chapman's mind. He could not fix it at first, but by-and-by he remembered that the place had cropped up in the Routh case. Routh's London headquarters had been at the restaurant in Antioch Street. As soon as he remembered this he got into a taxi and descended at the corner of the street, where by sheer luck he fell in with his Wensleydale friends.

He said he had marched into the restaurant and found it empty, but for an ill-favoured manager, who denied all knowledge of me. Then, fortunately, he chose to make certain by shouting my name, and heard my answer. After that he knocked the manager down, and was presently assaulted by several men whom he described as 'furrin muck'. They had knives, of which he made very little, for he seems to have swung a table as a battering-ram and left sore limbs behind him.

He was on the top of his form. 'I haven't enjoyed anything so much since I was a lad at school,' he informed me. 'I was beginning to think your Power-House was a wash-out, but Lord! it's been busy enough tonight. This is what I call life!'

My spirits could not keep pace with his. The truth is that I was miserably puzzled – not afraid so much as mystified. I couldn't make out this sudden dead-set at me. Either they knew more than I bargained for, or I knew far too little.

'It's all very well,' I said, 'but I don't see how this is going to end. We can't keep up the pace long. At this rate it will be only a matter of hours till they get me.'

We pretty well barricaded ourselves in the flat, and, at his earnest request, I restored to Chapman his revolver.

Then I got the clue I had been longing for. It was about eleven o'clock, while we were sitting smoking, when the telephone bell rang. It was Felix who spoke.

'I have news for you,' he said. 'The hunters have met the hunted, and one of the hunters is dead. The other is a prisoner in our hands. He has confessed.'

It had been black murder in intent. The frontier police had shadowed the two men into the cup of a glen, where they met Tommy and Pitt-Heron. The four had spoken together for a little, and then Tuke had fired deliberately at Charles and had grazed his ear. Whereupon Tommy had charged him and knocked the pistol from his hand. The assailant had fled, but a long shot from the police on the hillside had toppled him over. Tommy had felled Saronov with his fists, and the man had abjectly surrendered. He had confessed, Felix said, but what the confession was he did not know.

CHAPTER 7

I FIND SANCTUARY

My nervousness and indecision dropped from me at the news. I had won the first round, and I would win the last, for it suddenly became clear to me that I had now evidence which would blast Lumley. I believed that it would not be hard to prove his identity with Pavia and his receipt of the telegram from Saronov; Tuke was his creature, and Tuke's murderous mission was his doing. No doubt I knew little and could prove nothing about the big thing, the Power-House, but conspiracy to murder is not the lightest of criminal charges. I was beginning to see my way to checkmating my friend, at least so far as Pitt-Heron was concerned. Provided – and it was a pretty big proviso – that he gave me the chance to use my knowledge.

That, I foresaw, was going to be the difficulty. What I knew now Lumley had known hours before. The reason of the affair at Antioch Street was now only too clear. If he believed that I had damning evidence against him – and there was no doubt he suspected it – then he would do his best to stop my mouth. I must get my statement lodged in the proper quarter at the earliest possible moment.

The next twenty-four hours, I feared, were going to be too sensational for comfort. And yet I cannot say that I was afraid. I was too full of pride to be in a funk. I had lost my awe of Lumley through scoring a point against him. Had I known more I should have been less at my ease. It was this confidence which prevented me doing the obvious safe thing – ringing up Macgillivray, telling him the gist of my story, and getting him to put me under police protection. I thought I was clever enough to see the thing through myself. And it must have been the same over-confidence which prevented Lumley getting at me that night. An organization like his could easily have got into the flat and done for us both. I suppose the explanation is that he did not yet know how much I knew, and was not ready to take the last steps in silencing me.

I sat up till the small hours, marshalling my evidence in a formal statement and making two copies of it. One was destined for Macgillivray and the other for Felix, for I was taking no risks. I went to bed and slept peacefully, and was awakened as usual by Waters. My man slept out, and used to turn up in the morning about seven. It was all so normal and homely that I could have believed my adventures of the night before a dream. In the summer sunlight the ways of darkness seemed very distant. I dressed in excellent spirits and made a hearty breakfast.

Then I gave the docile Chapman his instructions. He must take the document to Scotland Yard, ask to see Macgillivray, and put it into his hands. Then he must ring me up at once at Down Street and tell me that he had done this. I had already telephoned to my clerk that I would not be at the Temple that day.

It seems a simple thing to travel less than a mile in the most frequented part of London in broad daylight and perform an easy act like carrying a letter; but I knew that Lumley's spies would be active, and would connect Chapman sufficiently with me to think him worth following. In that case there might be an attempt at violence. I thought it my duty to tell him this, but he laughed me to scorn. He proposed to walk, and he begged to be shown the man who would meddle with him. Chapman, after last night, was prepared to take on all comers. He put my letter to Macgillivray in his inner pocket, buttoned his coat, crushed down his felt hat on his head, and defiantly set forth.

I expected a message from him in half an hour, for he was a rapid walker. But the half-hour passed, then the three-quarters, and nothing happened. At eleven I rang up Scotland Yard, but they had no news of him.

Then I became miserably anxious, for it was clear that some disaster had overtaken my messenger. My first impulse was to set out myself to look for him, but a moment's reflection convinced me that that would be playing into the enemy's hands. For an hour I wrestled with my impatience, and then a few minutes after twelve I was rung up by St Thomas's Hospital.

A young doctor spoke, and said that Mr Chapman had asked him to tell me what had happened. He had been run down by a motor-car at the corner of Whitehall – nothing serious – only a bad shake and some scalp wounds. In a day or so he would be able to leave.

Then he added what drove the blood from my heart. 'Mr Chapman personally wished me to tell you,' he said, 'that the letter has gone.' I stammered some reply asking his meaning. 'He said he thinks,' I was told, 'that, while he was being assisted to his feet, his pocket was picked and a letter taken. He said you would know what he meant.'

I knew only too well what he meant. Lumley had got my statement, and realized precisely how much I knew and what was the weight of evidence against him. Before he had only suspected, now he knew. He must know, too, that there would be a copy somewhere which I would try to deliver. It was going to be harder than I had fancied to get my news to the proper ears, and I had to anticipate the extreme of violence on the part of my opponents.

The thought of the peril restored my coolness. I locked the outer door of my flat, and telephoned to the garage where I kept my car, bidding Stagg call for me at two o'clock precisely. Then I lit a pipe and strove to banish the whole business from my thoughts, for fussing would do me no good.

Presently it occurred to me to ring up Felix and give him some notion of the position. But I found that my telephone was now broken and connection was impossible. The spoken as well as the written word was to be denied me. That had happened in the last half-hour, and I didn't believe it was by accident. Also my man Waters, whom I had sent out on an errand after breakfast, had never returned. The state of siege had begun.

It was a blazing hot midsummer day. The water-carts were sprinkling Piccadilly, and looking from my window I could see leisurely and elegant gentlemen taking their morning stroll. A florist's cart full of roses stood below me in the street. The summer smell of town – a mixture of tar, flowers, dust, and patchouli – rose in gusts through the hot air. It was the homely London I knew so well, and I was somehow an exile from it. I was being shepherded into a dismal isolation, which, unless I won help, might mean death. I was cool enough now, but I will not deny that I was miserably anxious. I cursed my false confidence the night before. By now I might have had Macgillivray and his men by my side. As it was, I wondered if I should ever see them.

I changed into a flannel suit, lunched off sandwiches and a whisky-and-soda, and at two o'clock looked for Stagg and my car. He was five minutes late, a thing which had never happened before. But I never welcomed anything so gladly as the sight of that car. I had hardly dared to hope that it would reach me.

My goal was the Embassy in Belgrave Square, but I was convinced that if I approached it directly I should share the fate of Chapman. Worse, for from me they would not merely snatch the letter. What I had once written I could write again, and if they wished to ensure my silence it must be by more drastic methods. I proposed to baffle my pursuers by taking a wide circuit round the western suburbs of London, returning to the Embassy when I thought the coast clear.

It was a tremendous relief to go down the stairs and emerge into the hot daylight. I gave Stagg his instructions, and lay back in the closed car with a curious fluttering sense of anticipation. I had begun the last round in the wild game. There was a man at the corner of Down Street who seemed to peer curiously at the car. He was doubtless one of my watchers.

We went up Park Lane into the Edgware Road, my instructions to Stagg being to make a circuit by Harrow and Brentford. Now that I was ensconced in my car I felt a trifle safer, and my tense nerves relaxed. I grew drowsy and allowed myself to sink into a half doze. The stolid back of Stagg filled my gaze, as it had filled it a fortnight ago on the western road, and I admired lazily the brick-red of his neck. He had been in the Guards, and a Boer bullet at Modder River had left a long scar at the nape of his neck, which gave to his hair the appearance of being badly cut. He had told me the story on Exmoor.

Suddenly I rubbed my eyes. There was no scar there; the hair of the chauffeur grew regularly down to his coat-collar. The resemblance had been perfect, the voice was Stagg's, but clearly it was not Stagg who now drove my car.

I pulled the blind down over the front window as if to shelter myself from the sun. Looking out, I saw that we were some distance up the Edgware Road, nearing the point where the Marylebone Road joins it. Now or never was my chance, for at the corner there is always a block in the traffic.

The car slowed down in obedience to a policeman's uplifted hand, and very gently I opened the door on the left side. Since the car was new it opened softly, and in two seconds I had stepped out, shut it again, and made a dive between a butcher's cart and a motor-bus for the side-walk. I gave one glance back and saw the unconscious chauffeur still rigid at the wheel.

I dodged unobtrusively through the crowd on the pavement, with my hand on my breast-pocket to see that my paper was still there. There was a little picture-shop near by to which I used to go occasionally, owned by a man who was an adept at cleaning and restoring. I had sent him customers and he was likely to prove a friend. So I dived into his doorway, which made a cool pit of shade after the glaring street, and found him, spectacles on nose, busy examining some dusty prints.

He greeted me cordially and followed me into the back shop.

'Mr Levison,' I said, 'have you a back door?'

He looked at me in some surprise. 'Why, yes; there is the door into the lane which runs from Edgeley Street into Connaught Mews.'

'Will you let me use it? There is a friend outside whom I wish to avoid. Such things happen, you know.'

He smiled comprehendingly. 'Certainly, sir. Come this way.' And he led me through a dark passage hung with dingy Old Masters to a little yard filled with the debris of picture frames. There he unlocked a door in the wall and I found myself in a narrow alley. As I emerged I heard the bell of the shop-door ring. 'If any one inquires, you have not seen me here, remember,' I said, and Mr Levison nodded. He was an artist in his small way and liked the scent of a mystery.

I ran down the lane and by various cross streets made my way into Bayswater. I believed that I had thrown my trackers for the moment off the scent, but I had got to get to the Embassy, and that neighbourhood was sure to be closely watched. I came out on the Bayswater Road pretty far west, and resolved to strike south-east across the Park. My reason was that the neighbourhood of Hyde Park Corner was certain at that time of day to be pretty well crowded, and I felt more security in a throng than in the empty streets of Kensington. Now that I come to think of it, it was a rash thing to do, for since Lumley knew the full extent of my knowledge, he was likely to deal more violently with me than with Chapman, and the seclusion of the Park offered him too good a chance.

I crossed the riding-track, and struck over the open space where the Sunday demonstrations are held. There was nothing there but nurses and perambulators, children at play, and dogs being exercised. Presently I reached Grosvenor Gate, where on the little green chairs well-dressed people were taking the air. I recognized several acquaintances, and stopped for a moment to talk to one of them. Then I emerged in Park Lane, and walked down it to Hamilton Place.

So far I thought I had not been followed, but now once more I had the indefinable but unerring sensation of being watched. I caught a man looking eagerly at me from the other side of the street, and it seemed to me that he made a sign to someone farther off. There was now less than a quarter of a mile between me and Belgrave Square, but I saw that it would be a hard course to cover.

Once in Piccadilly, there could be no doubt about my watchers. Lumley was doing the thing in style this time. Last night it had only been a trial trip, but now the whole energies of the Power-House were on the job. The place was filled with the usual mid-season crowd, and I had to take off my hat several times. Up in the bow-window of the Bachelors' Club a young friend of mine was writing a letter and sipping a long drink with an air of profound boredom. I would have given much for his ennui, for my life at the moment was painfully exciting. I was alone in that crowd, isolated and proscribed, and there was no help save in my own wits. If I spoke to a policeman he would think me drunk or mad, and yet I was on the edge of being made the victim of a far subtler crime than fell within the purview of the Metropolitan force.

Now I saw how thin is the protection of civilization. An accident and a bogus ambulance – a false charge and a bogus arrest – there were a dozen ways of spiriting me out of this gay, bustling world. I foresaw that, if I delayed, my nerve would break, so I boldly set off across the road.

I jolly nearly shared the fate of Chapman. A car which seemed about to draw up at a club door suddenly swerved across the street, and I had to dash to an island to escape it. It was no occasion to hesitate, so, dodging a bus and missing a motor-bicycle by a hair's-breadth, I rushed across the remaining distance and reached the railings of the Green Park.

Here there were fewer people, and several queer things began to happen. A little group of workmen with their tools were standing by the kerb, and they suddenly moved towards me. A pavement artist, who looked like a cripple, scrambled to his feet and moved in the same direction. There was a policeman at the corner, and I saw a well-dressed man go up to him, say something and nod in my direction, and the policeman too began to move towards me.

I did not await them. I took to my heels and ran for my life down Grosvenor Place.

Long ago at Eton I had won the school mile, and at Oxford I was a second string for the quarter. But never at Eton or at Oxford did I run as I ran then. It was blisteringly hot, but I did not feel it, for my hands were clammy and my heart felt like a cold stone. I do not know how the pursuit got on, for I did not think of it. I did not reflect what kind of spectacle I must afford running like a thief in a London thoroughfare on a June afternoon. I only knew that my enemies were around and behind me, and that in front, a few hundred yards away, lay safety.

But even as I ran I had the sense to think out my movements, and to realize that the front door of the Embassy was impossible. For one thing, it would be watched, and for another, before the solemn footmen opened it, my pursuers would be upon me. My only hope was the back door.

I twisted into the Mews behind the north side of the Square, and as I turned I saw two men run up from the Square as if to cut me off. A whistle was blown, and more men appeared – one entering from the far end of the Mews, one darting from a public-house door, and one sliding down a ladder from a stable-loft. This last was nearest me, and tried to trip me, but I rejoice to say that a left-hander on the chin sent him sprawling on the cobbles. I remembered that the Embassy was the fifth house from the end, and feverishly I tried to count the houses by their backs. It is not so easy as it sounds, for the modern London householder studs his back premises with excrescences which seem to melt into his neighbour's. In the end I had to make a guess at the door, which, to my joy, was unlocked. I rushed in and banged it behind me.

I found myself in a stone passage, with on one side a door opening on a garage. There was a wooden staircase leading to an upper floor, and a glass door in front, which opened into a large disused room full of boxes. Beyond were two doors, one of which was locked. The other abutted on a steep iron stairway, which obviously led to the lower regions of the house.

I ran down the stair – it was no more than a ladder – crossed a small courtyard, traversed a passage, and burst into the kitchen, where I confronted an astonished white-capped chef in the act of lifting a pot from the fire.

His face was red and wrathful, and I thought that he was going to fling the pot at my head. I had disturbed him in some delicate operation, and his artist's pride was outraged.

'Monsieur,' I stammered in French, 'I seek your pardon for my intrusion. There were circumstances which compelled me to enter this house by the back premises. I am an acquaintance of his Excellency, your patron, and an old friend of Monsieur Felix. I beg you of your kindness to direct me to Monsieur Felix's room, or to bid someone take me there.'

My abject apologies mollified him.

'It is a grave offence, monsieur,' he said, 'an unparalleled offence, to enter my kitchen at this hour. I fear you have irremediably spoiled the new casserole dish that I was endeavouring to compose.'

I was ready to go on my knees to the offended artist.

'It grieves me indeed to have interfered with so rare an art, which I have often admired at his Excellency's table. But there is danger behind me, and an urgent mission in front. Monsieur will forgive me? Necessity will sometimes overrule the finest sensibility.'

He bowed to me, and I bowed to him, and my pardon was assured.

Suddenly a door opened, another than that by which I had entered, and a man appeared whom I took to be a footman. He was struggling into his livery coat, but at the sight of me he dropped it. I thought I recognized the face as that of the man who had emerged from the public-house and tried to cut me off.

''Ere, Mister Alphonse,' he cried, ''elp me to collar this man. The police are after 'im.'

'You forget, my friend,' I said, 'that an Embassy is privileged ground which the police can't enter. I desire to be taken before his Excellency.'

'So that's yer game,' he shouted. 'But two can play at that. 'Ere, give me an 'and, moosoo, and we'll 'ave him in the street in a jiffey. There's two 'undred of the best in our pockets if we 'ands 'im over to them as wants 'im.'

The cook looked puzzled and a little frightened.

'Will you allow them to outrage your kitchen – an Embassy kitchen, too – without your consent?' I said.

'What have you done?' he asked in French.

'Only what your patron will approve,' I replied in the same tongue. 'Messieurs les assassins have a grudge against me.'

He still hesitated, while the young footman advanced on me. He was fingering something in his trousers-pocket which I did not like.

Now was the time when, as they say in America, I should have got busy with my gun; but alas! I had no gun. I feared supports for the enemy, for the footman at the first sight of me had run back the way he had come, and I had heard a low whistle.

What might have happened I do not know, had not the god appeared from the machine in the person of Hewins, the butler.

'Hewins,' I said, 'you know me. I have often dined here, and you know that I am a friend of Monsieur Felix. I am on my way to see him on an urgent matter, and for various reasons I had to enter by Monsieur Alphonse's kitchen. Will you take me at once to Monsieur Felix?'

Hewins bowed, and on his imperturbable face there appeared no sign of surprise. 'This way, sir,' was all he said.

As I followed him I saw the footman plucking nervously at the something in his trousers-pocket. Lumley's agents apparently had not always the courage to follow his instructions to the letter, for I made no doubt that the order had been to take me alive or dead.

I found Felix alone, and flung myself into an arm-chair. 'My dear chap,' I said, 'take my advice and advise his Excellency to sack the red-haired footman.'

From that moment I date that sense of mastery over a situation which drives out fear. I had been living for weeks under a dark pall, and suddenly the skies had lightened. I had found sanctuary. Whatever happened to me now the worst was past, for I had done my job.

Felix was looking at me curiously, for, jaded, scarlet, dishevelled, I was an odd figure for a London afternoon. 'Things seem to have been marching fast with you,' he said.

'They have, but I think the march is over. I want to ask several favours. First, here is a document which sets out certain facts. I shall ring up Macgillivray at Scotland Yard and ask him to come here at 9.30 this evening. When he comes I want you to give him this and ask him to read it at once. He will know how to act on it.'

Felix nodded. 'And the next?'

'Give me a telegraph form. I want a wire sent at once by someone who can be trusted.' He handed me a form and I wrote out a telegram to Lumley at the Albany, saying that I proposed to call upon him that evening at eight sharp, and asking him to receive me.

'Next?' said Felix.

'Next and last, I want a room with a door which will lock, a hot bath, and something to eat about seven. I might be permitted to taste Monsieur Alphonse's new casserole dish.'

I rang up Macgillivray, reminded him of his promise, and told him what awaited him at 9.30. Then I had a wash, and afterwards at my leisure gave Felix a sketch of the day's doings. I have never felt more completely at my ease, for whatever happened I was certain that I had spoiled Lumley's game. He would know by now that I had reached the Embassy, and that any further attempts on my life and liberty were futile. My telegram would show him that I was prepared to offer terms, and I would certainly be permitted to reach the Albany unmolested. To the meeting with my adversary I looked forward without qualms, but with the most lively interest. I had my own theories about that distinguished criminal, and I hoped to bring them to the proof.

Just before seven I had a reply to my wire. Mr Lumley said he would be delighted to see me. The telegram was directed to me at the Embassy, though I had put no address on the one I sent. Lumley, of course, knew all my movements. I could picture him sitting in his chair, like some Chief of Staff, receiving every few minutes the reports of his agents. All the same, Napoleon had fought his Waterloo.

CHAPTER 8

THE POWER-HOUSE

I left Belgrave Square about a quarter to eight and retraced my steps along the route which for me that afternoon had been so full of tremors. I was still being watched – a little observation told me that – but I would not be interfered with, provided my way lay in a certain direction. So completely without nervousness was I that at the top of Constitution Hill I struck into the Green Park and kept to the grass till I emerged into Piccadilly opposite Devonshire House. A light wind had risen, and the evening had grown pleasantly cool. I met several men I knew going out to dinner on foot, and stopped to exchange greetings. From my clothes they thought I had just returned from a day in the country.

I reached the Albany as the clock was striking eight. Lumley's rooms were on the first floor, and I was evidently expected, for the porter himself conducted me to them and waited by me till the door was opened by a man-servant.

You know those rococo, late Georgian, Albany rooms, large, square, clumsily corniced. Lumley's was lined with books, which I saw at a glance were of a different type from those in his working library at his country house. This was the collection of a bibliophile, and in the light of the summer evening the rows of tall volumes in vellum and morocco lined the walls like some rich tapestry.

The valet retired and shut the door, and presently from a little inner chamber came his master. He was dressed for dinner, and wore more than ever the air of the eminent diplomat. Again I had the old feeling of incredulity. It was the Lumley I had met two nights before at dinner, the friend of Viceroys and Cabinet Ministers. It was hard to connect him with Antioch Street or the red-haired footman with a pistol. Or with Tuke? Yes, I decided, Tuke fitted into the frame. Both were brains cut loose from the decencies that make life possible.

'Good evening, Mr Leithen,' he said pleasantly. 'As you have fixed the hour of eight, may I offer you dinner?'

'Thank you,' I replied, 'but I have already dined. I have chosen an awkward time, but my business need not take long.'

'So?' he said. 'I am always glad to see you at any hour.'

'And I prefer to see the master rather than the subordinates who have been infesting my life during the past week.'

We both laughed. 'I am afraid you have had some annoyance, Mr Leithen,' he said. 'But remember, I gave you fair warning.'

'True. And I have come to do the same kindness to you. That part of the game, at any rate, is over.'

'Over?' he queried, raising his eyebrows.

'Yes, over,' I said, and took out my watch. 'Let us be quite frank with each other, Mr Lumley. There is really very little time to waste. As you have doubtless read the paper which you stole from my friend this morning, you know more or less the extent of my information.'

'Let us have frankness by all means. Yes, I have read your paper. A very creditable piece of work, if I may say so. You will rise in your profession, Mr Leithen. But surely you must realize that it carries you a very little way.'

'In a sense you are right. I am not in a position to reveal the full extent of your misdeeds. Of the Power-House and its doings I can only guess. But Pitt-Heron is on his way home, and he will be carefully safeguarded on that journey. Your creature, Saronov, has confessed. We shall know more very soon, and meantime I have clear evidence which implicates you in a conspiracy to murder.'

He did not answer, but I wished I could see behind his tinted spectacles to the look in his eyes. I think he had not been quite prepared for the line I took.

'I need not tell you, as a lawyer, Mr Leithen,' he said at last, 'that what seems good evidence on paper is often feeble enough in Court. You cannot suppose that I will tamely plead guilty to your charges. On the contrary, I will fight them with all the force that brains and money can give. You are an ingenious young man, but you are not the brightest jewel of the English Bar.'

'That also is true. I do not deny that some of my evidence may be weakened at the trial. It is even conceivable that you may be acquitted on some technical doubt. But you have forgotten one thing. From the day you leave the Court you will be a suspected man. The police of all Europe will be on your trail. You have been highly successful in the past, and why? Because you have been above suspicion, an honourable and distinguished gentleman, belonging to the best clubs, counting as your acquaintances the flower of our society. Now you will be a suspect, a man with a past, a centre of strange stories. I put it to you – how far are you likely to succeed under these conditions?'

He laughed.

'You have a talent for character-drawing, my friend. What makes you think that I can work only if I live in the limelight of popularity?'

'The talent you mention,' I said. 'As I read your character – and I think I am right – you are an artist in crime. You are not the common cut-throat who acts out of passion or greed. No, I think you are something subtler than that. You love power, hidden power. You flatter your vanity by despising mankind and making them your tools. You scorn the smattering of inaccuracies which passes for human knowledge, and I will not venture to say you are wrong. Therefore, you use your brains to frustrate it. Unhappily the life of millions is built on that smattering, so you are a foe to society. But there would be no flavour in controlling subterranean things if you were yourself a mole working in the dark. To get the full flavour, the irony of it all, you must live in the light. I can imagine you laughing in your soul as you move about our world, praising it with your lips, patting it with your hands, and kicking its props away with your feet. I can see the charm of it. But it is over now.'

'Over?' he asked.

'Over,' I repeated. 'The end has come – the utter, final, and absolute end.'

He made a sudden, odd, nervous movement, pushing his glasses close back upon his eyes.

'What about yourself?' he said hoarsely. 'Do you think you can play against me without suffering desperate penalties?'

He was holding a cord in his hand with a knob on the end of it. He now touched a button in the knob, and there came the faint sound of a bell.

The door was behind me, and he was looking beyond me towards it.

I was entirely at his mercy, but I never budged an inch. I do not know how I managed to keep calm, but I did it, and without much effort. I went on speaking, conscious that the door had opened and that someone was behind me.

'It is really quite useless trying to frighten me. I am safe because I am dealing with an intelligent man, and not with the ordinary half-witted criminal. You do not want my life in silly revenge. If you call in your man and strangle me between you what earthly good would it do you?'

He was looking beyond me, and the passion – a sudden white-hot passion like an epilepsy – was dying out of his face.

'A mistake, James,' he said. 'You can go.'

The door closed softly at my back.

'Yes. A mistake. I have a considerable admiration for you, Mr Lumley, and should be sorry to be disappointed.'

He laughed quite like an ordinary mortal. 'I am glad this affair is to be conducted on a basis of mutual respect. Now that the melodramatic overture is finished let us get to the business.'

'By all means,' I said. 'I promised to deal with you frankly. Well, let me put my last cards on the table. At half-past nine precisely the duplicate of that statement of mine which you annexed this morning will be handed to Scotland Yard. I may add that the authorities there know me, and are proceeding under my advice. When they read that statement they will act on it. You have therefore about one hour and a half, or say one and three-quarters, to make up your mind. You can still secure your freedom, but it must be elsewhere than in England.'

He had risen to his feet, and was pacing up and down the room.

'Will you oblige me by telling me one thing,' he said. 'If you believe me to be, as you say, a dangerous criminal, how do you reconcile it with your conscience to give me a chance of escape? It is your duty to bring me to justice.'

'I will tell you why,' I said. 'I, too, have a weak joint in my armour. Yours is that you can only succeed under the disguise of high respectability. That disguise, in any case, will be stripped from you. Mine is Pitt-Heron. I do not know how far he has entangled himself with you, but I know something of his weakness, and I don't want his career ruined and his wife's heart broken. He has learned his lesson, and will never mention you and your schemes to a mortal soul. Indeed, if I can help it, he will never know that anyone shares his secret. The price of the chance of escape I offer you is that Pitt-Heron's past be buried for ever.'

He did not answer. He had his arms folded, walking up and down the room, and suddenly seemed to have aged enormously. I had the impression that I was dealing with a very old man.

'Mr Leithen,' he said at last, 'you are bold. You have a frankness which almost amounts to genius. You are wasted in your stupid profession, but your speculative powers are not equal to your other endowments, so you will probably remain in it, deterred by an illogical scruple from following your true bent. Your true *métier*, believe me, is what shallow people call crime. Speaking "without prejudice", as the idiot solicitors say, it would appear that we have both weak spots in our cases. Mine, you say, is that I can only work by using the conventions of what we agreed to call the Machine. There may be truth in that. Yours is that you have a friend who lacks your iron-clad discretion. You offer a plan which saves both our weaknesses. By the way, what is it?'

I looked at my watch again. 'You have ample time to catch the night express to Paris.'

'And if not?'

'Then I am afraid there may be trouble with the police between ten and eleven o'clock.'

'Which, for all our sakes, would be a pity. Do you know you interest me uncommonly, for you confirm the accuracy of my judgment. I have always had a notion that some day I should run across, to my sorrow, just such a man as you. A man of very great intellectual power I can deal with, for that kind of brain is usually combined with the sort of high-strung imagination on which I can work. The same with your over-imaginative man. Yes, Pitt-Heron was of that type. Ordinary brains do not trouble me, for I puzzle them. Now, you are a man of good commonplace intelligence. Pray forgive the lukewarmness of the phrase; it is really a high compliment, for I am an austere critic. If you were that and no more you would not have succeeded. But you possess also a quite irrelevant gift of imagination. Not enough to upset your balance, but enough to do what your mere lawyer's talent could never have done. You have achieved a feat which is given to few – you have partially understood me. Believe me, I rate you high. You are the kind of foursquare being bedded in the concrete of our civilization, on whom I have always felt I might some day come to grief... No, no, I am not trying to wheedle you. If I thought I could do that I should be sorry, for my discernment would have been at fault.'

'I warn you,' I said, 'that you are wasting precious time.'

He laughed quite cheerfully.

'I believe you are really anxious about my interests,' he said. 'That is a triumph indeed. Do you know, Mr Leithen, it is a mere whimsy of fate that you are not my disciple. If we had met earlier, and under other circumstances, I should have captured you. It is because you have in you a capacity for discipleship that you have succeeded in your opposition.'

'I abominate you and all your works,' I said, 'but I admire your courage.'

He shook his head gently.

'It is the wrong word. I am not courageous. To be brave means that you have conquered fear, but I have never had any fear to conquer. Believe me, Mr Leithen, I am quite impervious to threats. You come to me tonight and hold a pistol to my head. You offer me two alternatives, both of which mean failure. But how do you know that I regard them as failure? I have had what they call a good run for my money. No man since Napoleon has tasted such power. I may be willing to end it. Age creeps on and power may grow burdensome. I have always sat loose from common ambitions and common affections. For all you know I may regard you as a benefactor.'

All this talk looks futile when it is written down, but it was skilful enough, for it was taking every atom of exhilaration out of my victory. It was not idle brag. Every syllable rang true, as I knew in my bones. I felt myself in the presence of something enormously big, as if a small barbarian was desecrating the colossal Zeus of Pheidias with a coal hammer. But I also felt it inhuman, and I hated it, and I clung to that hatred.

'You fear nothing and you believe nothing,' I said. 'Man, you should never have been allowed to live.'

He raised a deprecating hand. 'I am a sceptic about most things,' he said, 'but, believe me, I have my own worship. I venerate the intellect of man. I believe in its undreamed-of possibilities, when it grows free like an oak in the forest and is not dwarfed in a flower-pot. From that allegiance I have never wavered. That is the God I have never forsworn.'

I took out my watch.

'Permit me again to remind you that time presses.'

'True,' he said, smiling. 'The continental express will not wait upon my confession. Your plan is certainly conceivable. There may be other and easier ways. I am not certain. I must think... Perhaps it would be wiser if you left me now, Mr Leithen. If I take your advice there will be various things to do... In any case there will be much to do...'

He led me to the door as if he were an ordinary host speeding an ordinary guest. I remember that on my way he pointed out a set of Aldines and called my attention to their beauty. He shook hands quite cordially and remarked on the fineness of the weather. That was the last I saw of this amazing man.

It was with profound relief that I found myself in Piccadilly in the wholesome company of my kind. I had carried myself boldly enough in the last hour, but I would not have gone through it again for a king's ransom. Do you know what it is to deal with a pure intelligence, a brain stripped of every shred of humanity? It is like being in the company of a snake.

I drove to the club and telephoned to Macgillivray, asking him to take no notice of my statement till he heard from me in the morning. Then I went to the hospital to see Chapman.

That Leader of the People was in a furious temper, and he was scarcely to be appeased by my narrative of the day's doings. Your Labour Member is the greatest of all sticklers for legality, and the outrage he had suffered that morning had grievously weakened his trust in public security. The Antioch Street business had seemed to him eminently right; if you once got mixed up in melodrama you had to expect such things. But for a Member of Parliament to be robbed in broad daylight next door to the House of Commons upset the foundations of his faith. There was little the matter with his body, and the doctor promised that he would be allowed up next day, but his soul was a mass of bruises.

It took me a lot of persuasion to get him to keep quiet. He wanted a public exposure of Lumley, a big trial, a general ferreting out of secret agents, the whole winding up with a speech in Parliament by himself on this latest outrage of Capitalism. Gloomily he listened to my injunction to silence. But he saw the reason of it, and promised to hold his tongue out of loyalty to Tommy. I knew that Pitt-Heron's secret was safe with him.

As I crossed Westminster Bridge on my way home, the night express to the Continent rumbled over the river. I wondered if Lumley was on board, or if he had taken one of the other ways of which he had spoken...

CHAPTER 9

RETURN OF THE WILD GEESE

I do not think I was surprised at the news I read in *The Times* next morning.

Mr Andrew Lumley had died suddenly in the night of heart failure, and the newspapers woke up to the fact that we had been entertaining a great man unawares. There was an obituary in 'leader' type of nearly two columns. He had been older than I thought – close on seventy – and *The Times* spoke of him as a man who might have done anything he pleased in public life, but had chosen to give to a small coterie of friends what was due to the country. I read of his wit and learning, his amazing connoisseurship, his social gifts, his personal charm. According to the writer, he was the finest type of cultivated amateur, a Beckford with more than a Beckford's wealth and none of his folly. Large private charities were hinted at, and a hope was expressed that some part at least of his collections might come to the nation.

The halfpenny papers said the same thing in their own way. One declared he reminded it of Atticus, another of Mæcenas, another of Lord Houghton. There must have been a great run on biographical dictionaries in the various offices. Chapman's own particular rag said that, although this kind of philanthropist was a dilettante and a back number, yet Mr Lumley was a good specimen of the class and had been a true friend to the poor. I thought Chapman would have a fit when he read this. After that he took in the *Morning Post*.

It was no business of mine to explode the myth. Indeed I couldn't even if I had wanted to, for no one would have believed me unless I produced proofs, and these proofs were not to be made public. Besides, I had an honest compunction. He had had, as he expressed it, a good run for his money, and I wanted the run to be properly rounded off.

Three days later I went to the funeral. It was a wonderful occasion. Two eminent statesmen were among the pall-bearers, Royalty was represented, and there were wreaths from learned societies and scores of notable people. It was a queer business to listen to that stately service, which was never read over stranger dust. I was thinking all the time of the vast subterranean machine which he had controlled, and which now was so much old iron. I could dimly imagine what his death meant to the hosts who had worked blindly at his discretion. He was a Napoleon who left no Marshals behind him. From the Power-House came no wreaths or newspaper tributes, but I knew that it had lost its power…

De mortuis, &c. My task was done, and it only remained to get Pitt-Heron home.

Of the three people in London besides myself who knew the story – Macgillivray, Chapman, and Felix – the two last might be trusted to be silent, and Scotland Yard is not in the habit of publishing its information. Tommy, of course, must some time or other be told; it was his right; but I knew that Tommy would never breathe a word of it. I wanted Charles to believe that his secret died with Lumley, for otherwise I don't think he would have ever come back to England.

The thing took some arranging, for we could not tell him directly about Lumley's death without giving away the fact that we knew of the connection between the two. We had to approach it by a roundabout road. I got Felix to arrange to have the news telegraphed to and inserted by special order in a Russian paper which Charles could not avoid seeing.

The device was successful. Calling at Portman Square a few days later, I learned from Ethel Pitt-Heron's glowing face that her troubles were over. That same evening a cable to me from Tommy announced the return of the wanderers.

It was the year of the Chilian Arbitration, in which I held a junior brief for the British Government, and that and the late sitting of Parliament kept me in London after the end of the term. I had had a bad reaction from the excitements of the summer, and in these days I was feeling pretty well hipped and overdone. On a hot August afternoon I met Tommy again.

The sun was shining through my Temple chambers, much as it had done when he started. So far as I remember, the West Ham brief which had aroused his contempt was still adorning my table. I was very hot and cross and fagged, for I had been engaged in the beastly job of comparing half a dozen maps of a despicable little bit of South American frontier.

Suddenly the door opened, and Tommy, lean and sunburnt, stalked in.

'Still at the old grind,' he cried, after we had shaken hands. 'Fellows like you give me a notion of the meaning of Eternity.'

'The same uneventful, sedentary life,' I replied. 'Nothing happens except that my scale of fees grows. I suppose nothing *will* happen till the conductor comes to take the tickets. I shall soon grow fat.'

'I notice it already, my lad. You want a bit of waking up or you'll get a liver. A little sensation would do you a pot of good.'

'And you?' I asked. 'I congratulate you on your success. I hear you have retrieved Pitt-Heron for his mourning family.'

Tommy's laughing eyes grew solemn.

'I have had the time of my life,' he said. 'It was like a chapter out of the Arabian Nights with a dash of Fenimore Cooper. I feel as if I had lived years since I left England in May. While you have been sitting among your musty papers we have been riding like moss-troopers and seeing men die. Come and dine tonight and hear about our adventures. I can't tell you the full story, for I don't know it, but there is enough to curl your hair.'

Then I achieved my first and last score at the expense of Tommy Deloraine.

'No,' I said, 'you will dine with me instead, and *I* will tell you the full story. All the papers on the subject are over there in my safe.'